CAROLINE

'The deed is done, Caro. The land is mine. We haven't got anything on it yet — but the land is mine.' William couldn't hide the pride in his voice from his fiancée. The trek to remote north-east South Australia was soon to begin for this pioneering couple. But disaster was to strike Caroline, leaving in its wake a haunting legacy of pain and guilt. A present-day researcher, looking into these past events, has the task of getting to the bottom of it all. To her surprise, she finds herself bringing release and peace 'across time'.

DAPHNE SAXBY TAYLOR

◆

CAROLINE

Complete and Unabridged

ULVERSCROFT
Leicester

First published in Great Britain in 1995

First Large Print Edition
published 2006

British Library CIP Data

Taylor, Daphne Saxby
    Caroline.—Large print ed.—
    Ulverscroft large print series: romance
    1.Love stories
    2. Large type books
    I. Title
    823.9'14 [F]

    ISBN 1–84617–369–8

Published by
F. A. Thorpe (Publishing)
Anstey, Leicestershire
Set by Words & Graphics Ltd.
Anstey, Leicestershire
Printed and bound in Great Britain by
T. J. International Ltd., Padstow, Cornwall

This book is printed on acid-free paper

To the women who braved isolation and loneliness, who bore children and lost children and knew heartache, but endured with courage and fortitude against all odds in the early settlement of Australia

Contents

Acknowledgements

My thanks to all those who have encouraged and assisted me in the writing of this book — to Felicity and John for taking us on a fact-finding, atmosphere-experiencing, four-wheel-drive trip through the country of 'Bibbaringa', camping under the wide skies and gazing to the far horizons; to Anne for her help in seeking research material and to the Queensland State Library officers who provided such valuable material; to Justin for instructing me in the workings of the word processor, introducing me to its wonders; and to my husband Harry for his assistance in research, proofreading and encouragement — I deeply appreciate it all.

1

The quest

The heat haze shimmered across the plains.

She could see the house now — or what remained of it. Her pulse quickened with excitement. The trip had been fascinating, each part of it. But this for her was the culmination, the climax.

The journey through the Gammon Ranges, mountains of stark grandeur where the earth strata had in some primaeval upsurge been thrown up until now the layers of rock were tilted to almost the vertical, had left her in a state of awe-inspired wonder. Then yesterday Lake Callabonna had equally stirred her with its evidence of the very real existence of great prehistoric creatures.

She gazed across the never-ending plain. The vastness, the antiquity was overwhelming. There was a timelessness about the place — as if removed from the world.

Her gaze came back to the house. There was an ethereal quality about the way the building appeared to float above the mirage, the huge illusory expanse of water.

How remote it was. How much more remote over a hundred years ago, when this run had been selected. It had been taken up in 1866 and the house built in 1868 by William Bartlett. It was stated in records that three graves were to be found in the garden. His grave bore the latest date. This had been his home until his death.

Further research in libraries and family sources had revealed his later years had been lonely and sad, he becoming almost a recluse after the tragic death of first his two-year-old son and then his adored wife. The deaths had occurred while he was away droving cattle from 'Nockatunga' in far south-west Queensland to 'Bibbaringa', the name he had given this property.

As she gazed, the whole scene seemed to be moving. It would be so easy to get lost out here — to become confused. The heat waves, the shimmering glare and the gibber plain seemed to go on into infinity.

Angela sighed. Picking up her bag again, she flung it over her shoulder. It was hot. She trudged on over the gibber stones.

How far had Robert got up the creek? He was fired up all right with excitement and inspiration in his archaeological investigations. He had gone off before sun-up with his little pick and bag of goods. She smiled, remembering — and came back to thinking of her own research. It was hard walking. Had she been foolish to leave the four-wheel-drive back where they had made camp at the creek?

But then if this trip was to be really worthwhile, if it was to provide the intimate understanding she needed, she wanted to get the full atmosphere of the old place; to enter into the events of long ago; to be as far as was possible part of the lives of these people, Caroline and William, whose home this had been; to experience something of their persons, their feelings, the events that had so shaped the course of their lives and left a legend of courage and daring. Of endurance. Of conquering isolation, the unknown. Of dreams and fulfilment. Of death and an enduring love.

The throb of the vehicle's motor — its very presence — would shatter that atmosphere, an atmosphere she was now experiencing.

Of course, it would all have been very different when Willie first rode into the area with McDouall Stuart's party. The land had been fertile then. It had won his love and awakened the burning desire to own it, to make it his own, to build his kingdom here.

It was a fascinating, haunting story of how he had used his inheritance to buy this land: land beyond settlement — unknown, uncharted land — untried. He had risked his all and won — in land and assets, at least. The records had shown only facts — facts on which she wanted to build in order to fill in the human, the life elements.

Angela pushed hard against the gate. It hung lopsidedly on one rusty hinge. The sand piled up behind it made it hard to open. It was a long time since it had been opened.

She looked curiously at the old house. It was waiting. She had the distinct sensation that the house was waiting for her. It was supposed to be haunted. There were tales of encounters. Believe them or not, it did add colour to the venture.

With an extra heave, the gate opened and she was able to squeeze through. She could see three headstones in the far corner of the yard, the remains of a wrought iron fence enclosing them. This garden was reported to have once been beautiful. The only remaining evidence was the yellow Banksia rose twining around the verandah posts, its hardy little flowers flaunting its brave spirit of survival in the devastated surroundings.

She picked her way through the stones and piles of sand, past the saltbush to the little cemetery.

After several minutes, she turned back to the house. Wide broken steps led up to the verandah. She mounted the steps hesitantly and approached the front door, feeling suddenly like an intruder. She grasped the large door knob. It turned, grating as the latch lifted.

She opened the door and entered the house with rising curiosity and a strange sense of expectation. The spacious vestibule was wide and inviting. A feeling of welcome lingered, despite its derelict condition. The curve of the wide timber-framed archway facing her, presumably leading to a central hall, was gracious and lovely.

The soft glow of cream, pink and salmon sandstone walls was mellow in the sunlight now filtering in through the half open front door.

Peering round the corner, she saw that the hall continued to both the left and the right. This hall was not so wide as the entrance. That had been quite wide, the ceiling high in the style of the homes of the early settlement years. This hall being narrower gave the impression of being much higher. She looked up at the patterned ceiling with the circular fittings where each lamp had once hung. It must have been beautiful in its day.

She moved down the passageway, carefully avoiding the broken floorboards, and looked into the rooms opening off either side. Hardly anything remained to bring to her imagination the people who had once lived and loved, laughed and died in this far-flung homestead, gracious in its day, but now pathetically in a state of dereliction and decay. French doors opened from these rooms onto the verandah. Some of these were still covered by shutters, making the rooms cool and shaded.

She walked back out onto the verandah that encircled the house. Here the floor was in worse repair. A row of swallows' nests, where fledgelings had been sheltered over many springs, was visible beside the stone wall, high up under the sloping roof.

She looked out over the paddocks once so fertile, supporting thousands of head of cattle. The years had taken their toll. White settlement had not been kind. The land, cleared of too many trees, had been left with nothing to bind the soil. As the trees had gone, so had the herbage and grass coverings. They had been unable to withstand the hardfoot animals, the cattle and sheep moved in by settlers unused to the fragile balance of this strange new land. Then the scourge of rabbits had completed the devastation.

This land that had nurtured the soft-footed animals — the 'roos, wallabies, kangaroos and all their kind for thousands of years — had in the space of one hundred years been decimated by the onslaught of foreign animals and ignorance. The winds had brought the dust and sand from the desert. Now the land was barren, stony and desolate, the topsoil long since gone, the only sign of green on the top of the distant sand ridges — and the saltbush struggling to survive in the forbidding landscape.

'How sad,' she murmured. The gibber plain stretched away to a seemingly endless horizon, the sun picking up the red-purple glow of the stone.

She turned to re-enter the vestibule. As she did so, she thought she caught a glimpse of movement. Or was it a trick of light in the long central hall? She moved quickly to the arched doorway and looked both ways. Nothing there. She went slowly down the hall. A board creaked behind her. She looked back, alert, her scalp rising. Again nothing.

She turned into one of the rooms. The tiled fireplace with its ornate surround was dust-covered, the timber mantel cracked and sagging. She had the feeling she was not alone. She swung round involuntarily.

Suddenly, she was conscious of a sound. In the heavy silence, her hearing alerted, her own breathing sounded distinctly. It had sounded like moaning. She listened again. There was no sound. Not even a bird. No stir of breeze. Nothing broke the silence. The thudding of her heart sounded in her ears. Every sense strained to capacity.

Where had it come from? Or had she imagined it? There it was again. It seemed to come from across the hall. Yet again she doubted her own sensitivity. Had the desire to experience these people and long-gone events, the expectations, made her vulnerable to flights of her own imagination?

Glancing hastily around the room, she took a few silent, hesitant steps towards the door and listened again. She paused a moment, gathering all her courage. Then she left the room quickly and crossed the hall.

2

The encounter

The room was in deep shadow. The wide verandah with its deep, overhanging roof sheltered the interior from the intense light of the afternoon sun. In this deep shadow, the glass panels of the French doors provided slits of vision of the blinding glare across the gibber plain.

Angela stopped short in the doorway, catching her breath in astonishment. Beside the French door, her hand on the tattered remains of curtain stood a girl, a young woman. The girl did not move; she made no sign that she was aware of Angela's presence.

She was slim, with long fair hair — or it would have been fair, had it been clean. It was pulled back roughly in an unkempt fashion. It looked as though it had not seen company with a comb for a long time. Loose strands fell around her eyes. Her shirt was open at the neck. The sleeves were torn off above the elbow. The heavy skirt she wore was mid-calf length, but this, too, had a torn bottom. Her feet were bare.

Pulling herself together, Angela spoke. 'Hullo,' she said.

The girl turned her head. A wave of shock swept over Angela. The girl looked positively haggard. Her face was drawn, the cheeks sunken and her eyes deep hollows.

Whatever could be the matter? Could she be on drugs? Without knowledge of drug addicts, she had no way of knowing. But there was certainly something wrong. 'You surprised me,' Angela said, advancing into the room a few paces. 'I thought there was no-one around for miles and miles.' She gave a little laugh.

The girl looked at her. 'I am here,' she said unsmilingly. She turned back to the window and continued gazing out.

Well, she was certainly a strange one. What was she doing just standing silently there?

Possibly just like I am, Angela thought wryly. She may also be a student trying to experience the atmosphere of the place — though she didn't really have that appearance. But then, some students and writers were a bit way out and didn't pay any attention to their appearance.

But her face! Her emaciated look! She certainly needed a few good meals.

'I've come on a research visit to try to really get to know as much as I can of the original people here — so I can make them come alive in my writing,' Angela ventured. 'Are you doing something like that?'

The girl continued gazing out the window. Then she half-turned. 'I know it here,' she said softly.

Odd. She was not giving anything away. Well, she didn't want to pry, but it would be interesting to know what she was doing and why she was here. She must be camped on the creek somewhere just as she and Robert were. They had seen no signs of a vehicle, though — or tracks of one. And how she could have walked across the gibber stones barefoot was a mystery.

'Do you know the story of William and Caroline Bartlett?' she asked, moving closer.

The young woman retreated. 'I know it well,' she replied shortly.

Trying to have a conversation, to get a little information from her was like getting blood out of a stone. 'It is a very sad story after such a wonderful beginning, isn't it?'

There was no reply. Her eyes were fixed on something Angela could not see in the far distance. She seemed again lost in contemplation.

'I wish I could go back in time and change the story,' Angela said softly. 'Just to get Willie to stay at home — not to go himself to get the

11

cattle.' She paused. 'Or get Wan Loo and the Blacks to stay.'

Angela's companion lapsed into thought. 'Nobody can do anything. There's nothing anyone can do.' The young voice had a hopeless quality.

Angela looked quickly at her. Where she stood in the shadow beside the glare visible through the glass panel it was hard to see the expression. This girl seemed as interested as she herself and as involved in the heart-rending story. But why wasn't she more forthcoming about it?

'Willie will never forgive her! He couldn't! And little Jamie! She'll never be forgiven.' The words cut through the silence.

'Oh, but Willie didn't think of it like that! Really he didn't. Anyway, there's always forgiveness. Life wouldn't be worth living if there was no forgiveness. We'd never know any peace.'

If she was going to talk now, at least they could discuss the story and perhaps it may be beneficial to them both. But she was a strange sort of person. She must have some hangups about something to be so taciturn and yet so interested in a story like this. It must hit a personal chord somewhere.

'Peace!' She was talking again, harshly. 'Oh, she'll have no peace. Her father used to say,

'Peace be with you, my Carry." There was a strange note in her voice. 'But she'll never know peace,' she repeated. She moved her hands over her face and pushed her hair back.

Angela waited.

As the moments ticked by, she remembered the little cemetery with the three headstones and their inscriptions:

Jamie William
Beloved son of William and Caroline Bartlett
Born 1876   Died 1878

Underneath, the text 'Of such is the kingdom of Heaven' was clear on the small stone. This was obviously the work of a stonemason, done with precision: work to last on a white stone; a rock that endured.

The headstone in the far corner was dark marble, the lettering clearly visible in white. This surmounted the grave of William Henry Bartlett, the first owner of the property.

The central stone was the one which captured her interest and curiosity. She remembered the words:

Caroline Mary
Cherished, Beloved wife of
William Henry Bartlett
Born 1845   Died 1878

And then the text: Genesis 2, verse 23. Underneath the verse were the words:

Bone of my bone, flesh of my flesh
My heart doth safely trust in her,
Her price is far above rubies,
My wife, my beloved, my own.

This was a soft, pink-grained sandstone of once beautiful colours and pattern, now weathered and pitted with time and the wind-blown sand: a stone that had not stood the test of time.

Angela had traced the letters with her fingers in order to understand some of the words. So ravaged were they that it was almost impossible to decipher some letters.

Historical records had stated this had been carved by William Bartlett himself. He had learned of the death of his son and his wife a few days before his arrival home with the cattle from 'Nockatunga'. Angela could only guess at the love and heartache this had wrought: his devastation on returning to the homestead, his haven of love and peace, now so empty.

What love must have gone into the choosing and the carving of this stone: the emotion behind the deed; the need for some personal service to put into tangible form for this beloved wife all the love and adoration he felt for her.

The girl stirred from her reverie. 'Peace,' she whispered fiercely. 'She'll never find peace.' She passed her hand again over her hair, catching at the loose strands, pulling them back impatiently.

Did she have some personal antipathy towards the woman of long ago? She sounded almost belligerent. The girl thrust her hand into her skirt pocket and withdrew two combs. She jabbed them roughly into her hair, securing it untidily.

Angela said, 'It all started so happily, didn't it? Willie selected the property, their wedding and the excitement of coming here. It was a tremendously adventurous under-taking. Caroline was very brave to come all this way like that.'

'Do you think so?' The girl's voice was strained.

'I think she was wonderfully brave,' Angela replied, surprised by the unexpected response. 'She must have loved Willie very much.'

The girl nodded without looking at her.

'The naming of the property, building this house — oh, it must have been so exciting!'

Again the girl merely nodded, although her

15

demeanour seemed less rigid.

Encouraged, Angela ventured further. 'This must have been a beautiful homestead.' She glanced around the room. 'This would have been Caroline's bedroom.' She took a few steps towards the wall. 'And this would have been where her duchess stood. It had a lovely wide mirror.' She noticed the girl's eyes were now following her. 'And here the bureau.'

Angela turned back to her companion. 'I saw a family history album with a plan of the house. An artist had re-created an impression of this room from letters from the Bartlett family archives. It was very beautiful and reflected Caroline's gentle nature.'

She took a few steps back towards the wall. 'Caroline would have brushed her hair here, sitting on a little tapestry stool.' She moved her hands, indicating. She could see it all. 'And on the dressing table, her silver brush, comb and mirror would have been on the crocheted mat. And beside them, the ivory side combs that she always wore, because they had been Willie's wedding gift to her.'

Angela stood gazing into space, rapt in the story. 'They were so much in love — and so happy.'

'But that was all gone when Jamie died.' The girl's voice held a different quality.

There was a silence Angela dared not break.

Then the voice lashed out, full of repugnance, loathing. 'And she — she let him die. It was her fault.'

3

The question

The wind teased at the lone figure silhouetted against the sky. He seemed oblivious of the wind or anything else about him. He was gazing out over the gulf waters, but he did not appear to be watching anything. He leaned on the rail skirting the esplanade. Suddenly, the wind whipped his hat from his head and he was obliged to chase it. His reverie broken, he returned to his place at the rail. The gulf waters surged below him.

William Bartlett looked at the surging water. It really didn't excite him, he thought. Funny; some people were thrilled and inspired by this sight: to sail to faraway lands; to set off on the surging sea for a life of adventure on the ocean waves. Yet here he stood, unmoved by this splendour, dreaming of land, with horizons as wide as the sea: land still and silent till you tuned to its melody; land with majesty to equal the rolling, surging sea.

This was what life was about: to own such land. Ownership meant to ride over its vastness free as the wind itself; to round up your stock and move them over the grass and sweet herbage; to water them at the fresh water creeks and camp under a coolabah tree with the wide sky dark above you; to lie on your back in your swag and pick out the familiar stars and pinpoint where you were (The Southern Cross would be high at this time of the year); then, to rise with the first rays of the sun, sending arrows of flame across the arc of the sky, the sound of the cattle grazing clear in the silence.

It was possible. Thanks to Grandfather Bartlett's generosity, he had the means to purchase land. To buy freehold land would be the thing; to own it; to feel the soil beneath your feet and know that 'this land is mine'.

What a wonderful old man Grandfather had been — invited to hold the post of Chief Justice of the colony for so many years and respected and revered by not only his peers, but the ordinary men, hard-working settlers from England, Germany, China and other places, as well. He had a reputation for justice — 'fair play', as the local idiom would have it. He had truly been a man who would give a man a 'fair go', a man to be proud of.

That made it all the more important, of course, to use this legacy wisely. If he decided to invest it in a dream, then he had to be as sure as it was possible to be that the dream flourished and did not become a nightmare. He must make all the enquiries possible, check titles, look at rainfall likelihoods, calculate costs of stock, drovers, materials, bullock-waggon transport willing to go into unknown country without roads. He must go over and over to see if it was feasible. But oh, the excitement of it!

Of course, the reward for discovering that rich silver deposit in Mt Lofty Range would help greatly. He had been so lucky — lucky to have noticed that particular formation in the topography and lucky to have had such teachers — teachers like old Cheneworth who had opened his mind to the wonders of all beneath the surface of the land.

It was a flourishing field now, the Mt Lofty mine. It would bring wealth to the colony, wealth that was surely needed after the early years of financial chaos.

Still, the colony was progressing now. There would be expansion and development in many directions soon. It was happening now. That's why he must make his move now. What was the use of money tied up in investment? Interest rates were not such as to make a man's fortune. And where was the accomplishment, the thrill?

William's thoughts turned to the land of

his dreams; land he had seen and fallen in love with; land that drew out all the passionate desire to work and strive for; land that claimed an affinity with his soul. Surely, surely it would be his land.

There was always a risk, even in settled country. The man on the land depended on the seasons, the right markets. Even those with holdings close to Adelaide still were dependent on these things. But oh, the excitement, the adventure of pushing out, of taking up land where no-one had yet been — and making a go of it. That would be something!

He drew himself up. He couldn't keep going round and round like this. Soon he must make a decision. Would he risk his entire legacy and his reward in the fulfilling of this dream? Vision, he corrected himself with a wry smile, not dream.

He would go and have a talk with Grandmother Henrietta. She was a wise as well as an astute lady. She had all the German resourcefulness and ingenuity of her people, as well as the thriftiness, and could no doubt help him to sort out his thoughts and intentions. At any rate, she would be a willing and enthusiastic sounding-board.

William turned away from the seashore and headed down the road. Cottages now lined the road, each with its own garden in front. Some had quite a commendable display of flowers and trees. Further up the hill there were three gentlemen's residences. These were more imposing and commanded a spectacular view across the gulf and the surrounding countryside.

What a pity so many of the cottages — and even one of the larger houses — still faced their windows to the south as had been the custom in the northern lands! This was Australia — and new exciting times. The old lands had to be left behind. The past needed to be put aside and the new and different needs identified and met. How many of the homes here had wide verandahs — or verandahs at all to shelter the rooms from this stronger sun?

When he had secured his land, he would give great thought to the house he would build. They were calling houses on rural properties 'homesteads'. That had a good ring about it: the place where you returned to for rest and refreshment.

He supposed Caroline would have ideas about the sort of house she would like, too. He would provide well for her. What a beautiful girl, what a wonderful girl she was! No-one in the country could compare with her. Her charm, her beauty, her intelligence and gentleness left all the others like wallflowers at the bottom of the garden. He was the luckiest of fellows that she saw something in him and had accepted his proposal of marriage.

Walking thus on air, he almost fell over an Aborigine squatting at the side of the road as he turned round the last house in the row. The man was in the shade of the overhanging tree from the cottage garden. Jolted from his bemused state of mind, William stopped to apologise, then in surprise recognised the man. 'Yuelty!' he cried, clapping him on the back and wringing his hand. 'This is wonderful! Where have you come from?'

'Been Mutta Mutta, boss,' the Aborigine said.

'How about another trip up north? That lake country. Like last time you went, I went — with Stuart Boss. You showed the way. You go again?' The man's eyes lit up. 'You know that country.'

William looked at him, smiling, waiting for his answer. He looked at his feet. 'I know country. My country,' he said. Then he looked at William, a broad smile flashing across his face, his teeth startlingly white in his black face. 'I go,' he agreed.

William proceeded to wring his hand again. 'You here some time?' he asked.

The man nodded. 'I make ready. I see you again.' He turned and strode down the road that twisted away along the coast.

What a bit of luck to come across Yuelty just now! He would be crucial to the whole idea of taking up land. It could have taken months to locate him — then to actually contact him! And he had agreed to go.

He would keep his word. A good man, Yuelty — and what a guide! He knew that country well. He could take them just where he wanted to go. There'd be no worries about finding water — and a 'roo made a good meal. Yuelty had proved himself not only as a guide, but as a hunter and adviser on fresh food found in the bush on that other journey. It was almost too good to be true to have literally fallen over him in this way just at this time.

Surely it was meant to be — a good omen, some would say. How would Granny Etty see this? He was smiling as he swung into the drive leading up to the little house.

Henrietta Drabsch lifted her eyes from her mending and looked out the front window when she heard the footsteps coming up the path. She rose when she saw who her visitor was and hastened to the front door, throwing it wide open. 'Ah, my beautiful boy,' she cried, flinging her arms wide.

William's arms came round her in a great bear hug. 'How are you, Granny Etty? You're looking wonderful.'

'I'm very well, my dear. And so much the better for seeing you.' The old lady led him into the room where she had been sitting.

She was a tiny woman — barely one hundred and fifty centimetres. But her will and impact on her family and acquaintances made up for her stature. The eyes were bright and keen. Not much missed her scrutiny, though she did not always comment.

What did this dear boy want now, she wondered. He did not usually visit her mid-morning and there was something of subdued excitement — or perhaps controlled excitement — about him. No doubt he would tell her in his own good time.

How proud Johannes would be if he could see him now, a tall, broad-shouldered, clean-faced man. There was a look of Johannes about him — an expression, a gentleness she sometimes caught when she looked at him unobserved. Her heart swelled with pride and love for him.

There was an affinity between the young man and the old lady — the same high principles, the directness, the passionate love of freedom and tolerance of others.

William rose from the chair into which he

had dropped and, thrusting his hands into his pockets, strode to the window and looked out. Then turning, he looked at his grandmother and smiled. 'I want to talk to you, Gran. I want your advice. I'm thinking of buying land.'

'I thought there was something,' she said, lifting her eyebrows and smiling. 'Where is this land you are thinking of buying?'

'That's the thing. You see, when I went on that excursion with John McDouall Stuart — you know, before he went off on his big expedition — I saw land that would thrill you to the core.' He had in his growing excitement and desire to impress her strode over to her chair and stood looking earnestly into her eyes. 'There's miles and miles of beautiful country no-one has touched. There's good water and, oh, just the immensity of it. The vastness. It makes you feel free and oh,' he paused, 'like a king. To look over that land and think of the possibility of owning it just makes me feel drunk with excitement!' He laughed, then continued: 'To own that land as far as you can see. What a kingdom!'

The old lady smiled, calm, serene. 'You are certainly taken with this land. But you still haven't told me where it is.'

'When I went with Mr Stuart's party on

that foray — you remember?' She nodded. 'We took a course north, pushing along as quickly as possible. Then he changed course to a direction north-north-east. We came to a land that would delight your heart. There's mile after mile stretching as far as the eye can see. A wide creek teeming with bird life winds its way through the pasture, eventually going into a lake. In the spring, when we reached that country, the great expanse covered with all kinds of wildflowers was breathtaking.

'This is the land I want to own. I say I want to buy it. I desperately want to make it mine. I want to take my cattle to that creek to water. I want to sit in the shade under those trees by the creek. I want to buy it, Gran. I *can* buy it. I've got the money to do it and to stock it initially. But should I?'

4

The decision

William stood straight, all his prudence conflicting with his passionate desire.

'I've fallen in love with that land, Gran, but I've got to be wise. Grandfather Bartlett trusted me with that legacy and, of course, I've got the reward for the Mt Lofty find. But I can't let impetuosity ruin me. That's why I wanted to talk it out with you. Should I risk all I have on this that I see as an opportunity to build an empire? These are adventurous times and I believe if we grasp the opportunities, there is room for limitless possibilities.'

He paused. Henrietta took a deep breath. The boy certainly was in a state of high excitement and enthusiasm. No doubt he was right about the opportunities prevalent at this stage of the development of the colony for those daring and reckless enough to grasp them and risk their all. But had he looked at the pitfalls?

'So the land is north-north-east of here?' she asked. 'How far north-north-east?'

'I can't tell you in miles,' he replied, 'but I estimate it will take about twenty-one days to get there for a small party with pack horses.'

'Oh William! What a long, long way it must be! Are you sure you want to go so far for your land? What of getting your stock there? No doubt you will want to build a house sooner or later. What about materials for the house? Can you get men to work the place, to go so far away from civilisation?' She looked keenly at him. 'Can you even find your way there again?'

William told her of his chance meeting with Yuelty. 'He's a great guide, Gran. And, besides that, I kept a journal and charted our route on that other journey. Mr Stuart taught me a great deal. He was a strict leader, but he was wise and a superb bushman. I learned more — to chart both with the compass and the stars and to pinpoint my position. I can give you those positions of the land, but that will not, I think, mean a great deal to you.

'I have three friends who I think will accompany me on a journey to formally select the run I envisage and, with Yuelty, that will be a reasonable party. When I buy stock, they will have to be driven there. That will take some months, but should not prove too difficult if I set out at the right time of the year, knowing the availability of water.

'I feel sure there are fellows, good fellows willing to adventure and come as drovers, then stay on and help me work the place. It's a man's world in the frontier properties in this country, Gran. It's exciting. Think of the adventure. No, no. I'm sure I can get stockmen.'

She smiled gently at him. 'You say it is a man's world in this place, William. I had thought you were going to marry Caroline. What are you planning to do about her?'

William looked at her, shocked by the question. 'Of course I'm going to marry Caroline. You know that. She'll come too, of course, if and when I've got it all fixed.'

'And have you discussed this idea with her? Can she visualise life as the only woman — white woman, that is — for hundreds of miles? Don't you think she will be lonely?' She lifted her eyebrows.

'But she'll have me!' he exclaimed, astonished that his grandmother could think Caro would desire more. 'I've talked to her about it. She knows how keen I am and she's willing to come with me. We love each other, Gran. I'll provide well for her. I'm quite conscious of my responsibility and I certainly want to make her happy.

'I'll try to build her just the sort of homestead she'll like. I saw stone on the south-western edge of the area I have in mind that I believe would be suitable and make a beautiful building material. Of course, we'd have to get stonemasons and builders, but the other materials could be taken up by bullock-waggon. I think that could all be arranged. It will all take time, of course, but it will be fun. I don't see any problems that can't be solved.'

'Then what are you asking me, my boy?' The old lady looked quizzically at him. 'You seem to have all the answers.'

'I suppose it's mainly the right use of Grandfather's legacy.' He paced up and down the room again. 'I don't want to make a hash of it.'

'You are convinced this is good land that will fatten your cattle? There is good permanent water? You have no doubts about this? Have you checked this is completely freehold country with no strings attached?'

He nodded.

'Then perhaps it is just the leap out in faith in your own judgment that concerns you.'

She hesitated a minute. 'Do you believe God means you to take this step, William?' she said softly.

'I just know that land stirs me as nothing else has ever done. I dream about it: Caro and I making our life there, growing and thriving. And when I almost fell over Yuelty I thought, 'This is meant to be'.'

Henrietta remembered the great step she and Johannes had taken so many years ago. They had a young family in their homeland, they suffered religious persecution and they made the great decision to emigrate to Australia where they believed they could worship as they desired, grow their grapes and make their wine in peace and freedom.

It had been the right decision. They had prospered. Their family had grown and taken their place in the new land. And they had grown old together until Johannes had gone to be with his Maker. Her eyes misted over.

She held out her hand to William. 'Your grandfather Johannes and I had to make an even greater decision in leaving our homeland and coming to this country, William. We prayed. We made the right decision. And God prospered us. Ask God to take your hand, my boy, and step out in faith. And God be with you.'

When he left his grandmother's house, William strode briskly down the road to the stables where he had left his horse. Calling to the stable boy, he collected his horse, paid his account and headed for the first call on this round to see the friends he felt confident would come with him to make his selection.

After half-an-hour's ride, he drew rein at the gate of an imposing residence on the outskirts of town. The paddocks around the house were dotted with mares and foals, beautiful horses. George was a good judge of horses and an able veterinary on his father's property. So long as he could be spared just now, he would make a valuable member of his party.

They each had their areas of speciality. Tom would be a good man to consult regarding the land as a pastoral holding. His family were involved with cattle — and had been for many years. They were even importing new strains from overseas to improve their herds and were becoming renowned for their breeders. Tom would advise him if he saw any difficulties.

Of course, you just didn't know for sure till you had cattle on the place. There were none for many hundreds of miles, he knew, but it wouldn't be long before the pastoralists reached out. He wanted to be there first.

He alighted before the door and, taking his horse around the house, tied him up, then retraced his steps to the front door. A young man came to the door in answer to his knock. 'William!' he cried. 'Come in. We were just talking about you. Come in. Come in. Let me have your hat and whip.'

He turned from the hall stand and, ushering William into the sitting room where his mother was pouring tea said, 'Here's Will, Mother. This must be your tea party for your son's friends.'

His mother looked up. 'Come and have some tea, William.' Then to her son: 'When my son has such fine young men for friends, it is my pleasure to give them tea. They are most welcome.'

When he entered, William had not noticed two other young men in riding habit standing by the window poring over a large map. They looked up now, coming forward eagerly to shake hands.

'Will, this is just wonderful. We have just been trying to decide where this land is you are so keen about. George has a good map over here, but of course you don't get very far in a north-north-easterly direction before you run out of any charted territory. You said there was a creek, but there don't seem to be any creeks or rivers coming from that direction.'

It was the shorter of the two men talking. He was a thick-set young fellow with dark, curly hair and flashing brown eyes.

The four friends, taking their tea to the table by the window, gathered round the large map there spread out. 'The creek doesn't come anywhere near this far south,' William said. 'It runs into a lake.'

He calculated the latitude and longitude readings on the map. 'It would be somewhere about here,' he said, placing his finger on the map. 'Mr Stuart may not have found an inland sea, but he certainly found water — creeks, lakes — and water that doesn't flow into the ocean. I'm still very inclined to the theory of an inland sea at some stage. The country really enthralls me. It's so different, yet so beautiful.

'This is the greatest bit of luck finding you both here. I was just on my way to see each of you. You see,' he said, straightening up, his face glowing as he looked at each of his friends, 'I've decided to buy land there and I wanted to see each of you and ask you whether you will come with me to make my formal selection.'

The effect on each of the young men was electric. Excitement, adventure flashed before their eyes. There were crows of eager response.

'I know none of you have been on any of these expeditions like I was when I went with Mr Stuart, but you are all good horsemen, know the bush and are hale and hearty, I believe.'

The exhilaration was mounting.

'I charted the course we took. I have all the readings both by compass and star sitings. And,' he said, striking the table with his open palm in his excitement, 'by the greatest piece of good luck today I ran into' — he laughed — 'nearly fell over, actually, Yuelty, an Aboriginal fellow who was a guide on that first expedition. He's a great fellow and he's agreed to come with us. I have no doubts about finding the place and water on the way. With Yuelty with us, it just about puts a seal of approval on the whole venture.'

The four young heads were bent over the map, eagerly talking of possible routes, what was needed, how many pack horses, what provisions, how long the whole enterprise would take.

'George, you're the one who's the horse expert. Can you take responsibility for the horses? Tom, you know more about cattle and pastures, markets and the droving to markets than any of us. Can you give me the benefit of your advice in this area?

'Herb, can I count on your knowledge of watercourses, plants and bird movement, all the things that can help me be sure I'm not going to end up in bankruptcy courts? I'm fascinated by the place, but I've got to be sure before I commit myself. Will you all come with me?'

The babble of excited voices was answer enough. George looked at his friend seriously. 'I'll have to consult Father before I make it definite, Will, but all being well there, you couldn't keep me away from it.' He turned to his mother at the tea table. 'What do you think, Mother?'

'I think it is so unfair,' his mother replied. 'Why is it men do all the exciting things and have all the fun? If I was young and a man, wild horses wouldn't keep me out of an opportunity like this. I think your father will agree to spare you for a few months.'

It was almost dark before the four friends parted and William made his way home. He would see Caroline in the morning and tell her of his decision.

George, Tom and Herb, who all worked on family holdings, would consult their fathers. They would meet again the next afternoon with their decisions and, if all went well, start preparations for the trip. He should be able to arrange it all in two or three days. He hoped Yuelty would stay close by and not get restless. He didn't like being in town for long. He was a man of the bush.

It was an excited but purposeful man who turned into the drive of his home. He had made his decision. Now he would see what tomorrow would bring. That would determine his next move.

The sun made a dappled pattern as William walked up the tree-lined drive to the rectory next morning. Caroline with a flat basket on her arm was picking flowers for the house. She came to meet him when she saw him approaching.

'Willie, how lovely to see you so early,' she cried. William greeted her lovingly, his heart beating faster at the sight of her. He told her of his conversation with his friends, their keenness to accompany him and the earlier chance meeting with Yuelty.

'After meeting Yuelty, I went to have a talk with Granny Etty. She helped me to think clearly about it and we came to the conclusion I am as sure as I can be — depending on this journey, of course.' He paused. 'Caro, Gran did raise one point that's bothered me. You are happy about this venture, aren't you? I thought you were as keen as I am.' He looked earnestly at her.

'Of course, Willie. I know you can make a success of it. I have every confidence in your judgment,' she answered, surprised.

'Yes, but what about you? What about living there with no other women? I thought you'd be happy just with my company, our being together, but Gran seemed to think you might be lonely.' His concerned expression drew on Caroline's heartstrings and, at the same time, made her want to laugh.

'Of course I'll be happy, my darling,' she replied, smiling. 'We'll be together, as you say, and I'll have so many things to do to interest me and so many things to learn. We plan to come to Adelaide once a year, don't we? And Mother and Father say they must come to visit us and see it all. Please don't worry.' Willie visibly relaxed on hearing her answer. They talked for some time of Willie's plans for his journey before he went off to make enquiries about packhorses suitable for the long distance.

That afternoon, when the four friends met at the appointed time, the plan was definite. All were able to be spared for the two months thought necessary for the journey and the close investigation of the proposed property, William being conscious of the need to search out materials suitable for buildings and fences as well as examining the property from a grazing point of view.

It was decided, if all could be made ready, they would set out in two days' time. They would travel light, taking only what was really necessary. They parted each to make his preparations, William going off in search of Yuelty to acquaint him of their plans.

The late afternoon sun was casting long shadows as William searched up and down the streets of town for Yuelty. No-one had seen him. He decided to ride out to the area where he had seen him the day before. He rode up past his grandmother's house, up past the corner where he had almost fallen over him and on to the point where he had looked out over the gulf.

No sign of the lithe black figure. He asked a few passers-by, but no-one had seen him that day. One remembered seeing him sit in the shade of the tree the day before.

William was becoming concerned. What if Yuelty had got tired of the town and decided to go bush? It could ruin his plans. He'd have to postpone the journey until he found the old fellow. That could take time — and would his friends be free to go then?

Of course he could go without Yuelty, relying on his own knowledge and calculations, but it would be a great deal easier and safer with the black man's expertise.

He was riding back out across the bridge, when he saw a familiar figure step out of the bush onto the road a hundred metres ahead. 'Yuelty,' he called. 'I've been looking everywhere for you. You had me worried.'

'Get bush tucker, Boss,' grinned Yuelty, patting his stomach.

William communicated all his plans to Yuelty and arranged to meet him in two days' time. They parted each in his own way, excited by the prospect of the coming trip.

The following days were filled with preparations, busy from dawn till dark. Maps, instruments, records were packed. Supplies, clothing and medications for men and horses were all put together, then stringently reduced. All except the bare essentials were left behind to facilitate the light, fast travelling planned.

At sun-up on the third day, their plans materialised and, after fond farewells and many admonitions for care and caution, the little party set out on the great adventure north-north-east.

5

The selecting of 'Bibbaringa'

With fine conditions and clear sunny days, the rate of progress was very good. It was not yet that time of the year when the temperature rises above the century and the sun beats down mercilessly on all it touches. The dawn start and long days in the saddle soon dropped into an efficient routine for the accomplishment of the project.

The four young men, fit and enthusiastic for the purpose, relished the challenge and marvelled at their black guide's knowledge and expertise. For William's three friends, it was wholly a new experience — to conserve their waterbag contents; to ensure the replenishment of their contents before moving off in the morning. These were vital lessons to be learned for survival in this uninhabited region.

The settled area with its little farms and fenced paddocks had long since been left behind. The country opened out. The horizon receded. A trail was blazed, a further precaution for safety on the return journey.

The sky was now a predominantly clear, deep blue as sunrise followed sunset.

Their course north, ever north brought them eventually to the ranges Willie had seen on his earlier foray. 'The colours in those mountains are unbelievable,' Herb said one evening as they approached a spot where Yuelty had planned to make camp. 'There's a whole range of colours from the deepest purple. There would be some interesting plant and bird life in those mountains, I reckon.'

'Could be all sorts of interesting things. One day I'll go and investigate them. Could very easily be some interesting minerals. Might even be gold.' William gazed at the mountains in the distance. 'Who knows? We might even start some more mining activity.' He laughed, thinking of the Mt Lofty mine and the silver now being extracted.

He glanced at Yuelty. What was the black man thinking? There was an odd expression on his face. Had something disturbed him? 'What do you say, Yuelty?' he asked directly.

'Very important, those mountains,' he replied solemnly.

'Are they?' He now had the attention of the others.

'Many paintings my people.' He looked at the ground.

What was up with old Yuelty? He was usually bright and, for a black man in the company of whites, quite talkative. Did he not like the idea of mining for gold, the influx of prospectors and the disruption to the countryside?

'Do you think gold mining would be a bad thing?' Tom asked.

'Many special paintings, my people,' Yuelty repeated. 'Many very special. Very old, long, long time.'

'Your people value them very much, eh?'

'Very much. Must care for them. Teach them to our children's children.'

The young men were silent before the solemnity of their guide. What was the significance of those paintings in the mountains? Were they sacred objects? Obviously they were of great antiquity and importance in the life of these people. How little they knew of the culture of the Aboriginal people! Perhaps one day they would learn more. But for now, they must stick to the project in hand.

They followed the line of the mountains now, veering more to the north-east. The country to the east levelled out. The creeks from the mountains dispersed as they came down to the more sandy country, the water apparently soaking away as it spread out.

They passed a lake to the east.

Yuelty drew their attention to filling their waterbags at creeks when the lake was already in sight. 'Why fill our bags here, Yuelty?' Herb asked. 'There's water in plenty over there.'

'Water no good for drink,' Yuelty replied.

'Is it brackish or what?' Tom asked. 'Poisoned?'

'You see,' Yuelty replied as he led the way.

They dismounted at the edge of the water and gazed out over the great expanse. This must be where the waters from the mountains flowed to when there were flood rains.

George reached down and, scooping up a handful, lifted it to his lips and tasted it. 'Urgh!' he spluttered as he spat it out. 'It's salty.'

Yuelty laughed. 'I tell you, no good for drink.'

'Salt water, here in the inland?' cried Herb incredulously. 'So far from the sea! Your mountains don't send us good water, Yuelty.'

'Water good for drink in mountains. Just not here,' Yuelty replied.

How much there was to learn about this land! Perhaps the theory of an inland sea was right, after all. Perhaps those who had gone exploring for it just hadn't searched in the right places.

The party moved on quickly. They had

almost reached the area William was so excited about. There was good feed here — not the pastures they were familiar with, but the horses relished it. Low shrubby plants they were — fleshy. Some were almost velvety when you ran your fingers along the stems. The soil beneath was stony, the surface between and around the plants being covered with small red to purple stones where they showed through.

They could still see the sheen of another smaller lake one day, as William drew rein. He alighted and pulled out his compass, instruments and charts. 'This is where the land I think of as mine begins,' he said. 'I plan to select the land as far as you can see to the east and north . . . and a bit further. To the west you will see a creek with good waterholes. Permanent holes. You can't see the water from here, but you might see the line of trees.'

They gazed out across the country. The horizons seemed to stretch away into infinity. How on earth would you keep track of your stock? It was so vast, so incredibly vast! It was beautiful, too, in its own way.

Here the soil was more springy, more sandy. It was not like the stony country they had passed earlier. Everywhere was green here. It must have rained not long ago. Away in the distance they could see ridges which seemed to go off to the north.

So this was the country Will was so fired up about. It took a bit of getting used to. It wasn't quite what they had expected. But then nothing had prepared them for the experience of this new kind of country.

'Well, it certainly is vast. Almost takes my breath away,' Herb said at last. William had been eagerly awaiting their response.

'I see what you mean about feeling like a king looking out over your kingdom,' George said, waving his arm. 'It's,' he paused, 'stupendous.'

'What about you, Tom?'

'I don't know what to say. I can't find words to express my feelings. It's not what I was expecting. Mind you, I don't know quite what I was expecting.' He paused. 'But the more I look, the more excited I become.'

William smiled, well satisfied with his friends' responses.

'Well, come on.' He mounted his horse again. 'We'll go to the creek.'

It was cool and shaded by the creek. The beautiful smooth trunks of the coolabah trees curled and twisted upwards, the limbs supporting the thick canopy of leaves that provided the welcome shade.

The long waterhole stretched wide at this

point. Pelicans and other long-legged, red-crowned water birds were revelling in its freshness. The banks were sandy, the tracks of many of the smaller forms of life clearly visible among the footprints of birds of many species.

Herb is in his element, William thought. He would be recording all those tracks and weighing up their significance in relation to the prospect of the land as a grazing property.

'Here are some dingo tracks,' Herb called from the other side of the creek. 'Just as well you're not contemplating a sheep property.'

The water was fresh and clear, with a sandy bottom. Rainbow birds darted from branch to branch in the canopy above. William looked for and found the burrows to their nests in the sandy banks. A hawk circled above, soaring on the air currents, its great wings stretched wide. 'This place certainly is different,' Tom said. ' 'Majestic', I suppose, is a word to describe it. It stretches your mind.'

In the next week, they made a thorough survey of the land.

Water was a vital consideration and this was investigated and discussed at length. After following the course of the creek for kilometres in its twists and turns and the finding of other shallow waterholes, it was decided this would be adequate.

In some sections to the north-east, the flat stretches between the ridges were covered with water — obviously not permanent water, but at present almost forming lakes. As this soaked away, it would produce wonderful pasture. The red, sandy soil gleamed back in the light of the sun.

There was an abundance of pasture. These strange plants were apparently good feed. The 'roos they had seen were fat and sleek and abundant. And the horses grazed contentedly. It appeared feed would not be a problem and, going on the condition of the wild life, cattle should fatten well.

'The potential of the place seems first class,' Tom remarked one evening as they sat around the camp fire. 'My main concern is the long distance to market. It's a long, long way to Adelaide.'

'That's true,' William agreed, 'but if they are taken slowly and spelled on the way in several strategic places, I think that will not be a great disadvantage. At present, there are great areas of unsettled lands to be utilised and, by the time more people are venturing further out, there will be roads and stock routes formed, I feel sure. This is the very fringe, the thrust out into the unknown.' He paused. 'I guess that is part of my excitement about the whole thing.'

'I can see that. It's certainly an exciting prospect. As you say, you are, to some extent, gambling on the future. If you are willing to risk all you have to grasp this opportunity, you might end up building an empire. On the other hand, you could lose everything.' There was silence for a few minutes. 'These are adventurous times; and it could lead to limitless possibilities.' Tom gave a little laugh. 'I envy you your position in having such a decision to make.'

They must keep steady heads. William was asking their opinion, their guidance in the assessment of this property. They must put prudence to the fore. Will's enthusiasm was infectious and, now they had seen the place, all were convinced that, in their friend's position, they would have no doubt. They would take the gamble; risk whatever it took. To take up this land, to own it, to look over the vast expanse and know that this is mine was almost beyond imagination.

But they must be a constraining influence on Will. He had asked them to help in his decision-making. Now they must be objective and fulfil their function and not be carried along by excitement. They must give considered advice based on facts, their knowledge and their experience in their separate fields.

'If you decide to buy, where do you intend getting building materials for a homestead?' It was George speaking, George whose home was very important to him. 'Caroline has been used to a very nice home. The rectory is a good solid house, roomy and comfortable. This will certainly be a change for her.'

'Oh, I'm very aware of that,' William cut in. 'She's keen about this whole thing, but of course has no concept of what it's like here. I have suggested we live in a small hut while I get the place established — possibly for two years. Then we will choose a spot and build a homestead; a really good building. Stone I plan, as I said earlier. It is cool and solid.'

'That sounds all right. Where do you get this stone?'

'On the western side. We will go there tomorrow. I'm not sure, mind you, that it will be suitable. I saw it only briefly, but I do think it should make a beautiful building material. Of course, we will have to bring stonemasons from Adelaide for an extended stay, but I think this is feasible.'

'What about floors and doors and any framework? Are there any large trees, big enough to provide timber that will be needed? There don't seem to be many in the parts we have seen.' Herb with his interest in the watercourses and plant life had noted the lack of big trees. 'You couldn't take the coolabah trees from beside the creek, even if they made good timber for building.'

William agreed.

'We will have to bring the necessary timber from Adelaide,' he said. 'What we will need for yards and the hut I think we can get from around here. The huts and store will be temporary, only having to last till we build in stone. So they won't have to withstand the elements for any great length of time.'

The enthusiasm of the advisers was mounting. They could not hold back forever. Their approach had been cautious so far. How much longer before they could give rein to their feelings?

There seemed to be no insurmountable difficulties. Tomorrow they would look at the stone and determine if it was a feasible building material and could be transported to the homestead site without undue problems.

The last self-imposed reservations were vanquished when William's friends gazed at the stone suggested for the homestead. 'The colours in this stone are unbelievable!' George was picking up the various coloured pieces. 'A wall of this will be a painting in itself. You are fortunate beyond words to have this beautiful material to work with.' He chipped various pieces with the little pick he had brought. 'It seems eminently suitable for a building material. I suggest we take a few small pieces back with us to have this confirmed by a stonemason.'

Their jubilation was beyond bounds.

'So you agree I am not being overly impulsive, unrealistic, in proposing to buy this land?' William looked at his friends. 'My dream is not just a romantic fantasy?'

Tom gave their considered opinion. He studied a rock as he spoke. 'There is a risk. It is untried as grazing land.' He looked up. 'But if I had the decision to make, I couldn't get to the Lands Office quickly enough to make it mine.'

6

The deeds secured

It was an excited William who set off to finalise the purchase of the land he had selected. He had all the details in his pocket. He put his hand inside his coat to assure himself he had put the papers there. Yes. He could feel them there. He knew he had picked them up. He'd better calm down or he'd be making a mistake or a fool of himself.

He glanced at his watch. Five minutes to ten. He would call at the bank and just make certain there would be no hold-up with the payment and have a word with the manager.

He turned in at the door of the bank, striding across the polished wood floor. A clerk came to the desk. 'Could I see Mr Fisher for a few minutes, please?' he asked the clerk.

'I'll just see if he is in, sir,' the clerk replied. 'Please take a seat.' He indicated some chairs by the wall.

William had hardly sat down when the glass-panelled door opened and the manager came out briskly. 'Good morning, Mr

Bartlett. A pleasure to see you.'

William rose and shook hands with him. 'Just a few minutes of your time, Mr Fisher, to elaborate on the short note I sent you regarding my plans.'

The manager led the way into the office and motioned William to a chair. 'You are planning to buy some land and so will be drawing on your capital. You will not be reinvesting the money?'

'Not all of it,' William replied. He went on to acquaint the man of his intentions. After fifteen minutes, when they had discussed the matter enthusiastically, William rose to go. 'Thank you for your cooperation,' he said, shaking hands. 'And I value your judgment and advice.'

He left the bank and headed down the street for the government offices. Just this formality now and the first step would be complete. The land would be his.

The transaction in the government office was almost an anticlimax. It all happened so quickly and passed through without any hitches. William gave the details of the land. It was marked on the map. The deed was made out. He handed over his cheque and received the deeds. It was his. He was now a landowner. He had taken his first leap out in faith.

He remembered Granny Etty's words: 'Ask God to take your hand, my boy, and step out in faith. And God be with you.' He must go and tell Caro.

Caroline was sewing in the parlour. She had chosen this room because it had a good view of the drive and she had had one eye in that direction since ten o'clock. What if someone else had already taken out title on that land? Willy would be so disappointed. But that was really most unlikely. Besides, who else would want to go so far into unknown (unproven, too, she thought) territory?

She smiled, thinking of Willie's enthusiasm. He would make a go of it. She had no doubts.

As the clock struck half-past eleven, she looked up to see William approaching the house. She dropped her work and ran to the door. William bounded up the steps and grasped her hands. 'The deed is done, Caro. I've bought it.' He fished in his pocket and pulled out the deed, waving it before her. 'The land is mine. We haven't got anything on it yet, apart from 'roos, emus and natives maybe, but the land is mine.'

They hugged each other and twirled around in excitement. Caroline's mother, hearing the excitement, hurried down the hall. William released Caroline and waved the deeds to her. 'Mrs Hilliard, I've done it. It's all signed and sealed and delivered. The land is mine,' he cried.

She clasped her hands in pleasure. 'Oh William, I'm so pleased. Congratulations.'

There was much talk and questions and excitement. When Caroline's father came in, it had to be all gone over again and the map taken out and pored over to see just where the land was and how one got there. It continued over lunch and well into the afternoon.

Eventually William said, 'Caro, we can't go on calling it 'the land'. That's got no character. We've got to give it a name.'

The rest of the afternoon was taken up with suggestions and rejections from all and sundry. At last, after still coming to no conclusion, William took his leave, promising to call again on Sunday and asking all to please think of something suitable, something with feeling in it.

The bell was ringing for the eleven o'clock service when Caroline, tarrying by the rectory steps, saw William turn into the drive. He turned his horse into the little paddock and they hurried across to the church. The choir was just processing in from the vestry singing 'Thy hand, O God, has guided'. William and Caroline looked at each other. He squeezed her hand. 'I believe I was guided, Caro,' he whispered. 'It will be well.'

It was late that evening when they had almost talked themselves out — all the plans, all the things to be done — that William said, 'And we still don't have a name for it.'

The suggestions had included names of places enjoyed overseas. Caroline's father had suggested names of places he had loved in England. His wife added more — the ancestral names of Willie's grandfather and so on. But none had seemed to them just right.

William said, 'You know, Caro, we'll have a mountain to climb. It will be a long pull up. We'll be a long way from friends and family. We won't even have a proper house for a couple of years or so and there'll be a lot of work. We really are starting from scratch.'

Suddenly he threw up his hand. 'I know. We'll call the place 'Bibbaringa'. It's an Aboriginal word meaning 'mountain'. We'll climb to the top of the mountain together and survey our kingdom.'

And so it was decided. The newly acquired property of Mr William Bartlett as recorded in the Titles Office of the South Australian government was officially named 'Bibbaringa'.

7

Nuptials

The day dawned clear and sunny. Caroline stretched her toes to the bottom of the bed. Today she would become Mrs William Bartlett, wife of the owner of 'Bibbaringa', an extensive property in the north-east of the colony of South Australia. She hugged herself with excitement.

How grand it all seemed. She lay daydreaming of hypothetical meetings with ladies during her honeymoon.

'Good morning, Mrs Bartlett. Now where do you come from, my dear? Where is your home?'

'Oh my husband's property is up north, Mrs Fitzwilliam.'

'Indeed! Is it a very large holding?'

'Oh yes, to be sure. We can stand at our garden gate and the land as far as we can see is ours. I can't remember how many square miles it covers.'

'Goodness me! It must be extremely large! I do not recall having heard a holding described in square miles before. Now tell me, is it a sheep or cattle property? Or do you run both?'

'At the moment, Mrs Fitzwilliam, we run kangaroos, wallaroos, emus and Aborigines . . . '

She broke off her little fantasy, giggling at the absurdity of it.

Annabella, sleeping on the other side of the bed, stirred and rose up on one elbow, looking at Caroline. 'What are you laughing about?' she said. Then she added, 'This is it, Carry. This is your wedding day.' She dropped back onto her pillow and was silent.

After a moment Caroline, sensing something was amiss, turned and looked at her sister. Was that a tear on her lashes? 'What is it, Bella?' she said softly.

Annabella brushed her hand across her eyes and took a quick, shaky breath. 'It's just that I shall miss you so much,' she whispered.

Caroline hugged her sister. 'I shall miss you, too. But I'll come home again, you know.'

'But you'll be so far away and letters will take for ever to get to you. I won't see you for a whole year when you go.'

The tears really flowed now. The two girls lay clasped in each other's arms. 'I do want you to be happy. I know you love Willie and want to marry him. And I think he'll make a lovely brother. But oh! I wish you weren't going so far away.'

For a few minutes, the separation seemed insurmountable.

Caroline reached for her handkerchief and, blowing her nose and wiping her eyes, scolded her sister. 'Now come on. Stop it now. Here, wipe your eyes or we'll have red noses and eyes for the wedding. Let's get up now and go and pick the flowers before the sun touches them.'

Caroline slipped out of bed and began dressing. Annabella followed and soon the mood had passed, the excitement of the present day overshadowing future loneliness.

'Let's just have one more look at our dresses. They are beautiful,' Annabella cried. They tiptoed to the room where Caroline's bridal dress and the bridesmaids' dresses were hanging.

Annabella was to be chief bridesmaid and two of their cousins were also to be bridesmaids.

They gazed at Caroline's dress. How lovely it was. All the wedding attire had been lain out in readiness, the veil hanging from the wardrobe's carved top, spread out in soft folds across the carpet. On the duchess were the gloves and jewellery and all the necessities for their coiffure.

Caroline picked up the little velvet box Willie had given her the previous night. She lifted the lid and took out the two dainty, carved ivory side combs.

How beautiful they were. Willie had secured them from someone who dealt in curios and beautiful things from the East. What artistry was in the delicate carving. She would wear them always, all through their years of life together. It was just like Willie to think of a wedding gift so practical, so beautiful and so personal.

She tucked them back into their places in the box and, closing the lid, placed it back beside the brush and comb. 'Come on, Bella. The sun will be on those flowers and Mother will be up in a minute.'

The two girls tiptoed down the hall and, taking baskets and secateurs, opened the heavy front door and hurried down the garden.

Elizabeth Hilliard woke as the door latch slipped into place. This is the day, she thought. This is my daughter's wedding day. My baby is grown up. She is a woman about to set up her own home. My family is breaking up. She felt a little ache around her heart — if only she wasn't going so far away.

She pulled herself up sharply. This line of thought would very soon lead to tears — she must put aside her own feelings. The tightness in her throat made it hard to swallow. She must show a happy face to Caroline and enter into her joy. Her husband stirred beside her. 'Oh, it's morning already,' he yawned. 'Well, my dear, are you ready for the big event?'

'As ready as I can be,' she replied. 'The tables are all set for the reception after the ceremony and the food is prepared. There are just the flowers to be done. But, James!' She turned to him. 'Our little girl is grown up and leaving the nest.' She stifled a tear.

'But you are happy about it, aren't you? William is a fine young man. You are fond of him?'

'Oh yes. It's not that. It's just she's going so far away. The years have gone so quickly. It only seems like yesterday she was born and all that joy and love came into our lives. And now she's leaving us. But there. I must get up and see to things and stop feeling sorry for myself. I think the girls have gone out to pick the flowers. Wasn't it lovely to have all those flowers come last night from our parishioners? May is coming at eight o'clock to do the church flowers.'

She swung her legs over the side of the bed and gave him a playful slap. 'Come on. Rise and shine. 'This is the day the Lord has made. Let us rejoice and be glad in it.''

As the family finished breakfast in the sun room (the dining room was already set for the wedding reception), a carriage was heard approaching the house. Annabella ran to the door when the heavy knocker fell. She came back to the sun room, her arms laden with flowers, her face glowing.

'These are from Government House,' she gasped. 'Sir Edmund sent them in his own carriage.'

'Oh how kind, how thoughtful!' exclaimed Elizabeth.

'He really is a kind man. A wonderful friend,' agreed her husband. 'Put them in the scullery where they'll be cool, my dear. I suppose you will soon be starting on the arranging.'

There was much ado and excitement.

He rose and went off to his study to make sure again that he himself had everything ready for the ceremony. He would welcome young William as a son-in-law — a fine young fellow with a good head on his shoulders. His grandfather's legacy hadn't spoiled him, either. This venture with the land was a risk, but he was young and not afraid of work. Yes. He would be a fine addition to their family.

In the business of preparation, time flew. There had been a stream of people calling to wish the young couple well, to leave gifts and offer assistance in many ways.

James had a call to a sick bed, but thankfully was not away too long. The extra help engaged for the reception had arrived and they were ensconced in the kitchen, taking care of the food.

Elizabeth stood at the door of the dining room surveying her handiwork. It really did look nice, she congratulated herself. The long trestle tables borrowed for the occasion were covered with starched white damask cloths. Matching serviettes were folded at each place with a small rose tucked in the folds. The cutlery, silver dishes and jugs loaned by various members of the family sparkled and gleamed, all polished to a mirror finish. Chairs from all these family homes were lined up on each side in readiness.

At the middle of each table, May had arranged a high epergne filled with flowers, trails of ivy and fern flowing out along the snowy cloths. Trails of greenery had been wound along the curtain rods with small garlands of flowers in the centre. A huge bowl of massed flowers stood on the table under the front window. The silver serving dishes gleamed on the sideboard ready for the hot food.

Yes. It really did look beautiful. Elizabeth

was pleased. She was lucky to have this lovely big room.

The folding doors between the dining and sitting rooms had been opened and pushed back by the wall. This created a very large room, a good setting for the reception. The parish council had been wise when they built this house and thought of the future. The parish was growing. Settlement had extended out a long way in the two decades since she and James had arrived in Adelaide — and the town was still growing. It would not be many years before St Augustine's would be in the centre instead of the outskirts of Adelaide.

At this moment of her musing, there was a thunderous knock on the door. She could hear one of the girls going down the hall in answer to it. She heard voices and the study door open — obviously someone to see James.

Annabella came up behind her. 'That man nearly knocked the door down, didn't he?' she said. 'Ahh! Can you smell him? He's drunk and wanting to see Father. Today of all days! Why do they always come at these times?'

James Hilliard put his head round the door. 'There you are, my dear. This fellow wants some food. He's under the weather, but I guess he still gets hungry — says he has no money to buy anything. Would it be too much trouble for you to put something together for him?'

'No, of course not. I'll make him some sandwiches and a pot of tea.' Elizabeth hurried off to the kitchen.

'He had money to buy the drink he wanted,' commented Annabella.

Her father sighed. 'Yes. Unfortunately, his kind of people aren't always wise with their money. Or their lives,' he said. 'I think I'll take him out under the pepper tree to have it. He'll be comfortable there and the house won't smell like a bad brewery for the reception. Tell Mother I'll put the garden table and chair there for him.'

Annabella laughed. 'Really, you know it is rather appropriate him coming just now when we are about to get dressed for Carry's wedding. It's what we've grown up with, isn't it? All the unexpected interruptions to our plans and programs!' She turned to the door. 'It brings you down to earth, doesn't it?' she called over her shoulder as she followed her mother to the kitchen.

At a quarter to eleven, they were almost ready.

Elizabeth could hear the organ. She had seen members of the choir hurrying up the path to the vestry door. Old Mr Peters, the verger, had been hovering around the church door and was no doubt now supervising the ushers in their duties.

How well May had done the flowers in the church! Each pew had its ribbon bow and posy of flowers — and the arch where the bride and groom would stand was a work of art. There were four brass vases on the altar and a large brass jardinière supporting a huge arrangement on the little table near the front at the entrance to the church.

She glanced out of the window. There was the bishop arriving with his wife. How good of them to come and for him to consent to take part in the ceremony.

She turned from the window. She must see if all was well in the kitchen, then check on the girls. Caroline would perhaps need her to help with her veil.

As she came back towards the girls' bedroom, she heard a carriage pull up outside the church. She looked out. Sir Edmund's coach with the vice-regal crest on the door was at the church. His groom had opened the door and was just letting down the steps. It was an honour to have the governor of the colony as a guest at the wedding.

She hurried along to her daughters' bedroom. She could hear a titter of excited voices behind the closed door. She opened the door and caught her breath at the sight she beheld. Caroline, her fair golden hair gleaming in a beam of sunlight coming in the window, was breathtaking.

The dress had been right. She was glad she had spent the time on all that beading. The pearls and crystals lent a soft glow and sparkle to the organza and lace. Then there was the satin ribbon bows with the clusters of orange blossoms catching up the lace tiers at the sides of the dress, the graceful train, the wide neck on the edge of her shoulders, the lace falling gently almost to her elbows, the tight-fitting bodice. Oh, it was all a sight to behold.

Annabella and the other girls were beautiful, too. The gold taffeta was the colour of sunlight, she thought. They really complemented Caroline's appearance.

She stood there for perhaps a minute before Caroline caught sight of her.

'Oh Mother, thank goodness you are here. Will you fix my veil, please? I don't want to catch the tulle on the orange blossoms.' She moved carefully to the duchess and sat on the stool.

Elizabeth took the soft veil in her hands and, placing it on the curls piled high on her head, secured it in position. As she stepped back to view the effect, she heard the door knocker. 'Who on earth just now?' she cried. 'It's almost eleven o'clock!'

A knock came on the bedroom door. A head appeared around the door. 'There's a lady would like to see you, Mrs Hilliard,' the girl said.

Elizabeth hurried to the front hall to see Henrietta Drabsch waiting for her. She held out her hand in greeting. What on earth did William's grandmother want at this time? Surely there was no trouble?

Henrietta came forward. 'I'm so sorry to come so late, Elizabeth. I hope I am not inconveniencing you. I was delayed.' She opened her bag. 'I have a locket here. It is very old and very precious in my family. It belonged to my grandmother and the women in my family have worn it at their wedding ever since. I should like Caroline, if she is willing, to wear it today.'

She withdrew a little parcel from a velvet bag and unrolled it while she was speaking. She held out her open hand. On her palm lay a round locket. There was a glass-enclosed portrait of a young bride, surrounded by dainty gold filigree work set with pearls.

'Do you think it will be in keeping with her ensemble?' she asked.

'I think it is perfect,' Elizabeth smiled. 'Come along to the bedroom. You must clasp it round her neck yourself.' The expression on the old lady's face amply rewarded Elizabeth for her thoughtful suggestion.

The two women hurried back to the room where the bride was ready. Henrietta placed the locket around Caroline's neck. 'You are right, Elizabeth. It is perfect. Thank you, my dear, for letting me have a little share in your wedding day — and for making an old woman happy,' she added. She kissed Caroline's cheek gently. 'I must go over to the church or I shall be late.'

They all rose, pausing a moment to let her be seated before the bridal party arrived at the church door. Elizabeth led the way and entered the church. The head usher escorted her to her seat.

The crucifer and acolytes were waiting with the bishop and James at the door, as the bride and her maids, with her Uncle John, who was to give her away, came across the lawn from the rectory.

The signal was given.

The organ swelled to the Bridal March.

The congregation rose.

The bridegroom turned and the bridal procession entered the church.

The ceremony of the Solemnization of Matrimony began.

8

A beginning

He was a fine beast, no doubt about that. The handler led him round the ring, moving slowly to show off his points. He moved well, carried himself well.

The auctioneer was reeling off the spiel of virtues. Owned by G. Messenger and Co. of Gawler, he was from a superior herd renowned for quality. Their cattle had the reputation of being good foragers on open range, resulting in good weight gain. Good doers. They were fertile, giving good results in calving. Calving troubles were rare.

The auctioneer had started the bidding. The bids were coming thick and fast. The bull was being paraded again. Once, twice round the ring.

The men on the stands were intent. Tension was mounting. He would have some fierce competition for this bull. But what a prize for his herd! He'd hold off a bit longer till the bidding was drawing to a close.

'The gentleman on my right has the bid. Going once . . . '

William raised his hand. The auctioneer's offsider took the bid. It started again. The price rose with each nod of the head. The jumps were smaller now.

How much further should he go? It was imperative to have the best bulls he could muster in this initial stage of his venture. There were four hundred cows he had bought, two hundred from Tom's father and 100 from two other large, well-known cattle strains. The bulls he had already bought today were all good, but this fellow was a magnificent animal. The auctioneer's head jerked quickly from William to his rival bidder. The attention of the surrounding crowd was riveted on the spectacle of the fight for possession. The price was rising steeply. How far would they go? This fight would be told at bull sales for years to come.

'Any further bid? Am I offered any further rise? Going once . . . The bid is in favour of the gentleman at the back of the stand.' He glanced quickly from one bidder to the other. An almost imperceptible shake of the head came from one. He held up his hand. 'Any further bid? Going, going, gone. Sold to Mr William Bartlett of 'Bibbaringa.' '

There was a thunderous applause. For these cattlemen, the contest had been as good as a sideshow.

The auctioneer held up his hand for silence. 'It may be of interest to all assembled to know that Mr Bartlett has recently purchased a large holding in the north-east of this colony. It is in as yet uncharted land. He will be a pathfinder. He has already purchased good strains of females and today has bought bulls for the herd, finalising with this memorable purchase of 'Gawler Pride'. He will shortly set out on the mammoth journey, taking his cattle to 'Bibbaringa'. I am sure you would all want me to wish him well in his enterprise. It is on such intrepid daring that the growth of this country will depend.'

Again there was applause. William moved uncomfortably in his seat. There was a hubbub of voices. Men he had not met came up to him to give their congratulations and hear more of 'Bibbaringa'. 'Gawler Pride' was the last offering on the morning list. For the moment, business was over and the social time begun. The moving stream of male humanity made its way to the refreshment booth.

The next job for William was to check again the supplies list. Caroline had been through it and added considerably more items. All the family had joined in. The thing was, you might forget the most everyday things just because they were always there at hand. This list had to cover all they might need for the next six months. There would be no shops, no mail, no transport through which to procure anything they might forget. It was daunting, but at the same time daring and exciting. Especially for Caroline.

The bullocky with his teams had been hired to transport the supplies. He would follow the drovers with the cattle and one hundred horses. The horses were mostly stockhorses, with a sprinkling of draught-horses for the heavy work.

They must think of everything that would be needed. William had almost forgotten the harness for the draughthorses and the heavy chains for clearing.

He went over and over the list.

At last he set out for the Adelaide Pastoralists Supplies Company. There was a wave of excitement through the staff as William presented them with his long list of requirements. He explained his position and gave the date of departure. All must be packed and well secured in time for an orderly beginning.

Yuelty had been given the responsibility of securing three other Aboriginal stockmen. He could be trusted to find suitable fellows. There remained four experienced, reliable white stockmen to find.

William left the supplies company and stood on the footpath considering his next move. Where would he get hold of the type of men he wanted to employ? He could go to the labour exchange, but what assurance would he have? He needed men who were willing to stay in the bush for long stretches at a time, men who would not pack up and go at a moment's notice if they felt like it.

It would have to be single men. Later on, he might be able to employ married men with families, but to begin with, he and Caroline wouldn't have a house, let alone provide married quarters for workmen. They would need to be used to bush work, too — men who knew the bush, men who didn't get lost at the drop of a hat.

'Excuse me.' The voice came from behind him. William swung round. The man had just come from the supplies shop. 'I couldn't help overhearing what you said inside.' He jerked his head towards the door. 'Wouldn't be looking for some drovers, I suppose?'

William looked at the man. He guessed his age would be in the mid-forties. He looked as though he had been around the bush for a while — certainly didn't look like a city slicker.

'Well yes, I do need some drovers. You looking for a job?'

The man hitched his trousers. 'Yeah . . . like to get out in the bush again. Little bit of this town life goes a long way.' He spoke quietly, rather slowly. 'Been around here for a couple of years, but like to get right out again. Couldn't help hearing you say you were ordering six months' supplies. Must be well out you're going, eh?'

William was liking the man. He didn't know him from a bar of soap, but there was something about him he felt he could trust. 'You could say that. Well out.' William told him the general area. 'Can't run off to the town every week. No hotels or grog shops where I'm going. In fact, no shops or businesses of any kind.'

'Suits me.' He hitched his pants again and pushed his hat on the back of his head.

'Got any ties here in Adelaide or round about?'

William was surprised by the expression that crossed the man's face. His mouth tightened. 'No ties,' he said. 'No ties at all.'

'William Bartlett's my name. If you're willing to work for me and come into my part of this state, consider yourself hired.' He held out his hand.

'Wilkes. Ted Wilkes,' the man said, taking William's hand. 'I'll be glad to come. Thanks.' They shook hands and proceeded to talk about conditions and pay as they walked slowly along the street.

As they reached the end of the street, William stopped and turned to him. 'Would you by any chance know of a couple of other reliable fellows looking for work in the bush? Long-term bush. Three, actually, I want.'

'I know of two others,' he said. 'Worked with them a couple of years back. We'd find them at the 'Crown and Anchor'. They're not drunkards. Just looking for a bit of company and some fun while they're in town.'

'Don't begrudge a man that, or a drink,' William said. 'I've got no place for a man whose life is ruled by drink, though.'

'They're good fellows. I reckon you'd have no cause for complaint.'

They retraced their steps to the 'Crown and Anchor'. There was the usual babble of voices and gusts of male laughter as they entered. Ted looked through the door into the billiard room.

'There they are,' he said as he led the way into the room. One man was aiming, his cue moving slowly back and forth. He was of medium height, broad-shouldered with light brown hair — an athletic-looking fellow. He wore clean, tidy work gear and riding boots.

Another young man about the same age, possibly mid-twenties, was leaning on his cue watching. He was dressed in similar attire, but there the similarity ended. This man was tall and lean, with a shock of thick black hair. His skin was perhaps naturally dark, but tanned by the sun to almost black. William wondered what racial mixture made up his ancestry.

The cue hit the ball and it went straight into the pocket. 'Good shot,' said Ted stepping forward. The young man swung round.

'Good day, Ted,' he called. 'Come to have a game?'

'No. I've come to see if you want a job. A bush job. Way out.' He turned to William. 'This is Jacko, Mr Bartlett. And this hobo being held up by his cue is Snowy.' The men came forward to shake hands. 'They're good all-round workers. Can stay on a horse — and know one end of a cow from the other.'

'Are you interested in a job that will take you right out?' William asked. 'Into country not yet on the map?'

Both young faces were answer to the question. Here William could see the call of adventure and challenge in their faces. He talked for some time, explaining the position of the property, the job of droving the cattle over untamed terrain and then the establishing, from scratch, of his cattle station. Their eyes shone with excitement at the prospect.

'You're willing to take it on, then?' He smiled. 'The isolation doesn't bother you?'

They both emphatically asserted their keenness to accompany him and join in the task of setting up 'Bibbaringa'.

'There's just one thing,' William said as they were about to part. 'I've recently married and my wife will be accompanying us. We intend to build a hut first off when we get there and later, of course, build a homestead.'

The young men looked at each other and at Ted.

William lifted his eyebrows in question. 'I hope this will not bother you.' He turned to Ted. 'Sorry I forgot to mention this to you.'

Ted nodded, a strange serious expression on his face.

'This doesn't make any difference, does it?' he asked, concerned. 'My wife is a good horsewoman. She hasn't done a trip like this, of course, but she knows what to expect. She's keen to come with us and will do her part on the journey.'

'Will she be able to take the long day in the saddle?'

'And sleep on the ground?' added Snowy. 'Not the usual sort of caper for a woman.'

'What if she decides she can't take it when we're halfway there with all the cattle and drays and so on?' interjected Ted.

'I'm sure that won't happen. She's a very plucky lady. She's looking forward to it. I've got a small tent for a bit of privacy for her. It's easily erected when we get to camp each night. You won't have too many restrictions by her presence, I assure you. Just reasonable decency.'

Though obviously still doubtful, they relaxed somewhat at William's assurances. Taking a woman? On a trek that could involve all kinds of weather? What was she like? Couldn't be an English rose. Have to be tougher than that to take this sort of caper on. A woman joining a droving team — and no house or hut or anything when they got there! Hope this new boss knew what he was doing.

They parted, still shaking their heads. What would old Ted make of this, the young fellows wondered. He'd looked worried. But then women weren't all the same, any more than blokes were all the same.

Oh well! That's what the boss wanted, so they'd give it a go and see how it turned out.

9

The journey to 'Bibbaringa'

The air was crisp and cold as they gathered at the holding paddocks. The sun was not yet quite up, but it was going to be a clear day: good for their beginning. The cattle were quiet, having settled down in the yards. The feed and water had done their work.

When William and Caroline arrived, Yuelty and the three black stockmen he had secured were already there. They were watching the bullocky bring his beasts in to yoke them and connect up the waggon. Each bullock must be in his accustomed place. The two leaders were magnificent beasts. The drays stood to one side. William inspected the loads, talking to the drivers and repeating again the instructions for the journey.

He and the drovers would lead off with the mob of cattle and the horses. The drays would follow and then the bullock waggons. It was all orderly. The plans had all been made. All the men knew their responsibilities and now it was active, busy preparation for the departure.

Caroline sat with her parents and Annabelle in the carriage. Her horse was tied up close by, grazing quietly.

'So this is it, Carry. Do take care of yourself. This journey worries me a good deal. Do be careful to change if you get wet. Don't stay in wet clothes — and the same with your boots. There's nothing worse than staying in wet boots to give you a chill.'

'Don't worry, Mother. I'll take the greatest care. I know I must look after myself. I can't get sick on the way. That would be terrible.' She paused.

'I'll hear your voice scolding me and telling me to be careful every time a shower comes over.' She smiled lovingly at her mother.

Dear Mother. What would she do without her presence and surrounding love? But she was a big girl now — a married woman, in fact. She must accept responsibility for herself and not only care for herself, but for her husband's well-being, too.

She thought again of the medical kit she had prepared and the instructions from her mother and Aunt May as they tried to provide for any mishap or injury that may eventuate on the journey. But then, it wouldn't stop when they reached their destination. This would be an ongoing thing.

For the first time, Caroline began to realise

the enormity of what she was facing. Until now, the excitement of the purchase of the land, the wedding, the homecoming from their honeymoon and the preparation for the journey had blurred the reality of it all. This moment of parting brought it all suddenly and brilliantly into focus. She was leaving not only her home, her family, but everyone and everything that was familiar, all the means of support she had always known and taken for granted. And more, she was leaving the settled lands, heading out into the great immensity of isolation.

Her heart gave a great leap as panic welled up in her. What if she did get ill — not just on the trip, but when they arrived at Willie's precious land? What if Willie got sick? There would be no Mother, no Aunty May to consult, to guide her, advise her. In fact, there would be no other woman to talk to, even — about anything! What on earth was she doing? She must be mad!

'Almost ready to start off, Caro.' It was Willie beside her, his face aglow with excitement. He squeezed her hand. She looked up at him, all her love for him flooding back. This was why she was doing this crazy thing. 'Whither Thou goes I will go.' She would go with him wherever he went.

She swallowed the lump in her throat and

smiled. 'We'll say our goodbyes, then. The time will go quickly till we see you all again.'

Caroline mounted her horse. Suddenly there was movement. The gates were opened. The stockmen black and white, busy and intent on moving the cattle out quietly, headed them off along the stock route. This would be routine until they got beyond the extent of settlement into the unfenced, uninhabited areas. They'd think of that later. For now, they'd keep them moving, calmly but surely.

'God watch over you,' said Caroline's father as he kissed her tenderly. 'Peace be with you, my Carry.'

They moved off. The cavalcade was on its way. As the sun tipped over the horizon, the cattle streamed out. The creaking of the drays added to the pound of horses' hoofs, the plodding of the cattle. There was the crack of the bullocky's whip, his voice urging his beasts to action, the creaking and clanking of harness as the bullocks moved, straining to start the waggon wheels turning, falling into a rhythmic pattern as the whole symphony of sound swelled.

The little farewell party watched. The tears flowed. Silent prayers were offered for the thousandth time for safety on the journey and 'till we meet again'.

They watched until the last waggon disappeared, until only a haze of dust rose to indicate the whereabouts of the travellers. Then the farewelling party turned the carriage back towards St Augustine's. There was work to be done. Life must go on.

It was a long day. They had stopped for lunch by a river. For Caroline, the respite was more than welcome. Already she was stiff, but the morning had been wonderful. She had taken her place at the side where Willie had suggested. In a few days, she would really be able to pull her weight, she thought. The cook's dray had gone ahead then and, by the time the cavalcade had reached its destination for the first day, the campfire was burning and the smell of camp stew was wafting out to tease the appetites of the party.

As day followed day, they fell into a routine. In the pre-dawn, the cook would be stirring the fire to life, tossing on wood he had gathered the afternoon before, filling the billies and hanging them over the flames. Young Splinter, the fourth man of the white team of stockmen, had the job of bringing in the horses for the day's ride.

Caroline enjoyed this time — the day beginning but not yet under way. Willie was already up and out supervising. She lay thinking of this adventure and of the men

Willie had employed. He was pleased with them. They were proving their worth.

She smiled as she thought of their attitude to her. They had been wary of her at first, waiting for signs of discontent, expecting complaints. She had rubbed her muscles with oil and gradually they had grown accustomed to the day in the saddle. Her skin was becoming tanned as much as anyone with such fair skin could tan. She was careful to wear her sleeves long — and her wide hat. Though she was tired and looked it, she did not complain. The men's respect for her grew and there were many thoughtful little actions unmentioned, but kindly extended and gratefully accepted by Caroline.

She heard Willie's voice approaching, slid out of the swag and dressed quickly. 'You're up.' He put his head around the tent flap. 'We're just about leaving civilisation behind, Caro. Today we should see the last fences. Open range. Freedom.'

She looked at him, his face alight with the prospect. What a darling he was! The last fence was being left behind! No doubt he felt he had the rest of the world at his feet.

Her own heart skipped a beat as she contemplated what this meant. Suddenly, she felt very ill-equipped. She should have prepared herself so much more. Could she remember all Mother and Aunt May had instructed her in? She was well-trained in running a home with dignity and hospitality, but this was a different situation entirely. When was she likely to even see another woman to exchange a few words with?

She had thought she understood all the consequences of this adventure to go into the great unknown, uninhabited land. She was coming to realise she had not begun to be aware of even half the implications.

Oh well, she had made her decision. It was far too late to get cold feet now. She had just better pull herself together and face it all with confidence.

Willie had no such fears or anxieties. She must be equally positive. It was really very exciting. No doubt they would manage admirably — and, in a very short while, they might even have neighbours. She would not always be the only woman in a man's world.

Breakfast was over. Yuelty would now lead the party. This was where the value of his knowledge of the direction, feed and water for the cattle was beyond estimating. Without his leadership, the possibility of the successful completion of the journey would be very different.

Caroline paused beside him as she made her way to the waggon. 'You lead us now,

Yuelty?' she asked. He nodded.

'You see mountains way out today, Mrs? Big mountains. Many paintings my people those mountains.' He pointed north.

'Paintings? Your people's paintings?' questioned Caroline. He nodded again. 'In caves? On rock?' she continued.

'My people paint. Long time ago. Much my Dreaming those mountains.'

'They are special place for your people?' asked Caroline. He nodded again. 'Thank you for telling me. I would like to see them some time.'

'Some time I show you. Some painting very special. Dreaming painting. I can't show you.'

She nodded seriously, understanding some paintings were of such significance he was not at liberty to show her. 'One time, after we get these cattle to 'Bibbaringa' and we get settled, that one time you show me, eh?'

He lifted his head and smiled, his white teeth vivid in his black face. 'I show,' he said simply.

The sun was hot today. It was a clear sky. There was good feed. There must have been rain recently. The cattle were enjoying the fresh pick.

As afternoon wore on, they came out into more open country. Now they must keep the cattle together and not let them stray too wide. Having established their social order, the same leaders were always in front. The others would follow. Finding their cronies, they would travel in this order. What herd creatures they were.

Caroline could see now the distant mountains, majestic in their colour and grandeur. She would hold Yuelty to his promise one day when they were settled.

That night, as Caroline finished her meal, Snowy came and stood beside her. The fire had burned down and the others were filling their mugs from the billy. He squatted down, holding out a stirrup strap that had snapped that day.

'Oh thankyou, Snowy, you've fixed it,' Caroline said.

'Didn't take much doin', Mrs Bartlett. Glad to do it. You've been a real trooper on this trip. We were worried, you know, when the boss said he was bringing you along.'

Caroline looked up and laughed. 'I could see you were all expecting me to faint or something, that first week. Have I passed the test already? We're not there yet.'

'Aw, you'll be all right. Must have had some aches, though.' She nodded assent. 'Old Ted, he was really worried. See, his Mrs couldn't take the colony. Came out from

England, ya know. Never seen anything like this. They were out a way and, when she got cryin' and complainin', Ted came in to Adelaide. Got a job at the saleyards so she could be in town and have some social life. Wasn't his kind of work at all.

'But she still wasn't satisfied. Finally wanted to go back to the old country. Ted used all the money he'd saved to get a place of his own to buy her a ticket back and have enough to set up when she got there. Thing was, she took their two kids, too. Doesn't say much, but it must have knocked him about, I reckon.'

'Oh, I am sorry to hear that,' Caroline said. 'He seems a very fine man.'

'Yeah, good bloke, old Ted.'

'And you all thought I might be like that?' Caroline asked with a smile. 'I'm glad you think otherwise now. I'll leave you all to your men's talk now and I'll go and do a few things in my tent.' She stood up. 'Thank you again for fixing my strap and thankyou for telling me about Ted, Snowy. I appreciate your confidence in me.'

So that was why they had all been so anxious when she joined the party. Even so, they had not made her feel unwelcome. Of course, she was the boss's wife. But they could have made her feel uncomfortable. So she had passed the test. She smiled as she went to the tent.

They skirted the mountains, keeping them always in the distance. They had been weeks on the track now. Caroline had come to really enjoy the life — the fresh night air, the clear crisp mornings, the variety of the country as they travelled on. Perhaps she would even become infected with Willie's enthusiasm for these vast open spaces.

She wrote in her diary each night of the happenings with the cattle; the talk of the men; the birds, trees and wildflowers she saw on the way.

The slow pace of the journey had its charms — the lowing of the cattle as evening came on, the way a calf becoming separated from its mother would call and the cow answer. So it would go until the cow had located her calf — and then the rapturous sucking and tailwagging as the full teat of sweet, warm milk was found. Life was good.

For days they followed along the shores of a huge lake, crossing creeks and gullies that came down from the mountains. The variety of the country seemed endless.

At last one night, as they lay in their tent, Willie reached for her hand. 'Tomorrow, Mrs Bartlett, you and I will go ahead. I know the way now. Did you notice some of the trees marked with the axe?'

'No, I don't think I did. Did you mark them before?'

'We did blaze a trail when we came to select 'Bibbaringa', but not too closely. It was better to have Yuelty with us to lead us. But now I know where I'm going. We marked this part much more closely. We won't get lost now. We'll go ahead a couple of days, so we can find the spot by the creek where we'll build our hut.' He paused a minute. 'It will only be a temporary home — you realise that, don't you, Caro?'

'Of course. I've told you. I understand we can't do everything at once.'

'We can set out exactly where I want everything when the boys get there with the mob.' He was silent a minute.

'You know, I'm almost sad it's coming to an end,' Caroline said quietly.

'What? The camping and riding and smell of the cattle, the dust and everything?' Willie cried incredulously. 'I thought you'd hate all that. I was scared you'd be getting fed up with it all. And to think you've come to enjoy it! We'll make a drover of you yet!' He laughed happily.

The next morning, Willie and Caroline with their packhorses left the mob. There was some chayacking from the boys about not

93

getting lost as they headed north, ever north.

The days had merged into each other, dawn, noonday and sunset following, ever following the grand inexorable order of the universe. The pattern, the rhythm was coming to an end. Soon they would sleep in a hut in one place. There would not be the early call, the pound of the horses' feet as Splinter caught them and brought them in. The crackle of the camp fire and the cook's clanking would give way to settled domestic sounds.

How perverse I am, Caroline thought. Here I have been waiting to get to our destination. Now I'm getting sentimental about the trip coming to an end. But it has been good. Life is good. Now Willie and I can set up our 'Bibbaringa'.

They travelled quickly now, covering so much more territory just with their pack-horses. It was fun to have bursts of speed, urging their horses into a gallop, the wind taking her hat from her head and blowing through her hair. Oh, they could go on forever like this.

It was dusk on the third day when Willie drew rein. Caroline pulled up beside him. 'A little way along here now, Caro, we'll make camp. We've reached our destination. Welcome to 'Bibbaringa', Mrs Bartlett.'

10

Setting up

Caroline woke as the first tinge of light appeared on the faraway horizon. She lay in her bunk looking up at the dark sky above her. The stars were still bright. They had really arrived. This place was to be her home. Here she and Willie would build their homestead. Eventually, she reminded herself, then continued her daydream.

Here they would rear a family. How many children would they have — four, six, ten? She had a mental vision of herself surrounded by ten children, all looking like Willie — and she giggled to herself. Back to the present, she thought. Here they would build a kingdom, but today they must start at the beginning.

The camp fire had burned down and the morning air was cold. It would be warm when the sun came up. The air was so clear and fresh — lighter than Adelaide's. Perhaps this was because of the distance from the sea and the lower humidity. It was fresh, yet not clingy damp cold. There was a breeze blowing from the east.

She looked again at the horizon. A great glow of deep vermilion stretched the length of the eastern sky.

'Willie, are you awake?' She touched him softly.

He opened sleepy eyes. 'What are you doing awake so early? It's not light yet.'

'Look, Willie. Just look. I had to wake you.'

They sat up, pulling their clothes on. The breeze was cool. Over the ridges, the faraway horizon seemed to stretch away into infinity. The glow was spreading deeper into the sky, its expanse narrowing. The stars were still bright above.

As they watched, a golden glow appeared above the flush of vermilion. To the north and the south, the flush merged into blue, mauve, violet. The stars were fading. The feathers of cloud to the north were touched with pink.

A dash of cloud to the south turned wallaby grey, as soft as the animal's fur. Inexorably, the colours merged and changed. Still the morning star alone glowed above the converging source of light.

They watched transfixed, spellbound by the spectacle taking place before them.

Great flashes of colour pierced the blue above. The very air seemed diffused with flame, the land beneath a contrasting midnight purple. Like a glorious symphony, each element in the scene responded: ridges, tree tops, bushes and seed tops of grasses, reflecting the light, glowing with a transitory iridescent brilliance.

The colours softened to creams, pinks and lilacs and, as the great glowing orb of fire appeared, rising like Aphrodite from the sea, the immense kaleidoscope of wildflowers was seen in all its Spring glory.

'Oh,' Caroline breathed, 'it is so beautiful — so awe-inspiring.' She watched as the sun rose, the rays touching the elements beneath like a caress. 'It has a majesty, this land. It is beautiful. But it's a beauty of its own.' She groped for words. 'It's a different beauty. Strong. Overwhelming. Oh, I can't put it into words. The immensity, the vastness. I sense something of the majesty of God, watching this. It stirs me.'

'Now you know why it has enslaved me so, Caro. Why I am intoxicated by this land. Perhaps this whole thing is a gamble, but I just have to do it.'

'Oh yes, I do understand.' They were silent for a few minutes. 'I love it, too, already Willie,' she said softly.

He squeezed her hand, his face reflecting his love and delight. 'We'd better have breakfast and start work. This is a most important and auspicious day.' He laughed, joyful at the prospect and, clasping hands, they went to stir the fire and fry the bacon.

'I want to go looking,' Caroline said as they drank their cups of scalding tea. 'I didn't see a great deal last night. It was getting too dark.'

A bird chirped in a nearby tree. A willy wagtail alighted on an upturned saddle and flipped his tail as he danced around, calling to them his sweet pretty creature call.

They had camped last night on a high ridge above a creek. It commanded spectacular views, but the climb from each side would make it irksome for a permanent dwelling-place.

The sun now well up, they set off to choose the site for the centre of their enterprise. 'We need to be close to water. Somewhere with good waterholes. We need somewhere accessible for cattle to position the yards. We want it all fairly close together so it's all convenient.'

They rode over the place, along the creek, looking for the larger waterholes. The sun was hot now, the heat relieved by an easterly breeze.

Eventually, they decided on a spot that seemed to fulfil all the requirements. The deep waterhole was long and wide, the creek lined by large, old, twisted coolabah trees and river red gums. The sandy soil was soft and had a spring in it as they walked over it.

They would build the hut close to the creek. The banks rose sharply on the eastern side and levelled off, forming a wide low ridge, rising from vast flood plains. Here they would make their centre.

The country stretched away as far as the eye could see, the horizon many, many miles distant. The herbage and wildflowers formed a seemingly endless carpet of colour.

'We'll have to search for timber close to hand and get a store up as soon as possible,' Willie said as they ate their dinner by the camp fire. 'I want to let the waggons and drays get away on their trip back as quickly as I can.'

'It's been a long trip for them,' Caroline said, gazing into the fire.

What a long, long way it seemed back to Adelaide. How were all those dear folk at home? When would she see them again?

She looked around. It was beautiful, but almost overwhelming when you realised all that had to be done.

The wind was cold. She shivered slightly. Even the tent was some protection, but that was still with the dray. She thought of the sitting room at home and the warm fire on chilly evenings.

'Where will you start?' she asked quietly.

William looked up. 'Like I said, we'll build the store first so that waggons and drays can be unpacked.' He looked searchingly at her. What was the matter? She seemed to have lost her sparkle. Perhaps she was feeling the enormity of it all. 'After that, when we've got a weatherproof place to put all we brought, we'll build the hut for you. Then you'll have to set up house.'

He smiled encouragingly at her. Surely Caro wasn't getting cold feet on this whole thing now they were here? What would he do if she lost heart and got like Ted's wife? No, no, surely that wouldn't happen. She was probably just tired. How wonderful she had been on the journey! No, she was no doubt tired and feeling the cold wind.

He stood up and poked the fire, adding another log. 'We'll put a nice big fireplace in the hut for you.' He picked up a coat and laid it round her shoulders. 'This wind across the wide open space is cold. The waggons will soon be here and then we'll put your tent up till we get the hut built.' There was a little worry crease between his eyes and a concerned note in his voice.

I must pull myself together, Caroline thought. Willie has a great deal to organise. He doesn't want a despondent, weepy woman on his hands. I mustn't dampen his thrill of actually being here and making a start.

She swallowed hard and, with an effort, spoke as brightly as she could muster. 'You know, it will really be an interesting challenge to make a home of a little bush hut.'

'It is only temporary,' Willie put in hastily. 'When we've got the essentials attended to here and things start moving, I'll take you out to see the stone I'm talking about for our homestead. That's another thing. We'll have to draw up a plan and look to the aspects. We want the cool breezes in the summer; it gets so very hot. And the walls will be thick to keep the interior cool. But we want shelter from this kind of wind.'

His enthusiasm cheered her. Time would soon pass. She must think of one thing at a time. The store was the first consideration. It would need to be a fair size to hold all their supplies for the next six months.

She smiled at Willie. No doubt he had it all in hand.

By the time the rest of the cavalcade reached the spot chosen, the site for the store, the huts and the yards had been marked out. William had secured an amount of bush timber and the erection of a store was begun without delay.

'Have to be a jack of all trades in this job,

101

Mrs Bartlett,' Snowy called as he perched on a pole, tying the roof battens in place. 'Take up building next job I get.' He laughed happily.

'You're doing very well, Snowy,' Caroline replied. 'I'll go into the peg-making business.' She had been occupied with the aid of a small tomahawk in making pegs to hold the logs in place.

This must certainly be something new for Mrs Bartlett, Snowy thought. She wouldn't have ever held a tomahawk before. Guess the hardest thing she'd ever cut before were stems of flowers. A real lady she was. Not stuck up, though. Fancy a lady like her cutting points on sticks for pegs. As he'd told her before, real trooper she'd been on this trip. And now, working like this!

Caroline was surprised how quickly the store was completed. It was roomy. Shelves had been improvised from the scrub timber available to keep the foodstuffs off the ground. I can organise the food anyway, she thought. She was marvelling at the ingenuity and knowledge of the men and feeling rather wanting in such expertise.

She would learn, though. She was learning. What would Mother and Aunty May and Bella think if they could see her now? It was good to see Willie happy and so pleased with her involvement.

The waggons and drays were being unloaded — bags of flour and sugar, tins of foodstuff, boxes of all kinds of things, parcels of everything from household goods to leather and chains. A few pieces of basic furniture were stored in one end of the big room.

At last, the waggons and drays stood empty. Everything had been put in the store. All was safe from the elements. The big covering sheets used on the long journey had been stowed away ready for the next journey.

The sun was just rising the next morning as the bullockies' voices rang out, calling their beasts into place. Slowly, stolidly, they fell into place and the yokes were secured. The drivers of the drays were preparing for departure, too. They would travel together.

The little company to make their home in this place, this speck in an ocean-wide land, gathered to see them off. 'You'll be happy to come back with our supplies in six months' time?' William asked the leader.

'More than happy, Mr Bartlett. Been good to do business with you.'

'My order will go by hand and the Pastoral Supplies people will contact you.'

With a blast of noise, the cracking of whips and shouts of the drivers, the bullocks moved off. This would be an easy trip with no load, an empty waggon to pull.

'See you in six months,' Caroline called, waving good-bye. They watched till the dust settled and they had moved down the track.

'Well, what are we all standing here for?' William called. He looked around the company with mock severity. 'There's work to be done.'

Ted grinned. No doubt about the boss. Bet he knew they were all feeling a bit strange seeing the others set off for Adelaide. That was their last link with the outside world for six months, really. Oh well, rather be here than Adelaide, anyway. They needed this bit of urging.

'What's the next building job?' he called over his shoulder.

'A mansion for Mrs Bartlett,' Snowy joked. 'A mansion with an earth floor. Mother earth. Nothing like it.'

'Best place sleep, earth bed,' Yuelty added.

They loaded up the timber to be used and proceeded to the site pegged out: a commodious room with a large fireplace to be built in stone across one end.

Caroline watched eagerly as the work began with a will.

11

Home-making

It really wouldn't be too bad at all, Caroline thought to herself. It was looking surprisingly roomy now the walls were going up.

It had been hard to find enough stone for the fireplace. Willie had promised her a big fireplace and that's what he intended to have. The stones were bonded with mud and the inside of the chimney smoothed with cow dung, added to the mixture to ensure a non-smoking draw.

Caroline sat in the shade watching the progress. She felt a surge of excitement as the hut neared completion. How strange to be getting excited about an earth-floored hut made of bush timber, she mused. Everything, after all, is relative. Compared with the last few months, this hut would be the ultimate in comfort and convenience.

The last peg was in. The last tie made. Tomorrow they would hang the doors and shutters. The stone oven looked like an igloo, conveniently close to the back of the hut. Tomorrow, when all was finished, the men would move on to their own hut, then to the building of the cattle yards.

And tomorrow she would set to work to make this home — and try out the stone oven. It was an exciting prospect.

The fire cast a warm glow of light through the hut. The flicker of flames made moving shadows on the bush timber walls and roof structure. The light reflected back from the stones of the big fireplace and the hearth.

Willie had been most particular about these stones. They had been chosen with the greatest care. Careless choice or the use of round river stones could result in stones exploding in the heat of a fire. This could be extremely dangerous. Anything of this nature was tested by building a fierce fire around samples of the stone. Only after such testing were they used.

The hearth was raised quite a few centimetres from the ground and on either side a seat had been built in a fashion rather as in some of the fireplaces in England. It would be a cosy place to sit and warm themselves in the cold weather.

Caroline hung the iron kettle on the big hook. Willie would soon be in for a cup of tea.

She looked around the room, pleased with what she saw. The table and chairs they had brought with them stood in the middle of the room. A blue bowl of wildflowers she had picked sat on a crocheted mat. Mother had made that for her. The food safe was by the front wall and along the back wall they had put shelves. Now her blue and white china, cups, saucers, plates and all the rest gleamed back in the flickering light.

The end of the room was curtained off for their bedroom. It was a pretty, rose-patterned curtain. Their iron bedstead just fitted between the curtain and the end wall. A wardrobe was fashioned by a matching curtain stretched on a rod across the other corner. It had a cosy feel. It was very intimate. And there was the flickering light from the fire! It was really quite romantic. They would be happy here.

The erection of the long hut for the men's quarters, workshop and saddle room occupied the following days. The cattle had spread out, seemingly contented, grazing on the abundant herbage. The building of the stockyards would mean the initial setting up was complete.

Caroline watched from the hut door. Snowy and Jacko were putting in the posts for the lasso rails in the centre of the yard where the calves were lassoed and held for branding and cutting.

Suddenly, Jacko stood upright. He spoke to

Snowy. They both looked down the track, shading their eyes. Young Splinter came running across the yard.

'See that?' he called, his face anxious. Caroline walked out to see what was causing the concern.

Down the track, a moving mass was approaching. As it drew closer, she could discern that it was made up of black men, women and children, some of them carrying very small children. What did this mean? Surely with women and children in their midst they were not bent on hostility. What a crowd there was! Their black skin shone in the strong sunlight. They looked fit and well fed.

What did they want? Where were they going?

The men had stopped work and were silently watching their approach. Many of the young men carried spears and boomerangs. The women had bags made from some type of bush string. They, too, were silent as they came nearer. The soft thuds and scuffles of many bare feet on the ground was the only indication of their presence.

They stopped a way off. The women with the children and the older men sat on the ground.

Movement from behind the men's quarters

caught Caroline's eye. Yuelty was walking towards this large group of his countrymen. It seemed he was able to communicate with them. Perhaps he knew their language. At any rate, there seemed to be no trouble.

Caroline's racing pulse steadied. There had been stories in Adelaide before they left of hostile Aborigines raiding settlers. There had even been some killed. The retaliation for these occurrences had sparked off bad feeling and fear between settlers and Aborigines in other areas.

Yuelty was coming back with one of the men. He was the one Yuelty had been talking to.

Willie had been watching the interchange from the store. Thank goodness it appeared to be all right. In the event of an attack, they would be grossly outnumbered. He let his breath out with a great sigh of relief as Yuelty approached. Made a man think how vulnerable he had allowed this little establishment to be, though. He should really have given more attention to the possibility of an attack.

Yuelty was bringing the man to see him. William stepped out to meet them. He held out his hands. The man laid his spear on the ground. 'Willie boss, these my people,' Yuelty said, pointing to the group back behind him.

'This one boss man.' Yuelty spoke to the

man in his own language. He looked at William's outstretched hands and grasped them.

'This good man. Good my people,' Yuelty said. 'I tell him you good man, too. You not hurt their women, their children.'

William shook hands, smiling. 'Friends,' he said pointing to the man and himself. 'You, me.' He seemed to understand.

'What are they doing? Are they going walkabout?' he asked Yuelty. 'Is this the whole tribe? There are many children.'

'They go big corroboree,' Yuelty replied. 'Much dance, sing. Long way. Near lake. More people come. They say I go, too.'

'Do you want to go?' William asked. This must be a very special sort of gathering.

'Many people. Big corroboree,' Yuelty repeated. He seemed to make up his mind. 'I go,' he stated.

During the interchange between their leader, Yuelty and William, the rest of the tribe had wandered down to the creek. Their splashing and calling to each other could now be heard.

What free people unencumbered by possessions they were, Caroline thought. She would certainly not like to be travelling with the sun beating down on her bare skin and sleeping in a hollowed bed on the ground. They seemed happy, though. And they somehow didn't look bare with their dark skin. They didn't seem to worry at all about having dirt on their skin from sitting or lying down.

She looked at her own white skin. My skin wouldn't stand too much of that treatment, she thought. But then I wasn't bred for this climate.

In a short while, Yuelty had said his goodbyes and joined the party by the creek. Towards late afternoon, they headed off again, the old guide now happily in their midst.

At last, the establishment of the home centre was complete. There would be the homestead, permanent quarters and store built later on but, for the moment, the plant for functioning efficiently was ready and work with the cattle could proceed. For the present, Caroline would cook the meals for the whole company. As the enterprise progressed and the staff increased, they would employ a cook, but that was a way off yet.

The oven was proving efficient and Caroline's efforts were applauded by the men. The fire was lit in the oven until the stones reached the desired heat. Then the ashes and coals were scraped out, the food put in and the doorway sealed up. Bread, pies and cakes were all cooked in this way. Caroline became quite proud of her results as her expertise grew.

Almost three months had passed before Willie fulfilled his promise to take Caroline to see the stone he proposed to use for the homestead. They set off at daybreak. The weather was now hot and they would rest in the middle of the day. By evening, they had covered the greater part of the journey. They camped beside a small creek. The country had changed. Riding westward, they were now in undulating country and could see mountains in the far distance.

By mid-morning the next day, they had reached the source of the proposed building material. They alighted and walked among the rocks. Caroline was entranced by the colours: colours that ranged from cream to deepest magenta. She picked up broken pieces, rubbing the dirt off to expose their glory.

'Oh Willie,' she exclaimed. 'This will make the most beautiful walls. The colours are unbelievable.' She picked up one stone after another. William watched, delighted at her obvious pleasure and enthusiasm.

'What colour do you think should be used for the mortar?' he asked.

'Oh, cream — whatever is suitable for use

with this stone. O yes, cream to highlight the colours.' She picked up a large piece of the magenta rock, veined, dappled with cream — and gazed at it, entranced. The sun sparkled on something — mineral or whatever — in the piece. This would be like living in a fairy castle, living in a house made of this stone — like being in a jewelled castle. It sparkled and shone as though magic was encased in it.

Whoever would have a house made of this? No-one in Adelaide. The stone houses there would pale into insignificance beside this sparkling gem-like material. 'I just can't believe it,' she said wonderingly. 'Do you really think there is enough of this here for a house?' She looked at Willie who was laughing at her.

'Just look around,' he replied. 'You can only see what's on top, uncovered by soil.'

She went back to examining the different colours and patterns. She would keep everything else in neutral or plains to show up this treasure. The building material, the rock walls would be the *piéce de résistance* of the whole place.

The ride back was uneventful. As always, the return journey did not seem as long as the outgoing one. As they approached the little settlement, Caroline felt a happy thrill of anticipation. Tonight they would sleep in their comfortable bed in the warm hut, with the firelight flickering its soft glow throughout the room, making the shadows dance on the walls and ceiling. It was good to be home.

The sun had set and the cool air of the night started to come in as they reached the hut. The boys had finished work for the day and were having their tea.

'Made a bit extra stew for you, boss. Thought you might be late.' Snowy lifted the pot off the fire. 'Just my cooking, but it's hot and not bad.' The men all endorsed this.

'Thank you very much,' William replied. 'I must admit we are hungry. Mrs Bartlett's just gone in to get things ready. This will be a welcome surprise.'

'Oh boss,' called Ted, coming to the door of the quarters. 'Forgot to tell you. We saw a snake today in the store. Don't know how he got in. Must have been when the shutter was open some time, I suppose. Some kind of carpet snake, I think. Diamond pattern on his back. Thought I'd better tell you so you keep your eyes open. Fair size he was. Greeny brown. Light colour.'

A snake, eh? They had been lucky not to have seen any snakes around the settlement. They had been seen out in the pastures several times, but none just here. What would

114

Caro say about this?

Caroline had the fire burning and the kettle on when William returned to the hut. 'The boys cooked enough for us, too,' he said from the doorway.

'Oh lovely. I'm starving.' William set the pot over the fire as Caroline put the plates on the table.

'You know, it's lovely to be home. This really feels like home, doesn't it?' Caroline chattered happily as she busied herself in preparation for the meal. 'It cools off so quickly when the sun goes down. It was so hot today and now I'm thankful for the fire. It's so cosy.'

They enjoyed their meal and, after clearing up, sat talking of the stone they had seen. What would they like in this homestead they would eventually build? How would they plan the rooms?

At length, Caroline yawned. After the long ride, they were tired. Tomorrow would again be a busy day. They would go to bed early.

Caroline pulled the rug up round her neck. The sheets smelled deliciously of lavender she had put in the big chest. Willie was already dropping off. His breathing was deep and steady. Caroline watched the flickering shadows. It was so peaceful; so restful — just what was needed to lull you off to sleep. She closed her eyes.

A slight rustle broke the silence. Was that something on the roof? She opened her eyes. Nothing to be seen. She turned over and closed her eyes again. As she slipped closer to slumber, the soft noise came again. Her eyes flew open. The shadows danced on the ceiling above the bed. The light gleamed on something. It wasn't just the shadows. Something was moving!

'Willie! Willie!' Caroline gasped. She shook his shoulder, pulling herself towards the side of the bed. 'Willie, there is something up there.' She pointed upwards with her finger. Her heart beat furiously. 'Willie, wake up. There's something in the roof.'

William opened his eyes, jerked awake now by the alarm in Caroline's voice. He looked to where she was pointing. A small, smooth-pointed, yellow-brown head appeared. He bounded from the bed. 'Look out, Caro!' he cried urgently. 'Pull the curtain back. Open the door.'

Caroline rushed to obey.

'Light the lamp,' he called. 'It's a snake!'

'A snake?' Caroline gasped. Her hands shook violently as she lit the lamp. 'What will we do?'

'Don't be frightened.' Must keep Caro calm and not terrify her. 'Just bring me that long rake by the back door. I'll keep my eye on him so we know just where he is.'

Caroline brought the long rake and the shovel that had been by the door. 'How can you get it out?' She could hardly speak.

'I'll try to get him down with the rake and get him out the door.'

The snake was coiled around the rafter, its little head appearing and disappearing back into the roof structure. After several unsuccessful attempts, William was able to dislodge the snake from the rafter. It fell with a thud onto the bed.

Caroline screamed. A snake on her bed! It slithered onto the floor, looking for escape. Caroline jumped away, her bare feet making her feel more vulnerable than ever. Running to the other end of the room, she huddled by the fireplace wall, hopefully away from the direction it would take.

Sensing or seeing the open door, the snake twisted and shot through the opening. 'Useless to try to follow it any further,' William said, closing the door. He put his arm around her. 'Are you all right? I'll look all around the place in the morning. The boys told me they had seen one today. It looks like some kind of carpet snake. They don't attack like some of the others.' Caroline's trembling was steadying. 'Don't want them for bed mates, though, do we?'

They searched the room to make sure their

visitor had no companions. They shone the lantern as best they could over the roof. All seemed well.

At last they settled down again. But the moon was high in the sky and the fire burned down to embers before Caroline's eyes closed and sleep finally came.

12

News from home

Two years passed in quick succession. The seasonal round of cattle work progressed. The cows calved. In due time, there was mustering; the cattle were brought in and the calves branded. This was a noisy, busy time. The bellowing as the calves in the yard were lassoed was deafening, the mothers outside adding their distress to the hullabaloo.

Caroline was continually busy, keeping up the food to the workers. They worked from dawn to dusk. All were infected with the excitement as the tally was made of the year's increase.

'We've done well this year, Caro,' Willie said as he sipped the tea she had brought to the yards. 'I just hope the prices stay high. I hope we can finish here and get the cattle back out again before the waggons arrive from Adelaide. This muster has really been good, but I don't want to have more to cope with at the moment.'

Caroline was thoughtful as she carried the tea things back to the hut. The waggons ought to be here in a week or two. It depended on the weather.

She thought again of all the things they had ordered. They had drawn up a plan of the house they wanted and taken it to an architect on their last visit to Adelaide. He had been commissioned to order the necessary material and, in conjunction with the Pastoral Supplies Company, arranged for them to be delivered, along with Caroline's many other purchases, by the bullock waggon driver who had brought their initial supplies and now regularly transported their requirements each six months.

She had ordered rugs and lamps and bolts of material for curtains. It was to be a big house, with plenty of room — for all their children to have room to move, Willie often said. There was no indication of anything like this yet, though.

It was strange. Some people had children right away after they married. She had been married two years. Oh well, there was plenty of time. Perhaps it would be better if she didn't have any until the house was built. It would be much more comfortable — and safer, she thought, remembering the snake in the hut in their early days.

The muster and branding were finished. The dust in the yards had settled and the men out in the outstations checked the water and feed and returned the cattle to their familiar places. The weather had turned cloudy, but no rain fell. There was still no sign of the waggons and all they were to bring.

It was another two weeks before Willie, coming back from looking at the waterholes along the creek, saw dust rising far down the track.

'Caro,' he called, 'this might be the waggons coming.'

Caroline ran out from the hut, her hands covered with flour. 'Oh, I want to go and meet them,' she cried.

Hastily, she put the bread she had been kneading into the oiled tins to rise and set them in the warmth near the fire. Her hands were washed and dried quickly and she came out, untying her apron and throwing it over a chair. 'Come on,' she called, 'let's go and meet them.'

They met the bullocky as he brought his team around the bend of the creek. 'Welcome, welcome!' Caroline called as they fell into step beside him.

'How have you been, Mrs Bartlett? I trust you are well.'

'Oh very well, thankyou.' Caroline almost skipped in her excitement. 'We've been looking and looking for you.'

'Yes. Unfortunately, I am later than expected, but we were held up by rain further south.'

'They've had good rain down there, then, have they?' William asked. 'I'm very glad to hear it. We could do with some again now.'

'Yes, they had good rain. In fact, the river flooded and we were held up for a week before we could get across. Then we had to wait for the approaches to dry out sufficiently so we wouldn't get bogged.' He smiled at Caroline. 'Couldn't have that happen when we have all these special things for your house on board, could we, Mrs Bartlett?'

'Dear me, no! And did you get everything we had ordered?' Caroline asked excitedly.

'Seems to me the orders were all filled,' the man replied. 'We've got a good load on.' He glanced back. 'It was necessary to bring the two teams this time because of the timber. But it's all on.'

'And tell me, what ships are in port? Are there many people still arriving? And have you got mail for us? I'm just dying to hear from Mama!'

'Yes. I've got a bag of mail. You will have to go on holiday to read it all.'

Caroline laughed with delight.

'And about the people coming in. Yes. They

are still coming in droves. Adelaide's population is growing daily. It is making some headaches for the authorities, I'm afraid.'

'I suppose accommodation is a problem,' William cut in.

'Yes, indeed. Many people are finding it very hard. But you will see for yourselves. I also brought you newspapers — a bit out of date now, of course, but the best I could do.'

And so the conversation continued as the bullocks plodded stolidly along, pulling their great burden. What houses were being built? What were they like? Were many of them being built of stone now? It didn't stop until the waggons had pulled up alongside the store and attention had to be given to the unpacking of the load.

Caroline took the bag of mail to the hut and, her heart thudding, untied the strings. Out fell letters from family, friends, accounts, letters from agents and solicitors, one printed with the bank's stamp. And many more.

She searched hastily through and, finding one from Mother, slit the top with trembling hands.

'My Darling Daughter,' it began. Dear Mother. How lovely it would be to talk to her. Father and Annabelle were well. Father had been very busy. His work as an archdeacon had taken him to many parishes during the last few months. There were new parishes being formed as the population grew. It meant a great deal of work determining where boundaries should be placed and provision had to be made for the housing of the incumbents. It all meant much time being spent in discussions and deliberations.

At the same time, there were many calls at the rectory for assistance of all kinds. 'Some people have made no prearrangement or enquiries for accommodation and find themselves with all their luggage on the streets,' Mother wrote. 'Others have come with little or no reserves in money and find themselves destitute when the little they have has been used up. We are kept constantly trying to care for these poor folk.'

Bella was helping at home and trying to assist the immigrants, but had found time to examine some new houses being built. 'She thought you would like to hear of the latest fashions in decorating and is writing to you separately.'

Caroline read and re-read, then searched for Bella's letter. She devoured all the descriptions of interior decoration. 'Of course, some of these things may not be possible or appropriate in your situation at 'Bibbaringa', but I thought you would be interested.'

Towards the end of the letter a short paragraph caught her attention. 'When I was in town today, I met Willie's friend, George. He invited me to partake of afternoon tea in 'Hatherways'. I had time to spare before Father would pick me up, so I accepted. He really is a very pleasant young man.'

So Bella had enjoyed George's company. Caroline smiled to herself. She must tell Willie. Now don't start trying to play Cupid, she told herself. Still, stranger things had happened. Bella was still very young. George was quite a lot older than her. She nodded and smiled as she read that section of the letter again. It would be quite nice.

Soon, parcels and wrappings were strewn all over the store. Caroline had unpacked much of the food supplies and stowed them appropriately on the shelves. Then she was anxiously opening the materials and goods that had been ordered for the house.

Carefully opening one end of the wrapping around a bolt of material, she turned back the last sheet. 'Oh, it is beautiful!' she exclaimed. The rich crimson velvet gleamed in its wrapping. This would be for the dining room. What a thrill it would be, seeing the house erected! And what a lovely time she would have decorating it. She moved to another similarly shaped parcel. This one revealed a rich, deep green velvet for the sitting room. Another parcel contained cream lace in a rose and bird design.

Caroline was clasping her hands in delight as Willie entered the store. 'Whatever are you doing, Caro?' He was surveying the disarray of objects and wrappings.

'Oh Willie, I'm having such fun. Look at these lovely materials.'

'They are beautiful,' he said. 'Won't be needed just yet, though.' He smiled. 'The house has to be built first.'

Laughing happily, Caroline said, 'Please help me wrap the materials again. I don't want to get any dirt on them.' Carefully, they rewrapped and tied the parcels.

One large box stood by the wall. Caroline looked hesitantly at Willie. 'I'll just open this one. The others I won't touch until we have the house built and I can unpack them and put them in their places.'

Willie shook his head at her and smiled indulgently. 'You'll help me pack it up again, won't you?' Carefully, she withdrew the contents of the box and assembled the pieces. It was a beautiful lamp surmounted by a coloured shade with a design of roses. From the metal frame hung glass drops such as are used in chandeliers. The sun shone on the glass prisms, flashing rainbow colours as they were turned as Willie held the lamp aloft.

Caroline's eyes shone with pleasure. How good it was to see Caro enjoying these things so much. She had been so wonderful, accepting the hut so readily all this time. Willie's love for her welled up within him. He would see she had all she could desire in this homestead. It wouldn't be very long now.

13

Established

Sounds rang out over the paddocks and along the creek: steel on steel and steel on stone.

The stonemasons and builders had arrived from Adelaide. Around the settlement, the air buzzed with noise and activity. Stonemasons, experienced and professional, had been to the site of the stone deposit, had quarried and had brought back the material that so excited Caroline. Builders were digging out the foundation. Now Caroline could see the outline of the floor plan.

How big it seemed after the little hut. They had put a great deal of thought into the plan. Then the architect had improved on the original idea. The entrance was to be by way of a wide vestibule. An expansive archway then led into a central hall which extended the length of the house with rooms opening from it. All the rooms had French doors opening to a verandah which encircled the house.

Caroline's days were full indeed. Catering for such a large company of men was a full-time job. Sometimes, Willie or young Splinter assisted her, carrying the food from the oven into the hut or the temporary bough shelter they had made as a dining area. Long trestle tops had been set on block legs and, around this, the men gathered when the cow-bell was rung.

'Gee, Mrs Bartlett, I didn't know we all put away so much food till I been helpin' you,' young Splinter commented as he carried a heavy pot of potatoes to the shelter. 'We got enough to last till the next order after this crew is finished the house and gone?'

Caroline laughed. 'I certainly hope so, Splinter. We'll all have to go hunting for bush tucker if we haven't.'

'Pity old Yuelty has gone,' Splinter observed.

'Yes, he could certainly find food where we wouldn't even think to look. But don't worry. I think we'll have plenty to last us. I did order a lot extra to cope with the added numbers, you know.'

Splinter's concern was somewhat abated by Caroline's assurances, but he still looked askance at the quantity of food lined up at the end of the table.

Progress was good on the building. Caroline's excitement grew with the walls. The pattern of colour was emerging as their height mounted. Willie will be so proud of this homestead, Caroline thought. He was so conscious of the confines of the hut. Certainly she had felt the restrictions, but she had always known it would be only for a limited time.

Each evening, the contractor brought out the plan and, with Willie at his side, checked the day's progress and detailed the work for the morrow.

At last the roof was on and the ceilings put in. The round-patterned ceiling centrepiece was in place in each room, complete with hook on which to hang the lamp. The ceilings and woodwork were painted and the floor polished.

The sheen of the wide beeswaxed floorboards really complemented the stone walls. The solid front door with its brass knocker and large door knob was hung. The wooden shutters to shield the rooms from the heat and glare were secured.

It was finished.

The builders and stonemasons packed their equipment and departed after many congratulations for their successful efforts.

'Oh, it is beyond my wildest dreams,' Caroline breathed as she and Willie looked at the building from a little way off. The sun had just dipped over the horizon and the sky was diffused with colour. Like a watercolour painting, one colour merging into another, it was a magnificent backdrop to the expansive solid homestead nestling on their land before them. The wide verandahs around the house exuded a feeling of comfort, shelter and space.

They walked to the steps and up onto the verandah. Willie opened the massive door and, with a swift movement, swept Caroline off her feet and up into his arms. 'Welcome to your home, Mrs Bartlett,' he cried, with large strides carrying her across the threshold.

'Oh Willie, I'm so thrilled.' He set her on her feet and, keeping his arms around her, drew her to him and kissed her long and tenderly.

The days that followed were exciting indeed. The many parcels and pieces of furniture already delivered were unpacked and put in position. The velvet and lace curtains were hung. The bed, table and chairs and safe were brought from the hut. How small they seemed now in these big rooms! The lamps were hung.

When they went to Adelaide again, they would choose the rest of the furniture. Then it could come straight into the house when it was delivered.

The big stone store, the permanent men's quarters, the saddle room and stables, the blacksmith's shop and all the buildings needed had now also been built. It had taken months for all the building activity to be completed. Now the whole place was established. These buildings would last for centuries. Everything had been planned for comfort, convenience and quality to last. The men were enthusiastic about their quarters and chiacked each other about their 'mansion'.

The silence of the bush was impressive after the long time of continual building noises — the sound of men's voices raised as they called to each other, the burst of song from one builder and the whistle of another as they chipped at stone or hammered or sawed timber. An era had passed — an epoch-making time of pioneering, thrusting out with the bare essentials of equipment and basic scrub-timber shelter.

William's venture was on the larger scale; his was not the experience of the lone settler with barely the resources to pay his lease, the lone settler who single-handed cleared his land, built a hut, planted a crop and shepherded his half-dozen cows if he was lucky.

But I've risked my all, William thought. And it's paying off. He was lucky — lucky to have the resources. But he could have lost it all. The men in his employ were still the men who had come with him. They were happy. This was home for them, too.

Now they would all start a new era: an era of established plant, of more and growing knowledge and understanding of the land, a land that was so different from the land further south — or any other place William had seen, for that matter.

It had its vastness, its magnitude. But it also exacted its demands. It could not be stocked as the familiar country was. Grazing could not be carried out in the same way. You had to think big, like the country out here, William thought. When the moisture came, it responded and held for so long. The cattle filled out and grew sleek and shiny.

This would be an era of more gracious living for Caroline, too. 'Bibbaringa' homestead would equal any of the Adelaide homes they knew. One day, perhaps, it may even be famous.

The future beckoned enticingly.

★ ★ ★

James Hilliard reclined in a cane chair on the verandah. What a vista this was! William had certainly done well and this house was something to be proud of. He had known

William was a fine young man who had a good head. He had been happy to have Caroline marry him and he become a member of the family. His judgment had been vindicated.

They had been married a while now. It was a wonder they hadn't started a family before now. But then, perhaps, they had wanted to get settled in the homestead first.

This really was a very impressive cluster of buildings here. Of course, it was necessary to have a good home base on such an extensive holding.

It was a pity they were so far away — and without a mail link or contact of any kind, except by the rare personal excursions. Still, no doubt that added to the atmosphere here. There was certainly a mystique about the place.

His eye scanned the far horizon. It seems to go on into infinity, he thought. The Lord has created with an expansive hand here. 'Lord, how glorious are Thy works!' It was awe-inspiring.

'Having a quiet time, Father?' Caroline came through from the sitting room.

'I'm just marvelling at all this.' He waved his arm to indicate. 'It is just overwhelming.'

'You must wake early and see the sunrise,' Caroline suggested. 'It is something not to be missed. It looks as though it will be a clear sky in the morning.'

It was so wonderful to have them here. She and Mother had hardly drawn breath since they arrived. There had been the tour over the whole establishment. Then the detailed inspection of the house. They had enthused about everything. Mother was particularly entranced with the lamp in the sitting room.

Elizabeth Hilliard glanced at her husband and Caroline in conversation on the verandah. She felt more rested now. The journey had been long and tiring. Still, it was wonderful to be here and see all this for herself. All the description in the world couldn't do this place justice.

Caroline was looking well. The unaccustomed work hadn't seemed to harm her. Her eyes were bright and she seemed very happy.

Looking up, Caroline caught her mother's eye. 'Mother, come and sit here in the cool. The nights cool so quickly when the sun sets.'

They sat for a while, hearing the news and sharing the doings. There were so many people to enquire after, so many things to tell.

'Your cousin Phillip's little boy Timothy is growing so quickly. He is such a joy to his parents, and his grandparents,' Elizabeth said. 'Aunty May is quite dotty about him.'

What was Mother saying? Was she hinting

about a grandchild. 'He must be six or seven months old now,' Caroline said. 'They are very lucky to have a contented baby to give them so much joy.' The conversation drifted to other members of the family.

The evening wore on and, after a hearty dinner in the handsome dining room, the older couple pleaded weariness from the journey and retired early.

Elizabeth blew out the light and pulled the quilt up over her, slipping gratefully between the lavender perfumed sheets. She sighed as she rested her head on the pillow. The moonlight streamed in the window, casting soft shadows on the wall. From somewhere far off, an eery wail wafted across the moonlit paddocks.

'James, what was that?' She sat bolt upright.

'That, my dear, is the howl of a dingo,' James replied. 'We are now in the bush.'

The call came again. 'Oh, it gives me the shivers.' Elizabeth glanced nervously towards the French doors.

'It's all right. You are quite safe here.' The moon rose higher. It was a full moon tonight. All kinds of things happened at full moon, Elizabeth thought.

The howl came again, wailing. She pictured the dingo, head raised, howling to the moon. It was answered somewhere in the distance. The sound stirred Elizabeth. This mournful yet menacing wail engendered fear, apprehension, foreboding. This was a wild, majestic, untamed land. What little specks they were in its midst. Chiding herself for her vivid imaginings, Elizabeth settled down. James was already asleep. She, too, would go to sleep.

In spite of her will, sleep would not come. The dingo did not sound again. The only sound was an owl hooting somewhere close by. Her last conscious awareness before sleep came was the mopoke calling somewhere down by the creek. Mo poke. Mo poke. What strange creatures inhabited this land.

As she drifted into sleep, she was back in her native England with the familiar sounds and nuances. Inland Australia was far away.

14

Fundamentals

Caroline wiped the tears from her eyes as the carriage taking her mother and father back to Adelaide disappeared in a cloud of dust down the track. Ted was going on leave now and travelling with them. He would look after them.

It had been wonderful to have them these last weeks. They had been most impressed with the homestead. A real gentleman's residence, her mother had said. She had loved the beauty of the sandstone, its soft glow.

Caroline closed the gate and walked back along the path. She must make herself busy or she would miss them too much. She would begin on her garden. The well was proving a wonderful boon and would make all the difference to being able to establish plants and trees. She went to collect her gloves.

I'll begin with the seeds Mother brought, she thought. There were some flower and some vegetable seeds. Ted would bring back more when he returned from leave. Pumpkins and squash, rockmelon and watermelon would be a good start. They were hardy, too.

Then she must plant the herbs. She could establish a herb garden near the back door. Perhaps one of the men would dig the ground for her. Then she could set to work.

Caroline opened the bag of seeds and sifted them through her fingers. Here was new life, reproduction of its kind. She dropped the seeds back in the bag and tied the top. She seemed to be rather slow at this reproduction in her kind. Why hadn't she started with a baby yet?

All the animals outside had their babies. The cows calved every Spring. They had no trouble. The birds mated, laid their eggs and hatched their young. The swallows were already nesting high up under the verandah roof. They had been busy building there all week, flying back and forth with twigs and skimming the dam for water to make the mud to hold it all together. They all had families — everything around her. Yet she had no baby.

Some girls when they married had a baby straight off, before a year was out. And some had them every Spring, like the cows. She didn't really want it quite like that. But just one to start with: just to have a child of her own, to feel that child grow within her, to give birth.

They said it was a travail, but they all seemed to forget that pretty quickly when the baby arrived: to feel that soft warmth snuggled against her neck, to gently caress that softness, to smell that delicious baby smell. Oh, there'd be dirty nappies and all that, but she wouldn't care about that.

What she would give to hold her own baby in her arms, to suckle that baby at her breast, nourishing it from her own body. She even envied the cows as they stood contentedly chewing their cud while their calves sucked delightedly and butted their mothers' udder. What a bond there was between mother and offspring.

How wonderful it would be to look at your baby and search for all the family likenesses. There would be family likeness. An indelible stamp on each one, some inheriting one feature likeness or trait, some another, but all having something of the complex mixture of the genes of their ancestors evident in their person.

'What are you thinking about, Caro? Is anything wrong?'

Willie was standing in the doorway. He came forward, putting his arm around her. Caroline gave a shaky little laugh and wiped the tears that his voice, full of concern, had brought forth. 'I'm just envying the cows,' she said.

'Envying the cows? Whatever do you mean?' He stood back, holding her at arms length, looking at her, his face creased with concern.

'I just do so want a baby, Willie,' she whispered.

William drew her close, cradling her head on his shoulder. 'You'll have a baby,' he said, stroking her hair with one hand. 'We'll have a family all in good time.'

'But I thought we'd have one straight away. Or even in the second year. But I still haven't started. What's wrong with me?'

'There's nothing wrong with you. We have each other for now. Be happy in that.'

'Oh, I am happy, Willie. I love you and you make me happy. It's not that I'm not happy with you.' She must make him understand that. He mustn't feel she was discontented or found their marriage lacking.

'I love you, Willie. Our marriage is wonderful. It's something different. Deeper or something. I don't know. I just get a yearning to hold my own, our own baby, to love it and care for it.' She paused. 'I guess it's something very fundamental in me stirring; the urge to reproduce after my kind.'

She stood, leaning against him. They were silent a moment.

'I didn't realise you felt quite so strongly

about this,' William said quietly. 'Would you like to have gone back with your mother and father for a change to take your mind off it? Get some social life?'

'No, no, my darling. I'm happy. Really.'

Willie continued, 'I've brought you out here with no company, with no women to talk to. You must get sick of men's voices and conversations. I've been thoughtless.'

'No really, Willie. I'm perfectly happy here. Really I am. I love it. Just like you do. And now there is this beautiful home. No, no. It's nothing like that.'

She picked up the bag of seed. 'I opened this bag of seed and started thinking about reproduction. You took me by surprise when you spoke to me. I didn't hear you coming. That's why I started to cry. I was just surprised.' She smiled. 'Then I thought about the cows having a baby every Spring. That's why I said I envied the cows.'

Willie's face broke into a smile. 'A baby every Spring? For how long? I'll have to enlarge the house if that happens too many Springs.'

Caroline laughed. 'Oh no, just one to start with.'

She was feeling better now. Dear Willie. How she loved him. 'I'll just have to be patient. I've got you, as you say. We are lucky to be so happy. It was just a line of thought I got caught in.'

Willie released her and they walked out onto the verandah. There was a line of clouds gathering along the horizon. There could be a storm later in the day. Perhaps this had contributed to Caro's mood. There was a mounting of tension in the atmosphere before a storm. This could have added to her concern. He'd have to be more thoughtful, more aware of her moods.

She was such a bright, happy person as a rule. He supposed he didn't think much about her having moods. If he was happy and contented, he rather took it for granted that she was, too. This thing had obviously been in her mind a good deal for her to speak as she did. 'Envy the cows', indeed! It must mean a great deal to her.

He wanted a son, children, but there was plenty of time. There was no hurry. Why had she got herself into this state? Oh well! Maybe it was just being a woman. No doubt they had deep feelings he couldn't quite understand. He couldn't expect her to see things from a man's point of view.

Suddenly, he realised this was exactly what he frequently did. He must mend his ways. If only there was a neighbour, a woman she could visit sometimes. He must find out if there were any more properties opening up. Ted would have some news when he got back.

'Looks like we could get a storm later in the day,' he said, pointing to the line of clouds.

'Yes. Some rain would be nice. Come and help me plan my garden.' They walked down the steps and along the path talking about her plans. 'I'd like some roses eventually if you think we can grow them — and some chrysanthemums, too. They make such a show. I'll put a yellow broom over on the fence and some lavender here.'

Caroline was waxing enthusiastic. Thank goodness. Willie relaxed. They stopped under a tree. 'Would you like a garden seat to put here in the shade?' he asked.

'Oh, yes. That would be lovely. And a bird bath for over here.' She walked quickly to the spot she had in mind.

'I'll put them on the next order south,' Willie said.

Caroline chattered happily as they went round the house. 'All I need now is a gardener to really get my vegetable garden under way,' she said. 'It will be wonderful if I can grow more fresh vegetables.'

'Well, we aren't exactly in town or on a road where we might be lucky enough to have a gardener passing or calling in. We'll just have to do our best and learn from our mistakes.'

Caro seemed her happy self again. She had no doubt felt the loneliness when her parents left. She was all right.

William took himself off to arrange for one of the boys to dig the gardens for her so she could make a start. She'd be happy if she kept busy. He must remember to think of her.

The storm hit late in the afternoon. The trees by the gate had turned their leaves, a sure sign of coming rain. The birds had hushed their song as the heavy clouds approached, blotting out the sun — great billowing clouds, black-grey purple, edged with green. Would there be hail in it?

The wind came. It picked up the sand from the dunes way out and stung all it blasted. Caroline fastened the doors and windows to keep out the gritty sand. The wind forced it through every crack and crevice.

When the rain came, it was fierce, heavy, driven by the wind. The heavens were rent by great flashes of forked lightning streaking across the sky and hurtling earthwards. Thunder rolled, deafening peals with each explosion of lightning, rumbling on and on.

It was over soon, passing on its way. A tree had been hit down by the creek, splintered like matchwood, the debris scattered across the paddock. What power there was in the elements! What force!

Another fundamental, Caroline thought to herself. We do many things, add many things to our lives. But the fundamental things: they remain.

15

Sights on far horizons

Willie emerged from his office and stretched his arms above his head. It was good, really good. Ted was home and had brought back the mail. It was a rare thing here to have mail. He had been going over the accounts, checking with his bank statement. It all agreed.

He had done well this last year — each year since he had been here, really. The seasons had been good. The demand for beef had kept the price of cattle up. Who knew? One day he might be exporting cattle or beef back to England. Things were progressing.

Of course, improvements could be made. The rainfall here wasn't as reliable as he would like it to be. One year he might be hit with drought. Water as well as feed could be a problem if that happened. What he needed to think about was the possibility of extending, buying land further south.

It was more reliable fattening country further south. Of course, nothing would entice him away from 'Bibbaringa'. His heart was here.

He wasn't dependent only on local rainfall. When the floods came from up north, the water spread out miles wide, bringing back the idea of an inland sea. As it soaked away, the miracle happened and the feed and wildflowers flourished.

Just where this water came from, where rain had fallen to send such volume of water, he was not sure. Some of the Aborigines had talked of rivers starting hundreds of miles north in Queensland and flowing south and west instead of emptying in the ocean to the east. These rivers, they said, joined into one as they came south, eventually spreading out into permanent waterholes and lakes. Some of this water fed the creeks and water holes on 'Bibbaringa'. But a man must be practical and see realities. A drought year throughout could bring real problems.

He walked out onto the verandah and leaned on the rail, gazing out over the paddocks. The spell hadn't lessened. His heart still swelled as it had the first time he saw it. Now this was his. How he would like Grandfather to see it. It was thanks to Grandfather that he had been able to buy it.

And now this house. It was a home to be proud of: large rooms, wide verandahs, the shutters over the French doors to shade and cool the house in the heat of summer. The summers did get hot here, no doubt about that. But this house should provide every comfort possible.

Caro had chosen the furnishings well. It was all just as she wanted it. And it was all paid for. The figures had all tallied. He could start looking to further progress.

William left the verandah and, walking past the men's quarters, went in search of Ted. Ted Wilkes was working in the blacksmith's shop. It was good to be back. This was home now. He soon got tired of town — didn't know how they could stand to settle down in all that noise and bustle and people and live there all their lives. It took all sorts to make a world. He'd enjoyed the break, but it was good to be back here where the fellas didn't talk your ears off, where there was peace and quiet.

Not that it was very quiet here at the moment! This hammer on the anvil sure split through your head.

His face saddened. The letter from Jessica had contained some good news of the boys. They were doing well. Both were growing tall, she said, growing out of their clothes. Bill's voice had deepened. It was hard to think of him growing into manhood.

Maybe they would come back to Australia some day. It didn't sound much like Jessica was ever thinking of coming back, though. He had still held onto that hope, a hope that when she had seen England and her old life again, her desire would be satisfied and she would see Australia with fresh eyes and want to come back. But it looked as though that was going to be a forlorn hope for a long time to come.

'There you are, Ted.' William came into the shop. 'Wanted to talk to you about a few things — first chance I've had since you got back.'

'Just about finished here,' Ted said.

William watched till Ted had finished his job. Then they walked out together. 'Come up and have a cup of tea,' he said.

When they were settled with their tea and William had enquired about the break, he said, 'What's the country to the south looking like now, Ted?'

'Looks good,' Ted replied. 'Some good country down that way a bit, you know. Wouldn't mind having a bit of it. Good fattening country.'

'That's what I've been thinking. More reliable rainfall, too. I wonder what a man would have to pay for a good place?'

Ted looked up. Surely the boss was not thinking of selling 'Bibbaringa' — thought he loved the place.

William was speaking again, cutting through Ted's thoughts. 'We've been lucky with the seasons, you know. But it can't last forever. We get a good drought!' He left the sentence unfinished.

'That's certainly the drawback here,' Ted said tentatively.

'We need a place for fattening should that happen — just to keep them going, really. And it would also be great to have two or three places on the route to Adelaide markets. Then we could get cattle there in top condition. There's good demand for beef. The influx of immigrants since the mining discoveries has done a great deal for the beef industry.'

Ted relaxed. Obviously the boss was not thinking of selling. Rather, he was planning further development, the purchase of more properties. No doubt about him. He was a planner. Progressive. He really thought things out. He was lucky, of course, to have the dough to do it.

'Great idea if you can do it,' he ventured.

'Have to look more carefully into it,' William responded, smiling.

'Come to think of it, there was a place in the ranges area. Looked good land. Don't know what it's worth, of course, or what they're asking for it. Bloke named Winchester owns it. Heard about it on the way back. Might be worth keeping your ear to the ground. You could sound out the agent if you can get onto him.'

William grinned.

'Reckon it would be worth a trip to Adelaide?' he mused.

'Could be,' Ted ventured. It looked like the boss was really serious about this. He must have been thinking about it for a while to take it up like this. Perhaps there had been something in the mail he had brought home to confirm his ideas.

'Another thing, Ted.' William again broke into Ted's thoughts. 'Have you heard of anybody taking up land out this way? Any other venturers into this part of the world? I'm wondering if we are likely to get any neighbours.'

What was the boss onto now?

'Did hear talk of someone taking up some land south of the lake further west than us, of course.' He looked at William, trying to discern where this question would lead. 'Don't know whether it was right, but it was talked about. Still a good way from us.'

'Yes.' William was silent a moment. 'I was hoping you might have heard of the possibility of neighbours for us.' He turned to Ted and spoke softly. 'I think Mrs Bartlett must get a bit lonely sometimes. Do her good to have a good talk to another woman sometimes, someone close enough for an overnight visit occasionally.' He paused, then added. 'Women do think differently, you know.'

Ted nodded. 'She did take to the life here, though, didn't she?'

'Oh yes, wonderfully,' William said.

Ted was obviously thinking of his wife and her failure to adjust.

'Have you heard lately from your wife? Any change there? Any chance of her coming back?'

Ted shook his head. 'Doesn't sound like it,' he said simply.

William nodded sympathetically. After a moment, he said, 'If she ever does, Ted, let me know. We're in a position now to build married quarters. I regard you as part of the enterprise now. We've been together a few years.' He paused.

Poor old Ted. He was such a good, reliable bloke. 'Just let me know,' he added.

★ ★ ★

'A trip to Adelaide? Oh Willie, that would be wonderful! But why?' Caroline was all excitement.

William told her of his conversation with Ted and his ideas regarding the advisability of securing land en route to Adelaide markets. He said nothing of his reference to possible neighbours. He fully intended making those enquiries, though, when he got to Adelaide.

If there was talk of anyone venturing out taking up more land, expanding out, he would hear of it. The colony, although population was growing, was still not so advanced that something like this would not be known.

He had been so occupied with building up 'Bibbaringa' that he had not taken time on his brief trips to Adelaide to make any such enquiries. The time had been fully occupied with necessary business and family activities. This extra visit would give the opportunity.

'So I thought we would take a bit of time off and go and see the family and see if there is any interesting land offering. I feel we'll be very lucky if we don't get hit by drought before too long.

'I want to be ready for that. The more I think about it, the more advantages I can see in it. You never know, if all goes well, we might end up owning several places on that track. Then we could move stock around. Very interesting challenge.'

Caroline hugged him, laughing. 'That

would really be something for the 'Bartlett and Sons' enterprise, wouldn't it?' he grinned, teasing her. 'We could put one son in charge of each place, couldn't we? How about that?' He counted off on his fingers. 'How many properties? How many sons? Now what about the daughters?'

'Oh Willie, stop. Stop,' Caroline cried. 'We haven't got even one son yet, or daughter.'

'Oh we will, we will,' he replied. 'The name will go on. And 'Bibbaringa' will be known for its stock.' He looked at her, his eyes sparkling with fun. 'Cattle and humans.'

Caroline grabbed a cushion and threw it at him. He dodged it and strode out the door. Dear Willie. He had such plans! William Bartlett and Sons! But it wasn't on the horizon yet.

Caroline lapsed into a more sombre mood. When would she have a baby? She was healthy. Happy. And her marriage was happy and fulfilling. What was stopping her?

Although Willie joked, she knew he wanted a family as much as she did. He may not be in a hurry, but this talk of Bartlett and Sons Enterprise showed his desire. He took it for granted that sooner or later they would have children.

What if she failed him? What if she grew older and older and never had a child?

Her heart missed a beat. A fear welled up in her. It did happen sometimes. There were couples she knew — not many certainly, but there were cases where people never had any children, even though they wanted them badly.

O God, don't let me fail Willie, she prayed silently. To bear the fruit of their love. That was her great desire.

But then, perhaps, Willie was right. She shouldn't worry. It would surely happen sooner or later. She would put it out of her mind and be happy. They hadn't been married so many years yet to get really worried. She was just being impatient. She was just anxious. She had plenty of childbearing years left yet.

She laughed at herself as she picked up the cushion, plumped it and put it back on the chair. She really did get into a rut sometimes when she got set in a line of thinking. She must be more objective and keep her thoughts and her emotions under control. Willie was right. There was plenty of time.

A little persistent voice in the back of her head whispered, 'But there's still no baby.'

16

Action and consultation

What a lovely wedding photograph it was! Caroline held it in her hands. The smiling faces looked back at her. It had been such a wonderful day. She studied each face, her dress, Willie's glowing expression, Father's pride. Polishing the glass with her cloth, she placed the photograph back on the credenza.

It had been eight years. What wonderful years they had been! She and Willie had grown closer and closer to each other until now it was hard to remember life without him. Of course, they had differences every now and then, but they were soon made up and their harmony restored.

How far they had come in their development of 'Bibbaringa'! — or, she corrected herself, the 'Bartlett Enterprise'.

Willie had bought the property Ted had told him about after the leave when he had escorted Mother and Father back to Adelaide. That trip to Adelaide had been the greatest fun. Willie had made all sorts of enquiries. She and Bella and Mother had gone shopping and visited so many friends. She had caught up on so much news.

Then, as they came back home, they had spent two days at the homestead of the property in the ranges. 'Onavale' it was called. Willie had inspected the place and liked what he saw. It was very different from 'Bibbaringa'. I must be acclimatised — prejudiced or something, she thought to herself. It was beautiful country. It would certainly be a more secure rainfall property. But it didn't have the openness, the vastness, the wide horizons of 'Bibbaringa'.

As they had travelled home, she had felt herself relaxing and looking expectantly for that wide sky, the distant vistas. Then there was the feeling of coming home as they came closer. There's a freedom, a bigness about this place I love, she thought. You could never feel shut in here.

It had proved a boon having the new place these last few years, too. Willie's vision had been vindicated. Now, when the drovers took cattle to Adelaide, they spent several weeks at 'Onavale' to finish for market.

She looked again at the photograph. Eight years. Eight years of happy marriage — but still no children. Suddenly, Caroline made her decision. She went in search of Willie. 'I want to talk to you,' she said when she found him. Willie looked at her in surprise. What was on her mind? He followed her back to the house. 'I want to make a trip to Adelaide,' Caroline said when they were seated.

'Oh? What's urgent?' Willie asked in surprise. Why had Caro come to find him to make this declaration? They could have talked about a trip over lunch if there was something she wanted to go to Adelaide to choose for herself.

'Well, I suppose it's not exactly urgent. But I've just come to a decision and I want to do it now.'

Willie waited. What was Caro talking about? It sounded as though it was important to her whatever was on her mind. 'I want to go to Adelaide and get some medical advice as to why I haven't started with a baby. There's been no sign of a baby. And it's eight years! It suddenly hit me this morning when I was looking at our wedding photograph. Eight years, Willie! And no sign!'

Willie let out his breath. So this was it. Caro was thinking again that perhaps there was something wrong with her.

She was speaking again. 'We've just been waiting and hoping. And nothing has happened! Year after year is going and still nothing!' Her voice was beginning to shake a little. 'I want to go and see someone about it. Now.'

She watched for his reaction. Would he take her seriously? He always said she was worrying about nothing. William put his hand over hers. 'If that's what you want, then that's what we'll do,' he said, looking earnestly into her eyes. 'I think you'll find all is well. I can't think there is anything wrong with you. You are very well and healthy. But if it will set your mind at ease, we will go.' He paused a moment. 'When did you have in mind? I need a little time to leave things in order.'

'Oh yes. Of course.' Caroline had relaxed now. She had opened the floodgates of her concern. 'Just as soon as possible. I just had to talk to you now about it and start making arrangements.' She paused, then continued. 'I just know we shouldn't wait, drifting along, any longer. I just came to a definite decision when I was dusting our wedding photograph.'

She looked up, smiling now. Willie shook his head. The ways of a woman, he thought. He kissed her gently. How precious she was. He sometimes found it hard to follow her thought pattern, but she was infinitely precious.

The journey to Adelaide was accomplished in the buggy Willie had bought the previous year. This was the first time Caroline had travelled any distance in it. It was a stylish vehicle with red wheels and brass trimming — too stylish, really, for their isolation, Willie had said. But times were changing and, when the new people who were buying land south of the lake were established, it would be good for Caroline to be able to drive herself in comfort and dignity to visit.

How thoughtful he was for her happiness, Caroline thought. Now that there was action regarding her long-held anxiety, she was feeling better.

They sped along happily, seated side by side, their luggage stowed behind. William handled the horses easily, talking of his plans for the country they passed through and stock they saw. They would spend a night at 'Onavale' on the way.

The miles sped by. There was quite a discernible track now with the passage of the bullock waggons bringing supplies, their own visits to Adelaide and the movement between 'Bibbaringa' and 'Onavale'. In a few years it could even be a road. How fast the country was opening up and developing!

The visit to 'Onavale' was most enjoyable. They were a pleasant couple, the manager and his wife. Willie had been fortunate to secure such a couple. The house was neat and had been arranged attractively. They had started a garden.

Willie was happy with what he saw as they travelled through the property. The cattle were looking good. Around the homestead, all looked cared for and well ordered. It would surely be an asset.

They said goodbye with light hearts. Willie approved the bookwork of the manager — and the company of another woman had done wonders for Caroline. They set their horses for the next stage of the journey.

As they left the ranges and moved south, Caroline was constantly exclaiming about the settlement that had taken place in the last twelve months. Where such a short time ago so much was still wild and uninhabited, cabins were springing up. Some were mere huts, shacks, shanties. But some were more substantial, with fences and gardens. The land in places was being fenced into paddocks.

Momentarily, she thought of trying to fence 'Bibbaringa'. This is a different world, she thought. I could never come back here. It's beautiful in its way, but it will become fenced in. 'Bibbaringa' will never be fenced in. There will always be room to move and breathe.

Caroline's excitement mounted as they swept up the hill to the rectory. Mother and

Father didn't know they were coming. This was a surprise visit. They rounded the corner and entered through the open gates of the drive, pulling up at the door. Willie jumped down and held out his hand to Caroline to help her descend.

The front door opened and James Hilliard peered out over his glasses to see who was coming. Suddenly, he realised who it was. He dropped his book and, calling to his wife, came hurriedly down the steps to throw his arms around his daughter and wring William's hand with much back thumping.

Elizabeth Hilliard, startled by her husband's call, came running and joined in the melee of surprise and joy. 'And what brings you to Adelaide just now?' James asked when they were all settled down sufficiently and enjoying a cup of tea.

Caroline told them of her decision. They had long known of her desire. They would understand. They would not think her foolish.

'So, we must find you the best doctor possible,' her father said. He looked at his wife. 'Have you any ideas? Any particular person to suggest?'

'We'll ask May,' she said definitely. 'She has far more knowledge in these things than I have. I feel sure she will have some views on the matter.'

Aunt May! Of course! She had brought lots and lots of babies into the world. She would know what to do and where to go. Her experience would be a wonderful help.

'And so we wondered if you could advise us, Aunt May,' Caroline concluded. Aunt May had come for the day after getting a surprise visit from her brother-in-law, acquainting her with the news of Caroline and Willie's visit.

'Oh yes, my dear,' May said. 'I have worked or had something to do with most of the doctors in town. I must say I think Mr Baddely will be the best person for you to see. He is very approachable and you will find him sympathetic. Would you like me to approach him for you?'

'Oh yes, please,' Caroline said quickly. 'As soon as possible.'

'I'll call on him when I'm in town after lunch and let you know how I get on, as I go home.'

Now that the time had come, Caroline was in conflict. It was what she had been wanting for so long, but hadn't brought herself to the point of decision. Now she might know from the doctor tomorrow.

What if he said she would never have

children? Her dreams and hopes would be shattered. Her resolve wavered. Did she really want to know for sure? Don't be a ninny, she chided herself. She had come all this way. Of course she wanted to know. Even if there was something wrong, there may be treatment available.

It was a tense and nervous wife that Willie escorted into Mr Baddely's rooms the next day. Aunt May had duly made the arrangement.

'Don't be nervous, my dear. Be quite truthful with him. Remember this is his vocation in life. He has had great experience and helped many women.' I must keep remembering Aunt May's words, Caroline reminded herself as they were ushered into the surgery.

A dark-haired man, greying at the temples, was seated behind the big desk. He smiled and motioned them to chairs as he stood up to greet them. 'Now, Mrs Bartlett, your aunt tells me you are very anxious to have a baby and that you have been married for eight years without yet anything happening in this area. Naturally you are anxious. It is a very big built-in desire in us.' He smiled as he added, 'Particularly for women.'

Caroline was relaxing. Obviously he didn't

think she was being foolish or over-anxious. He understood.

Dear Aunt May, for finding her someone like this! She poured out her heart to him — the longing; the great desire; the fear. Her voice faltered, the tears flowed, but she persisted. He listened silently, nodding his head occasionally. He questioned her for some time. At last he said, 'Well, my dear, come along now into the examination room.'

He rose and moved towards the connecting door. 'We'll just see how things are with you.' He looked reassuringly at Willie. 'It won't take very long,' he added. They disappeared through the doorway into the little room.

17

Trust and obey

Elizabeth Hilliard smoothed back the hair from Caroline's forehead as she sat beside her on the couch. 'Oh my darling, don't cry so.' She was nearly in tears herself. Her heart ached for this child of hers.

'But Mother, he said he doesn't think I will ever have a child. He said, 'I won't say it is impossible, but it is most unlikely.' Why Mother? Why? When there are children born every day who are not wanted, who are neglected — even ill-used. Why, oh why can't I have one when I want one so much?' Another wave of tears flowed.

Willie came into the room carrying a tray with drinks. 'And here's Willie building up our Bartlett and Sons Enterprise, and we're never going to have a son!'

Willie held a glass to her, his arm around her shoulders. 'Never mind the Bartlett and Sons Enterprise, Caro. It's not final that we won't have any children. He just said unlikely.' He paused, shattered himself, but trying to comfort Caroline. 'Anyway, the

167

important thing is we've got each other,' he added.

Elizabeth looked at him, her eyes showing her love and appreciation of this young man who was so good to her daughter. He was, indeed, a fine addition to their family as James so often said. He was no doubt feeling the impact of this news greatly, but he could still put his own feelings aside for Caroline's sake.

Caroline sipped her drink. It burned down her throat and sent a warm glow through her. Gradually she calmed. 'You remember that bad illness I had when I was about twelve?' she said. 'He said that may have had some lasting effect on me.'

James Hilliard came into the room. Obviously Carry's news from the doctor was not good. Young William also looked very crestfallen. 'Well, my dear, how did you get on?' he asked, trying to keep a cheerful note in his voice.

'Oh Father!' Caroline held out her arms to him. Her tears flowed again. He came to her, his arms around her comforting, resting her head on his shoulder.

The doorbell rang loudly through the house. 'I'll go,' Elizabeth said rising. She hurried from the room. Caroline, between sobs, told her father the outcome of her visit to Mr Baddely.

Elizabeth came back. 'I'm sorry, darling,' she said softly to Caroline. 'James, it is Ellen Travers. She's very upset. She got home to find a note from Phillip. He's gone off east somewhere and taken all their money. She has three children, you know. She wants to talk to you. She just doesn't know where to turn.'

James disengaged himself from his daughter. 'I'll be back as soon as I can, Carry. This is what comes of spoiling your children. Phillip was a very spoilt boy. Ellen is a good wife to him, but he just doesn't want to take any responsibility. I'd better see what can be done for the poor lass.' He went out, shaking his head.

Caroline reached out to Willie. He caught her hand. 'Poor Ellen,' she said. 'I know I'm lucky to have a husband like you, Willie.' His arms came round her, holding her close. This glimpse of some other person's reality had steadied her. She would be all right.

It was late afternoon before James had an opportunity to get back to a private family talk. Why did these things always happen at a moment of family importance? And yet, in a way, the knowledge of poor Ellen's predicament had helped Caroline.

Poor Carry, what a blow to her! She had so set her heart on a family. She was good with children and they always seemed to take to her. Why was it that she was not to be a mother? Not the physical reasons, but why had God decreed things this way? She would be a good mother. She would care well for her child.

How deep this longing for a child was with women. James' mind wandered to the biblical figure of Hannah, mother of Samuel. Then there was Elizabeth, mother of John the Baptist. Then there was also Sarah, away back in the Old Testament. All these characters of long ago had borne children even though it seemed unlikely. Thus ran James' thoughts as he came into the house. He found Caroline in the sitting room. 'Alone, my Carry?' he asked.

'Yes, Mother is seeing about tea and Willie has gone to see his grandmother.'

Her father eyed her keenly. 'Feeling better, my dear?'

'Oh yes. But oh, Father, it is more than a disappointment. I so want a baby of my own. I know I can perhaps find a child I can adopt — a child who has no parents or a child nobody wants — and I could love that child. Maybe I will come to that.' She paused. 'But it's not the same. I want a baby that's Willie's and mine — our own flesh and blood. I want it so much.'

James nodded. He understood.

'Why do you think God doesn't seem to be going to grant me my great desire?' Caroline lifted beseeching eyes to her father. 'I do try to live a good Christian life, Father.'

Her father's heart went out to her. He patted her hand. 'I know you do, my love,' he said. 'But all is not lost. You must not lose hope.'

Caroline lifted surprised eyes to him.

'Mr Baddely did not say irrevocably that you will not have a child. He said it was unlikely. I was thinking as I came in. You know, there are women in the Bible who desired just this thing you desire, a child of their own — a great desire. Good women, God-fearing women they were. Just you remember. Hannah, Samuel's mother — she had no child. She longed for a child. She prayed and God gave her a son, Samuel. And she gave him back to the Lord to serve him all his days.'

He had her attention as he went on to talk about Elizabeth and Sarah in the Bible. 'In all this, in reminding you of all this, my dear, I am saying nothing is impossible with God. Pray, my dear. Pray with all your heart, believing God will grant your request if it is for your good and it is his will. Trust him and follow all his promptings.'

Caroline was thoughtful for a few minutes.

The clock on the mantel shelf ticked loudly in the silence. Then Caroline lifted her eyes to her father. 'Do you really think there is hope, Father?' she said softly.

'Are you willing to accept God's decision for you, my dear?' he asked gently. 'If God's answer is 'No', are you willing to accept that, if for some reason it is not what God wills.'

Caroline thought a moment. 'Yes. Yes, I am willing. I've got to be honest. I don't want it to be 'No'. I want a child so badly. But yes, I know God knows best. I'm just likely to forget it.' She smiled ruefully.

'Aren't we all?' her father rejoined. 'If you can accept that, then, that God knows best, then you've crossed your greatest hurdle. That is trust. It doesn't mean you can't pray for what you want. Far from it. Pray with all your heart. Just remember to add 'but you know best, Lord!' That is trusting and obeying. It's also being honest and open with God — and yourself.'

Caroline nodded. Father was right. She hadn't thought about it like this. She had been asking Why: Why, God, don't you let me have a child? But she hadn't thought of it like this.

Come to think of it, she hadn't really prayed for a child. She had just been feeling aggrieved and afraid that she was never going to succeed. She hadn't come to God asking, like a little child asked his father for something. What a ninny she was. How could she forget all these things she had been taught for as long as she could remember?

'God is your loving heavenly Father,' Father had always said. 'Talk to him. Ask of him just as you would the most loving father you can ever imagine.'

How could she have forgotten? How lucky she was to have dear Father to talk to her like this. She wasn't old. She certainly wasn't past the age of having a child.

'God still works today. He is still active just as he was away back in those olden days.' Her father's voice cut into her thoughts. 'God loses nothing of his power. Nothing is impossible with God if it is his will.'

The clock struck six. There were footsteps approaching. The back door opened and closed. 'Here comes Mother to say tea is ready.' He stood up and looked down the passageway. 'And here is Willie back just in time for tea. He must have an inbuilt clock.'

'Oh, Willie is always on time for meals. He's always hungry, ready for his meal.' She stood up. Linking arms, they walked through into the dining room.

Elizabeth set the hot dishes down before James' place at the head of the table. 'Come along, now, before it gets cold,' she called. 'James, grace please.'

They held hands around the table:

> '*For what you have provided, Lord,*
> *For she who has prepared,*
> *For all we who are in trust*
> *and obedience about to receive,*
> *We thank you O Lord.*'

James smiled at his daughter across the table.

18

Day by day

The spinning wheel turned smoothly. The rhythmic treadling, the soft whir of the wheel was very relaxing. This was a task Caroline thoroughly enjoyed.

It was pleasant here on the verandah. The garden was progressing, though not as quickly as she would have liked. The wool being deftly spun into thread was soft, the oil smoothing her hands. She picked up a combed piece from the prepared basket and touched it softly. It was like thistledown, she thought; so soft and lovely.

What a dear Willie was to have bought those sheep. He had even thought of getting some black ones for her. They had arrived as a surprise. Now she had a yearly supply of white and black wool to spin, then make up for their needs. It would be fun to try out the weaving loom they had bought. It would be more suitable for certain garments than knitting or crocheting.

Her mind ran on as her foot moved up and down on the treadle. The wheel turned smoothly and the wool ran through her fingers, back and forth, back and forth, the spindle drawing it in. This wool had a creamy yolk. It would be soft enough — lovely, in fact, for baby clothes.

That's what she would do. She'd make some little jackets up in this finest wool. Then, if God granted her desire, she would have a start in preparation. She had some baby patterns somewhere. She'd look them out after lunch and see what was needed. She glowed with happy anticipation at the prospect.

Caroline lifted her eyes and looked out over the paddocks. What was that away out? A speck on the landscape appeared out of the haze, moving. She stopped treadling and shaded her eyes with her hand. No, it wasn't a rider. It looked like someone walking. But who would be walking down the track by the creek? That only went to the northern outstation. There was no track further on. There was thick scrub and no marked territory.

Even Willie hadn't been much further than their boundary. It was no man's land. It belonged to the government, she supposed, strictly speaking. It was crown land, but uninhabited and unknown — by whites, at least. Apparently, the Aborigines knew it and periodically travelled that way.

The figure was coming closer. He had an unusual gait. He didn't seem to be running, yet he covered the ground surprisingly quickly. It was a smooth, rhythmic movement.

She stood up to watch. He moved closer. Good heavens! It was a Chinaman. However did a Chinaman come to be here — to just appear down the track? She went back to her spinning, keeping an eye on the approaching figure. She waited until he was close, then walked down the path to meet him as he neared the gate.

He stopped and put down his bundle. 'Good morning, Missie. Wan Loo at your service.' He bowed as he spoke.

'Good morning, Wan Loo. I am Mrs Bartlett. Wherever have you come from? Where are you going?'

'Ah, Wan Loo foolish man. Come to find gold. Long way.' He drew out the word. 'No like mining camp. Go with drovers. Cook for them. Wan Loo no like move, move all a time. Wan Loo look for home.' There was much gesticulation as he spoke. His expression became solemn as he finished.

'You are looking for a home?' Whatever was to be made of this little man? He had come to find gold, left that because he didn't like life in the mining camp, went as cook with drovers, but didn't like moving all the time. Now he was looking for a home. Did this mean he was looking for work, somewhere to settle down? 'Do you want work, Wan Loo?'

'Work and home, Missie.'

'What work do you do? You can cook?'

The little man smiled. 'Very good cook, Missie. Wan Loo make good cooking.'

'Mmm. Maybe you like to cook dinner for me? Show me?'

Wan Loo smiled broadly. 'Make dinner for you, Missy.' Caroline led him round to the kitchen. How wonderful this would be if he was in any way a decent cook! Their last cook had got tired of the isolation and had packed up and left while they were in Adelaide. The whole responsibility for feeding all hands had fallen to Caroline since their return. It took up too much of her time to still cope with all her other activities.

Wan Loo pointed. 'Good stove,' he said approvingly. 'Where is meat house, Missie?' Caroline took him on a tour of inspection.

He looked disparagingly at the vegetable garden. 'Not much good vegetable,' he said with a wave of his hand. 'Need good vegetable.'

Caroline was rather taken aback. Not good? She had laboured over this little patch.

She was even rather proud of what she had been able to achieve. 'Not good?' she asked, her brow wrinkling.

Wan Loo shook his head. 'Nooo. Need water. Need dig. Need . . . ' He went on with an endless list of what was needed.

Suddenly, Caroline forgot her indignation. This Chinaman must be a gardener, a *real* gardener. He seemed to know all about it. And he wanted to settle down, to find a home? Oh, if only he would stay and take over the gardening — maybe the cooking, too, if he was any good in that direction. 'You like garden?' she asked.

'Ah — like very much to garden,' he nodded emphatically.

'You cook and garden for me?' Caroline asked.

He looked surprised, happy.

'You cook good dinner, we see what boss says.' Caroline led the way back to the kitchen. She left him there examining the contents of the cupboards and went back to her spinning.

What would Willie say? He'd certainly be surprised to find a Chinese cook at work in the kitchen. She smiled to herself. It was almost too good to be true, to get two in one, a cook and a gardener in the person of one round little Chinese man.

Wan Loo served a very presentable meal to Caroline at midday. As he had not had a great deal of time, Caroline was surprised and pleased. If he could do this well on short notice, he would certainly be adequate to meet the requirements of cook on the station. 'Wan Loo, you make dinner for boss tonight?' she asked when she took her plates to the scullery.

'Make dinner, make dinner,' chanted Wan Loo, smiling broadly and bowing. 'Wan Loo make Chinese dinner?'

Caroline considered this. Would Willie like Chinese food? Why not? They'd try it. It would certainly be a change. 'Yes, that would be nice, Wan Loo. But you can cook Australian meal, too?'

'Yes, yes, can cook.'

She nodded and left him to his preparations. As she turned the corner of the verandah, she noticed a piece of downpipe opened out at the top, leading from the edge of the verandah out onto the vegetable patch. The soil around the bottom of the downpipe was wet. Wan Loo must have put it there to carry water from the kitchen to the garden. Oh Willie, she thought, I hope you are as keen as I am about this little man.

'Caro, where are you? What on earth is going on in the kitchen? Who's in there?

180

There's all sorts of noises coming from there.' Willie came striding along the verandah.

'Come and sit down. I want to talk to you.' Caroline patted the chair beside her. She went on excitedly. 'Willie, the most wonderful thing has happened.'

Whatever had happened to so enthuse Caro? She was almost beside herself with excitement, her words tumbling out on top of each other. It was so good to see her like this, her eyes sparkling, her hands emphasising her words. He'd better pay attention to what she was saying.

'I saw him coming away up the track. I was sitting here spinning, you see. Oh yes, and I thought I'd spin some very fine wool and make up some little baby jackets. I know I've got some patterns. I'll have to look those out.'

She was nodding and gesticulating as she spoke. 'When he got closer, I could see he was a Chinaman — a little round fat man with a pigtail. I couldn't have been more surprised!' She went on to tell him what had happened.

'So you think you could have a cook and a gardener in one go, eh?' Willie smiled. No wonder she was so keyed up. This garden had become very important to her. She worked hard at it and was really doing very well under the circumstances.

'Yes, I'm hoping so. I've asked him to cook dinner for us, so you can see what sort of cook he is.' She hesitated. 'There's just one thing. He suggested cooking Chinese dinner. I don't know how you will like that, but he was so keen I didn't have the heart to say no. He cooks Australian meals, too, he said.'

'Well, we'll see, won't we?' William rose. 'I'll go and make his acquaintance.'

There were some appetising odours coming from the kitchen as William came around the verandah. Standing in front of the stove stirring onions in the pan was the man. What had Caro said was his name? Wan something. Oh yes, Wan Loo.

'Hullo there. Wan Loo, is it?' William said from the doorway. The little man turned sharply. 'William Bartlett.' He held out his hand. Wan Loo shook his hand, bowing as he did so. He really was very polite — just as Caro had said.

'My wife tells me you are looking for work.'

Wan Loo nodded. 'Work and home,' he said.

They talked for some time, William trying to ascertain his previous jobs and where he had come from. It appeared he had spent some time after the droving job with a tribe of Aborigines and had left them further north. They had told him of 'Bibbaringa' and told him if he followed the sand ridges he would come to the open country around the homestead.

'However did you find food when you were on your own after you left the blacks?' William asked.

'Oh, Wan Loo learn about bush tucker from black friends.' He smiled broadly, bowing and gesticulating with his hands. 'Wan Loo eat very well. Not Chinese food. But not go hungry.' He patted his stomach.

That was very obvious, William thought. Oh well, the fellow seemed all right. Quite an interesting, pleasant fellow, actually. He'd give him a go. It would certainly make Caro very happy if he turned out to be such a good gardener.

'Would you like to work for me? Cook and gardener?'

'Very much like. Wan Loo like garden. Like cook.' He looked around and waved his arm. 'Beautiful house,' he said. 'Wan Loo want to find home.'

'Well, you make good dinner and we'll call it settled.'

And so a new member was added to the establishment. Here's hoping he will settle down and stay, William thought as he went back to Caro to tell her what had been decided.

It would be just too bad if they got used to having him and Caro's garden did well, then he decided to move on. He thought about the prospect and the inability of replacement if such eventuated. Oh well, no use crossing your bridges till you came to them. It may not happen. They'd just have to wait and see.

19

Help and discernment

A spiral of smoke came from the creek bank. The blacks were back and camped there in their favourite spot. It looked as though they were intending to stay for some time. They had shown great interest in the new buildings and had ventured close to take in all the details when Willie had encouraged them to do so.

It was good to have them back, really. There were certain of the men who were anxious to try out stock work when Willie needed extra hands. They mounted a horse with much chatter and laughter but, once seated, were doing surprisingly well.

Would it be possible to train some of the girls in housework, Caroline wondered. There were some girls from tribes in other places who did housework and also looked after children. They seemed to like that kind of work. It would be a help to have a couple of girls' assistance. She would talk to Willie about it.

Perhaps it was the heat. She was feeling

rather tired and fell asleep if she sat down quietly for long. It would be good to offload some of the work.

Willie was most enthusiastic about the idea when she mentioned it later. He would go down to the camp and see if there was any interest. They were very curious about the inside of the house and all the things this white Mrs used. There may be more wanting jobs than they could cater for.

Just on dark, Willie came striding up the path. Caroline heard the gate slam shut and Willie's step on the verandah.

'Well, how did you get on?' she called.

'Very well,' he replied, sitting down to loosen his boots. 'There are two girls, Minnie and Polly. That's what we're to call them. Their tribal names are unpronounceable. Anyway, they want to try. You'll have a job, I think. They don't know anything about housework, but are anxious to learn. I've taken on a couple of the young men for regular work and they seem to be setting a fashion. I guess you'll have to dress the girls if they are coming into the house — for while they are here, anyway.'

Caroline considered all this. She found two dresses she thought sufficiently suitable. It depended on the size and shape of the girls. Willie had told them to come to the house the next morning.

186

Wan Loo was making a real racket washing the breakfast pots and pans, when Caroline noticed two of the black girls near the front gate. They hung back, scraping a toe in the dirt, looking at each other and giggling. Caroline opened the door and called to them. Hesitantly, urging each other, they opened the gate and made their way slowly up the path.

Caroline met them at the edge of the verandah. 'You like to work for me?' she asked, gesticulating to help them understand what she was saying.

Both girls nodded.

'You clean house?' Caroline picked up the broom to show them how to sweep. They watched attentively, then again nodded. She went through the antics of various cleaning jobs to demonstrate. They were happy to try.

Leaving them to try their hands at sweeping the verandah, she went into her room and picked up the dresses. She held them up as she came out onto the verandah. The girls looked up, their faces questioning, uncomprehending. Caroline pointed to the dresses and back to the girls.

'You put on?' she asked, raising her eyebrows and smiling. She pretended to pull the dress over her head and pointed to the girls.

Suddenly, one girl understood what she was proposing. Her eyes flew open as wide as saucers. She threw back her head and laughed then, putting her arm over her eyes and, pointing at the dress with her other hand, giggled. Her companion now grasped what was being suggested and joined in the hilarity.

After several attempts, hampered by the frivolity of the girls who obviously thought the whole thing absurd, each had donned the dress she had been given. I won't even suggest shoes, Caroline thought. That would be just too much.

She had established the girls' names. Minnie was a slim, lithe little miss, with a flashing smile and beautiful big dark brown eyes. Polly was shorter and plumper, possibly a couple of years older and of a gentler disposition, Caroline suspected.

The noise from the kitchen area had abated somewhat, so Caroline thought it an opportune time to introduce Wan Loo to the two new members of household staff. 'Wan Loo,' she said as she entered the kitchen. 'We have two new members of staff I want you to meet. They are going to learn to help me in the house — Polly and Minnie.' She indicated the girls as she spoke.

Wan Loo stepped forward, bowed; his

polite self. 'Very pleased to meet you,' he said in his sing-song voice. 'Wan Loo welcome you.'

Polly looked demurely at the floor and nodded her acknowledgement. Minnie, Caroline noticed with shock, dropped her eyes to the floor, then raised them directly at Wan Loo, and flashed a provocative look, her long eyelashes sweeping her cheeks. Her smile tipped her lips at the corners, a teasing smile.

The little minx, Caroline thought. She's flirting with Wan Loo already. She'd have to watch that one.

Suddenly, she felt a wave of giddiness wash over her. She clutched the wall for support. Wan Loo hastened to her aid. Helping her to a chair, he cried, 'You sick, Missie? What wrong?' Caroline was beginning to feel better already.

'No, no. I don't know, Wan Loo. I'll be right in a minute, I think.'

They left the kitchen a few minutes later, Caroline quite recovered. The girls handed back the dresses and promised to be back next morning.

Missie tired, Wan Loo thought as he saw Caroline in the garden next day. He would tell boss she needed to rest. Those girls could do work now.

He glanced away from the thought of the

silent interchange between Minnie and himself yesterday. Not modest, that girl. Not like Chinese girl. He shook his head and turned back to his preparations for dinner.

Polly and Minnie were quick to learn under Caroline's tuition. They were most interested in household things. Minnie was especially bright and forthright. When she swept the verandah, it didn't matter at all if she missed a few leaves. When Caroline corrected her in this, her eyes flew wide open in surprise. Even if she went ever so slowly and carefully, the wind would only blow more onto where she had swept.

Polly was not nearly so quick, but much more willing to be thorough and do her work well. She even took pride in it and glowed with satisfaction when Caroline praised her efforts.

Both girls were quickly picking up English words and communication became easier.

'Whatever is Wan Loo cooking?' Caroline said one day. 'That smell coming from the kitchen is making me feel sick.'

Minnie looked at her under her eyelids. The two girls exchanged glances. The cooking smell was making their mouths water. They were hungry for lunch.

Caroline picked at her lunch.

'Wan Loo is a good cook, isn't he?' Willie

said, finishing the last bits on his plate. 'That was good.' He looked at Caroline's plate. 'What's the matter, Caro? You've hardly touched your meal.'

'Oh, I can't eat it. The smell is enough. It makes me feel quite ill.'

Willie looked at her with concern. 'But it was good. I enjoyed it very much,' he said, puzzled. 'Wan Loo tells me you are tired. He says you do too much and that you had a little fainting turn in the kitchen one day recently.'

'Yes, I did, but it passed quickly. I was wondering if that bacon we've been having is all right.'

Willie insisted she rest for the afternoon. She had been lying down only a few minutes when she fell asleep and slept until the sun was down.

'You better, Missy?' Polly asked next day as they turned out the sitting room. Polly particularly liked this room with its dark green velvet curtains, padded chairs, soft cushions and rugs scattered on the polished floor boards.

'Yes, I think so, thankyou Polly,' Caroline replied. Minnie was on her knees rubbing the beeswax into the floor. She wasn't very keen about this job and could see little difference in spite of her desultory efforts.

Polly brushed the chairs and plumped the cushions. Caroline lifted her eyes to Polly brushing a lime-green plush cushion. A wave of nausea swept over her. She looked away hastily and went on with her polishing of glasses on the chiffonier.

After a few puzzled moments, she looked back at Polly. She was putting the cushion, one she greatly admired, back on the chair, sitting it upright. The limegreen pattern again sent the wave of nausea over Caroline. 'What on earth is wrong with me?' she cried in exasperation. 'Why should a cushion make me feel ill?'

Minnie sat up, still kneeling on the floor. 'You baby,' she said solemnly, patting her stomach. 'Baby,' she repeated, nodding her head knowingly.

Shocked, Caroline's eyes turned quickly to Polly. She nodded agreement, a little smile playing round her lips. Baby? They were suggesting she had a baby in her stomach! In shocked disbelief, Caroline stared at them both. Could it be possible? What was the date? Suddenly she realised, with incredulous certainty, that it could very well be so!

Not daring to believe the possibility, she sat down to go over the various odd little things that had happened of late. Could it be true? Could her dreams be about to be realised?

She had prayed for a baby, oh so earnestly and so long. Was God about to fulfil her desire? The enormity of it almost over-whelmed her.

'Didn't you believe God would answer your prayer?' a voice in the back of her mind asked. 'I thought you were believing and trusting.'

The rest of the morning passed in a haze for Caroline. Her mind was filled with the great question. A baby. She could be having a baby. It was almost ten years now they had been married. It could be a great dream was to be fulfilled. Willie's Bartlett and Sons Enterprise could yet be a reality.

It all went round and round in her mind. Oh, to have Mother at hand to talk to — or Aunty May. What would they say if this was true?

She would have to go to Adelaide to see Mr Baddely again to be sure. Oh, she must know as soon as possible. She'd wait just a little bit before saying anything to Willie, just in case.

Why hadn't she thought of this before? Why hadn't she noticed the dates? The days had been busy and interesting, filled with the company and getting to know the two girls who now helped her. And to think it was they who had brought it all to her attention! She hugged herself in anticipation, hardly daring to allow herself to become excited.

Willie was aware of a change in her. She was still not eating well, but she seemed happy. She was unusually quiet, but he caught her at times, a little smile playing about her lips. When she looked up, sometimes there was something in her eyes. She had almost a glow about her. There was something of suppressed excitement about her. Yet what was there to be particularly excited about? Perhaps she was just feeling the benefit of the help in the house and enjoying the company of the girls.

Unable to keep the secret to herself any longer, and wanting to share the excitement of the possibility, Caroline eventually revealed her thoughts to Willie.

His response of delight was beyond bounds. 'What did I tell you? You see, there is nothing wrong with you. I told you there wasn't,' he cried.

'Now don't get too excited. It's not confirmed yet. We'll have to go to Adelaide to see Mr Baddely again.'

Willie nodded. 'Of course. When do you suggest we go?' They talked far into the night, hugging each other when they visualised again the possibility of a dream fulfilled.

They must go as soon as possible. It was important to have it established. It was two years almost since Caroline had seen the doctor. They hoped he was still there and would be able to see her. They would contact him as soon as they arrived and make an appointment for the earliest opportunity.

A thrill — half excitement and happy anticipation and half apprehensive fear — ran through them.

What would be his diagnosis?

20

Confirmation

The trip to Adelaide was accomplished without difficulty. Caroline's parents had been overjoyed to see them and to hear the reason for this unscheduled visit. 'I am sure you are expecting,' Elizabeth told her daughter. She smiled. 'You have the look.'

'Whatever do you mean, Mother?' Caroline asked. 'The look! How can you tell by a look?'

Elizabeth laughed. 'Call it a sixth sense. I'm usually right.'

The appointment with Mr Baddely was duly made and Caroline and William again waited in his rooms. This time, there was excitement tinged with trepidation. Would his diagnosis confirm their hopes? Or could all the symptoms indicate some dire intractable difficulty requiring urgent solution?

'Mrs Bartlett, would you come through, please?' The receptionist ushered them in.

Mr Baddely addressed them heartily. 'Sit down, please. You have had a good journey, I trust.'

'Oh yes, very good.' Caroline's heart was thumping hard. The moment had come. Please God, let it be, she prayed inwardly. Let me be having a baby.

'And so you think you may be pregnant, Mrs Bartlett? That will be wonderful if it proves to be correct.'

He said 'if it proves to be correct'! Did he think it may not be correct? Oh please, God, please let it be true.

He was talking again. Caroline wrenched her attention back to the doctor. 'Now tell me, my dear, all that makes you think you may be pregnant.'

She detailed all the reasons, all that had happened to make her realise the possibility. 'And when I realised the date, I just couldn't believe it,' she finished.

Mr Baddely smiled. 'Well, come through and we will see what's happening.'

After the examination, he helped Caroline down from the table. He had said nothing more than 'Mmm, good, that's all right.' Now he led the way back to the surgery. What was he going to say? Why didn't he say something? Was she having a baby or not?

William looked up expectantly. He caught Caroline's eye and realised she had not been told she was pregnant. Was something wrong?

Caroline resumed her seat and Mr Baddely

sat down behind his desk. He leant forward leaning on his elbows, resting his chin on his hands. He smiled broadly. 'I am very pleased to tell you there is no doubt whatever you are pregnant. There is a very definite little body there, doing very nicely.'

Caroline burst into tears — tears of joy, of wonder, of incredulous acceptance of the wonderful fact. William's arms came round her. They were on their feet, overwhelmed. William fished in his pocket for his handkerchief to wipe away Caroline's tears and surreptitiously wiped the corners of his own eyes. Laughing, swallowing the great lump in his throat, he spoke huskily. 'Come on, Caro. What are you crying about? I thought you wanted a baby.'

The ride home in the carriage was quiet. Caroline leant against Willie's shoulder, exhausted after the great rush of emotion.

As they tumbled from the carriage, James and Elizabeth came hurrying out to meet them. 'Yes, yes,' Caroline called, waving her gloved hand. 'It's true. I can't believe it yet, but it's true. He says there's no doubt whatsoever!'

'Praise the Lord,' cried James joyously as he enfolded his daughter in his arms. 'Praise the Lord. You see? Didn't I say nothing is impossible with God?'

'Yes, yes, Father. I did as you said. At least I thought I did, until Minnie said I had a baby,' she patted her stomach. 'Then I realised I hadn't really been expecting it to come true. I didn't even recognise any of the signs!'

'Never mind. God is true to his promise always. You prayed and he heard your prayer. This child will be a special gift from God.' He patted his daughter and, putting his other arm around Willie's shoulder, led the way back inside.

Elizabeth wiped her eyes. Oh, the joy! Caroline was to have the baby she so desired. She and James were to have a grandchild. 'Thank you, thankyou Lord,' she prayed silently.

It was indeed a jubilant partaking of the midday meal. The young couple were ecstatic, only slightly exceeding the elation of James and Elizabeth. 'We must go and tell Granny Etty this afternoon,' Willie said as they concluded the meal.

'And I'll send word to May to come tomorrow for us to talk about arrangements for the birth of this baby,' Elizabeth added.

Caroline looked at her mother, suddenly serious. 'Goodness, I haven't dared think that far yet!' she exclaimed.

Henrietta Drabsch met them at the door.

'My darlings,' she cried. 'What is your news?'

'You are going to be a great grandmother,' Willie responded, smiling broadly. 'No doubt at all.'

Tears flowed down the old lady's cheeks. 'Oh my dears, I am so happy. Thank God for his goodness.' Excitement and happiness welled in her heart. How wonderful! How happy she was for this dear grandson and his wife. And what a dear girl Caroline was! She was blessed indeed.

Aunt May came the next day. The expert in the family in bringing babies into the world, her advice was needed. The three women, James and Willie were in the sitting room. It was pleasant there, private and comfortable.

'If Mr Baddely says there is no problem, I can't see any reason why you can't have the baby at home, Caroline,' Aunt May said, 'providing you have the ministrations of a competent midwife.'

'Do you think that will be quite safe, Aunty May?' Willie asked.

'The alternative is to come back here very early, which means a long extended time away from home, or come near the time, which I think would not be advisable. It would be very exhausting and might even bring on a premature birth to travel over such a distance on such a track, or lack of it, during that last time. I wouldn't recommend that at all.'

'Yes. I can see what you mean, Aunt,' Caroline said softly. How would they solve the problem?

Elizabeth caught James' eye. He nodded. 'I could come and stay with you a month before you are due, if you would like me to, dear,' she ventured.

'Oh Mother! That would be wonderful!' Caroline cried in relief. Then soberly she added, 'But can Father spare you?'

'I'll manage,' her father responded with a mock, long-suffering expression.

'That just leaves our need of a good, experienced midwife,' Willie observed.

There was silence for a moment as each considered this problem. Smiling gently, Aunt May looked at Caroline. 'If you consider me sufficiently experienced and competent, I could come with your mother, if you would like me to,' she said.

Caroline jumped to her feet, throwing her arms around her. Between laughter and tears she cried, 'Oh Aunty May, that would be just wonderful. To have you and Mother with me! Oh, I can't think of anything better.'

Relief engulfed William. 'Thank you, Mother. Thank you, Aunty May. I can't tell you what this means to me — how much I appreciate your offer.' He put his arm around Caroline. He swallowed hard. That lump was back in his throat and things had suddenly become misty. Forcing a jocular tone, he exclaimed, 'We'll make that Bartlett and Sons Enterprise yet, Caro!'

Eventually the talk settled down to practicalities; details of time, of travel, of what would be necessary.

Presently, the men left the three women together to discuss what would be necessary to purchase before Caroline and William started on their return journey. They must go shopping tomorrow for Caroline, for the baby, for other needs between now and the next order. All the things preferably chosen personally must be bought now.

'I'll get pen and paper. We must make lists so we have it all down. We'll never remember everything otherwise,' Elizabeth said.

It was a starry-eyed Caroline who returned from the shopping expedition the next day. The three ladies emerged from the carriage, their arms laden with parcels.

'Willie, where are you, Willie?' Caroline called, as they entered. 'Willie, I've had the most marvellous time. Come. You must see the things I've bought.'

She dumped the parcels on the couch and clasped her hands. 'And Willie, I've ordered the most beautiful cradle. It is carved and has the darlingest frills and flounces of muslin. Oh, it is beautiful!'

William was standing by the door, smiling at his excited wife. 'I'm glad you had such a wonderful day,' he said. 'I hope you have not overtired yourself.'

'Oh, no. I feel wonderful.' Caroline dropped into a chair. 'Though I would love a cup of tea.' William went off to fetch the required refreshment.

The days in Adelaide were now filled with purpose and plans. The advent of one small baby was of such import that the activities of the whole family hinged around it.

At the end of the week, Caroline and Willie took their departure. There were no tears now. The joyful realisation had penetrated. All energies were directed to the event only a few months away.

'Goodbye, my darlings,' Elizabeth called as she waved her handkerchief as they set off. 'We'll see you in a very short while. The time will go very quickly.'

'Goodbye. God be with you,' called James. He involuntarily followed a few steps, waving as the horses gathered pace.

They swept down the drive, through the big iron gates and out onto the road down the hill. It would be a long journey. Caroline would be very tired. But they had promised to take it easily.

One thing was certain. There would be much to talk of along the way. The time would not drag. The dream that had occupied so much of their thoughts and feelings was a dream no longer. It was a potential reality.

21

A dream fulfilled

Fleeting shadows danced across the quilt on Elizabeth's bed. The gentle glow of a shy crescent moon cast soft shadows. It seemed to peep between the branches and leaves of the tree beside the house, making a delicate tracery of infinite grace — like silhouette lace, she thought. The bush hush of night had settled over the house. Only the crickets chirping and the sounds of the wild ducks where they camped by the dam disturbed the silence.

A soft breeze played on her pillowed face. When would the baby arrive? They had been here three weeks now. Thank God Caroline was well and relaxed. The last stages of pregnancy were notoriously trying, but apart from that she was very well.

How was James managing? Annabelle would look after him. But they missed each other so much when they were parted. When the baby came, they would send word immediately. He would be so anxious. If only there were a mail service. But, of course, that was impossible in such an isolated region.

She heard a door open quietly down the hall. A soft knock sounded on her door. Then it opened and Caroline's head appeared around the door. 'Are you awake, Mother?'

'Yes, darling. Come in.' Elizabeth sat up. 'Are you all right?'

'Yes. But I woke up with a stitch in my back. Then I couldn't go back to sleep.'

'Did the stitch last long?'

'I rubbed it and eventually I could move again. It's quite gone now.' She paused. 'Could that mean anything?'

'Perhaps. If it is gone and there's nothing else, go back to bed and try to get some sleep. You never know. Things may be beginning to happen.'

Caroline went out and closed the door softly. She slid back into bed and snuggled up beside Willie.

So Mother thought it may be starting. Oh, my little baby, I'll soon be able to see you. I wonder what you are like. Are you a boy or a girl? I don't care at all which you are. I just love you so much. The baby moved. Yes, I can feel you. You are ready to come out into the big wide world, aren't you? Or just about.

She hugged Willie at the thought. He stirred, lifting his sleepy head. 'You all right, Caro?' he asked.

She patted his shoulder. 'Yes. Go back to sleep.'

★ ★ ★

The night light was still sitting on the verandah table as James returned to the rectory. He could see his way up the steps and to the door. He sighed as he turned his key in the lock. Picking up the lantern, he went inside.

It had been a hard call, this one. The baby he had just baptised was such a weak little thing. There seemed to be something wrong with it. The midwife had suggested they send for him when the baby was born.

Poor little thing. It would be surprising if it survived. Poor little mother, too. She had apparently had a bad time. It was the couple's first child, too. They seemed devoted to each other and so grateful he had come quickly to baptise their frail little son. He'd see them again in the morning.

How was Carry going? He hoped she would not have to endure to the degree this little mother had. And Lord, please grant the little one will be delivered safely.

He yawned as he pulled off his shoes and prepared again for bed. How long would Elizabeth be away? How he missed her!

Mustn't be selfish, though, he reminded himself. Carry needed her and he was happy for her to have her mother with her.

He was asleep very quickly.

★　★　★

By mid-morning, the girls were cleaning the dining room. They had been having a busy time — Mrs was wanting all kinds of things done today. Why did the table have to be polished today? And the globe of the lamp wasn't blackened. Why did it have to be cleaned when it wasn't dirty? All the lamps in the house had been filled with kerosene. Mrs had insisted.

Minnie was grudgingly putting some effort into getting a good shine on the table. 'Go round and round, Minnie. You rubbed the wax in along with the grain of the wood. Now make a pad of the cloth and go round and round.' She took the cloth from the girl and proceeded to demonstrate.

Suddenly she doubled over, a gigantic cramp ripping through her. 'Oh, oh!' she gasped.

Minnie rushed to her as she leant on the table. 'Baby come, Mrs,' she said excitedly. 'Baby come now.'

In a few moments, the pain had gone.

Caroline found her mother and Aunt May seated on the verandah. Mother was crocheting a little jacket from the hand-spun wool. Their calm was broken as Caroline told them what had just transpired.

As the day wore on, the contractions increased in severity and frequency. Aunt May accompanied her walking around the garden, walking around the house, resting a while, then walking again.

The room for the delivery had been prepared for some time. Now Aunt May checked again to see everything was ready. When evening came and the time for retiring to bed arrived, no-one was anxious for sleep. A much more important happening was imminent.

Two o'clock, Elizabeth thought as she heard the clock strike. She had surprised herself. She had actually slept a short while. She would go along to the room and see how Caroline was doing. Poor little darling. How she wished she could relieve her of the pain. But that is part of motherhood, she thought. No wonder we love our children so much.

She tiptoed quietly along the hall, her slippers making no sound. A soft glow showed under the door. She opened the door. May was just moving to the high bed where Caroline lay. Another contraction gripped her. Her breath came in heavy gasps. A little scream escaped her.

'Hush, my darling, hush. Don't make a noise.' She hurried to the bed.

'Nonsense, Elizabeth. Let the girl shout if she wants to — if it will help her,' May said firmly. 'Pull on the sheets, dear. Pull hard.' She stood by assisting Caroline. 'There you are, it's going again. Relax now. You're doing beautifully. It won't be long now.'

She took the ends of the sheets tied to the bedposts from Caroline's hands and helped her lean back. Almost immediately, Caroline was up again and the procedure continued.

The first light was creeping into the room as Aunt May cried, 'Just a little more, darling. Try hard. Just a little more. Here it comes!'

With a great burst, Caroline realised her baby was born. Time had ceased to exist. How long had it all gone on? A great whirling engulfed her for a split second. 'It's a boy, Caroline. It's a boy,' cried Aunt May. 'Here he is.' She laid the baby on Caroline's suddenly deflated abdomen. 'Here he is. Oh, he is beautiful. Elizabeth, did you ever see such a beautiful baby?'

Caroline raised her head. Her first glimpse of her little son! He had a shock of soft auburn hair, still wet. He was pink and round. Now he opened his mouth and cried lustily.

'Elizabeth, go and tell Willie. Tell him he has a beautiful son.'

Tears poured unchecked down Elizabeth's cheeks.

Willie was just near the door. He had heard the first cry and was almost beside himself. 'It's a boy, William. A beautiful boy!' Elizabeth cried, hugging him. 'Come and see him. May is just fixing Caroline up. The baby hasn't been bathed yet, but come and see.'

As William came to her, Caroline cradled the baby in her arms, her face aglow with elation. 'Willie, he's so beautiful. Look at him. Look at his little hands. They're your hands, Willie. We actually have our little son.'

William tried to speak. That lump was in his throat again. A man doesn't cry, he thought. Oh, to be a woman to have the release of tears! He put his arms around Caroline and his son. Overwhelming feelings of love, wonder and gratitude engulfed him. Momentarily, he laid his head against her and closed his eyes. Something shiny and wet fell on her hand. She reached up and caressed his cheek.

'Are you all right, my darling?' he whispered.

She nodded. 'It was all worth it,' she said,

laughing shakily. 'Now we have our little son. Now I'm a mother.'

'Thank God you are both safe,' he whispered.

'Time now to bathe this baby and put some clothes on him.' Aunt May bustled into the room with a little bath half-filled with warm water. She took the little bundle in his rug from Caroline.

Now Caroline and Willie enjoyed a brief moment together, trying to realise the wonder of their so-long-held dream's fulfilment. It was almost beyond comprehension. It was a miracle. It was true.

Polly and Minnie hung by the door. The Missus was sitting up in bed, beckoning them in. 'Come on. Come in and see the baby,' Caroline called. 'He won't bite.'

The girls giggled, urging each other to go in. Willie sat on a chair beside the bed. He stood up and moved across to the cradle, removing the mosquito net. 'Come on. Now you can see him,' he invited.

The girls came hesitantly forward and peeped in the cradle. With a quick indraw of breath, they giggled and Minnie pointed at the baby, then at Willie. 'Boss baby,' she laughed. 'Him boss baby.' Polly joined in the laughter and pointing.

'You think he's like the boss?' Caroline

asked, interpreting their reaction. They laughed and pointed again.

'Mmm, nice,' said Polly, putting her head on one side and smiling at the sleeping baby.

William replaced the net and turned to Caroline. 'I'll go now and arrange for Jacko to take the news to your father and the rest of the folk in Adelaide. What a pity we can't shout it from the treetops and make him hear it right away.'

He strode away down the hall. She heard the back door slam shut. He would be back presently for the letter he had just written.

Father would be pleased they were going to call the baby James after him and Willie's grandfather. The little man would have something to live up to, bearing the name of these two ancestors. Caroline, thinking fondly of her father, drifted into sleep. The girls had slipped quietly out on their bare feet. The household settled quietly down to siesta.

The rider left within the hour after the midday meal. He would travel a good way before dark. When he reached 'Onavale,' he would change his horse in order to shorten the time in getting the good news south.

★   ★   ★

213

At home at St Augustine's, James and Annabelle waited patiently for news. How much longer before the longed-for baby arrived? Or had he already arrived? Perhaps someone was already bringing news.

'How beautiful are the feet of he who brings good tidings,' James thought. 'Pray God it will be good tidings.'

22

A baptism and a Banksia rose

They gathered on the wide verandah, the overhanging roof providing a shady haven from the heat of the late morning sun. It would be a hot day before it was finished. The temperature was already climbing past the readings familiar to so many of the guests from Adelaide.

Henrietta Drabsch sat fanning herself in the cane chair. What a bustle there was. People were bringing chairs from every available quarter and men bringing drums and planks from the shed, making extra seats. What a good idea, putting the rugs over the planks when they laid them across between two drums. Really, there was no end to Willie's ingenuity.

How well he had done and how he had developed and matured. She had been right to encourage him in this venture. She had no doubts at the time, but it was very gratifying to find her confidence justified.

Now she had a great grandson. Her eyes saddened. How Johannes would have loved to see this beautiful little baby. Perhaps he could. She smiled to herself at the thought of the baby. What a dear little fellow he was. Fancy being a great grandmother. It made one feel quite ancient.

Jamie William they were calling him, after his grandfather, great grandfather and his father. James Hilliard was a good man, a good priest, a man his grandson might well admire and emulate. And his great grandfather, the former chief justice of the colony, was a fine example.

'Are you feeling the heat, Mrs Drabsch?' It was Elizabeth Hilliard beside her chair.

'Oh, not unduly,' Henrietta said, giving a little laugh. 'Though it is rather different from our weather in the south, isn't it?'

Elizabeth nodded. 'It is very beautiful here. It's all very different, but I think it would soon capture my heart were I here very long.' Elizabeth looked out over the paddocks. 'It's so immense: so silent, and yet so demanding.'

Henrietta nodded agreement. 'God is very evident,' she said.

'Careful now, don't bump it.' Caroline hovered behind the two men carrying the table onto the verandah. She emerged through the French doors with a tablecloth over her arm.

'What are they doing now?' asked Henrietta.

'They are using that table to put the silver bowl on,' replied Elizabeth. 'Everything has to be improvised, of course, there being no church. They are using the big silver bowl for a font. My parents sent it to them from England for their wedding present. It will make an excellent font.'

Henrietta smiled agreement. What a different setting this was for a baptism! How different from the ancient cathedrals and churches she had known in Germany. Certainly this was a new life, a new country, with new ways. God was still here, though. How fresh and natural it was compared with the rigidity she had known and the persecution of those last years in Germany. It was like the fresh breeze of the early evening across this sun-drenched country. The Wind of the Spirit, she thought. The wind bloweth where it listeth. God will not be thwarted.

Caroline put the large silver bowl on the table, it having duly been placed in an appropriate position and covered with the cloth. A silver candlestick and vase of flowers were added.

More family members and close friends being housed in the extension to the large store building were sauntering up the stone path, gathering for the service. The seats were filling up.

The men working on the property led by Ted Wilkes were coming across from their quarters in a little group. Good men, they were yet not exactly at ease in the company of this chattery group of the boss's people from Adelaide. It was a long time since they had talked to other white men — and as for white women! They came rather shyly, neatly dressed with clean, ironed shirts and their riding boots polished to the best shine possible, considering their customary condition.

Willie had been fortunate in his little group of hands. They respected him and were satisfied with their lot.

Aunt May bustled out, looking for Elizabeth. 'Oh, there you are, Elizabeth. Come and tell me what you think about the dining room. Have I enough plates and servers — and do you think the food is sufficient?' The two women hurried indoors.

Caroline came out, carrying baby Jamie. 'Granny, would you please hold him while I see if Father has everything he needs?'

'I would love to hold him, the darling.' Henrietta held up her arms and took the baby. He was looking particularly beautiful. Caroline was a dear girl to accept her offer of the loan of the christening robe. It had been one of the family treasures she had brought with her at that hard parting in Germany.

She fingered the soft silk. It had yellowed somewhat, but it was still beautiful. This child would be the fifth generation in the family to wear it.

They seemed to be just about ready now. Here was Caroline taking her baby again, making sure everyone was comfortable and had service books, as she made her way to her seat at the front.

The godparents were seated there with Caroline and Willie. The chairs had been lined up in rows as far as available numbers permitted, then came the drums and plank seats. Caroline's father had taken his place at the table and lit the candle. He took up his book.

' 'Lead us, Heavenly Father,' Number 56,' he said. Voices rose as he led the singing and so the service proceeded. At the appointed time, he motioned for the parents and godparents to move closer to the table, asked the questions from the prayer book and received the answers. He moved to Annabelle and took the baby on his arm, holding the baby's head over the font.

'Name this child,' he said clearly.

'Jamie William,' came the reply.

'Jamie William, I baptise thee in the name of the Father, and of the Son, and of the Holy Ghost.' His voice rang out as he scooped the water in his hand and three times poured it over his grandson's head.

Little Jamie blinked his eyes as the water was poured, then, as his grandfather wiped his head with his surplice sleeve, he looked up at him and smiled.

Caroline's eyes filled with tears. This was her baby, hers and Willie's. God had granted her desire. Now he had been baptised, dedicated to God. Her heart overflowed. Her throat was tight. The overwhelming emotions of love, joy, thankfulness welled up within her, penetrating her whole being.

Willie squeezed her hand. Taking his handkerchief from his pocket, he surreptitiously handed it to her. She dabbed her eyes and smiled.

Annabelle took the baby back from her father. She glanced at the three young men, Jamie's godfathers, taking up the chairs in the rest of the row. They seemed to be taking the service and their part in it very seriously. They were very nice men. But then these were Willie's special friends who had come with him when he selected the property. It would be good to get to know them again. George especially had such a pleasant, courteous way about him. He really was a very likeable man.

She brought her mind back to the service. Father was exhorting the godparents as to their responsibilities.

Jamie was looking directly at her, smiling. She cuddled him close. What a darling! What a beautiful baby smell! What soft tender sweetness! She would keep her promises well to teach him the faith and all he should know to be brought up a good Christian man. Children were so vulnerable, but he would have loving people to protect and care for him.

The service was concluding.

George, sitting beside her, turned and said, 'Now I had better get to know my godson better. Come here, young Jamie. Just feel your Uncle George's hands upon you.' He took the baby confidently. He seemed to be at ease. Some men were so awkward holding a young baby.

Jamie was the centre of attention, fussed over and admired by all present. The photographer who had travelled from Adelaide with the party was kept busy as one after another were posed and photographed holding him. At last all seemed satisfied and the photographer retired with his equipment.

William stood in the doorway to the dining

room and struck the dinner gong. 'Everything is ready for lunch,' he said when he had attention. 'But before we move into the dining room, we have another little ceremony. On this auspicious occasion, Caroline's father has something to say and to do.'

Smiling, he stepped aside and James Hilliard moved forward. In his hands he had a plant. 'This is a little ceremony I would like to perform,' he said. 'This beautiful country has in it growth, the elements of growth. Growth physical in the trees, pastures and this garden Caroline and William have established in the last ten years or so. It also has the elements of growth in person, as evidenced in this couple, Jamie William's parents, parents now of this beautiful child and owners, guardians of this majestic place.

'There is a blending, a marriage of the old and the new: the old ways of this land and the new brought by William when he selected this property. He has prospered through wisdom and work. There has been growth.

'I had the desire to mark these thoughts in a tangible way and so I have brought a rose, a yellow Banksia rose, a symbol of the old world so many of us have known in our homelands, to plant in this land new to us, but old in its own way — a symbol of that blending. It is a yellow rose, because yellow is the colour of hope, hope that springs eternal against all odds.

'I wish to plant this rose on this occasion of Jamie's baptism to symbolise a new life, and growth. All life comes from God, the Banksia rose will grow from God's earth and Jamie will grow from the fruit of God's earth. It will mark the years of his growing.'

There was a hushed silence as he stepped from the verandah to the spot beside a verandah post where a spade was ready for the planting. He took the rose from the pot and planted it. Someone carrying a tray of drinks offered drinks all round. Glasses were raised in toast. 'To Jamie.' 'To Jamie and his rose. Long may they live.' The voices rose in salute.

'May Jamie and his rose grow and bloom in hope and beauty,' called Henrietta, the matriarch of the company. Glasses were raised again. The mounting heat of the day was forgotten.

It was a happy, voluble party who trooped into the dining room for the celebration lunch.

23

The plan

'Jamie, Jamie,' called Caroline as she went through the garden looking for her son. Behind a shrub she found him squatting on the ground, his hands on his knees, watching a trail of ants, so engrossed he was oblivious to all around him.

He looked up and caught sight of her. 'Ants,' he said, pointing his finger at them, but not moving otherwise. Caroline squatted down beside him.

'Do you like ants?' she said.

He nodded vigorously. 'Jamie like ants.' They remained a few minutes, watching the miniature hive of activity, then Caroline held out her hand.

'Come along, lunch is ready. Daddy is back for lunch.'

The little boy jumped up at the mention of his father. They made their way into the house. Willie was waiting at the table. 'Well, what has my boy been doing?' he asked as he lifted Jamie into his chair.

'Ants. Jamie see ants,' he said, describing

with his fingers how the ants had been busy up and down the track.

'Ants have gone to have their dinner now. Jamie eat his dinner, too,' said William, starting him off on his meal.

When lunch was finished and Jamie put down for his afternoon sleep, Caroline came back to the table to enjoy a cup of tea with Willie before he started on the afternoon's work.

'You know, Caro, we've been very lucky. This has been a good year,' said William. 'Having the other property down the line has been a good investment. We can work them together. We've sold record numbers this year. That last mob of steers we sold in Adelaide just about topped the markets. It made a great difference not having to drove them all the way from here in one go. That's great fattening country down there. I just hope our luck holds out in the overseers we've been able to get.' He looked up and smiled. 'We'll make that 'Bartlett and Sons Enterprise' yet.'

Caroline sipped her tea. Life was good. What more could she want to make her happy? A beautiful home, a husband who loved her, a beautiful son, prosperity. Was there anything more she could wish for? Perhaps a little daughter one day. She smiled to herself. Willie was speaking. He was saying something about cattle for sale.

'They haven't had rain up there for nearly twelve months. It really is drought. So they are reducing their numbers. Ted was saying this fellow told him it would be a buyer's market. I believe there's about a thousand head they want to get rid of. A mixed mob, he said. Some cows and calves among them.'

Caroline brought her full attention back to William. 'Where did you say they were?' she asked.

' 'Nockatunga',' he replied. 'It's up north, in southwest Queensland. It's a big station. It's been going some time and they have good stock. I'd like to get hold of some of that strain to bring into our herds. It's hard on them, of course, having to part with that number of cattle, but that's the way it is on the land. You have to go with the seasons and the sooner they sell them the more chance they'll have of saving the rest. This unreliable rainfall makes it a bit difficult. That's where our places in different areas help so greatly. We were lucky to get in early, Caro.'

Caroline could see he had more than passing interest in the cattle he was describing. She felt a little clutch of anxiety round her heart. Ted Wilkes had been south recently and she had heard him telling one of the other men about them.

'It's a pity they are so far away. It would be very difficult and a long way round to bring them down through New South Wales and across to us, wouldn't it? It would take months. Otherwise, you might consider buying some.'

'Unless they were brought direct down the Cooper and then down Strzelecki Creek,' he said. 'We could do with increasing our stock now after the recent sales and, as I said, I would like to try introducing some of the 'Nockatunga' strain into our herd. I think it would be a good thing. If we brought them down the Cooper and Strzelecki, it would cut off weeks of travelling.'

He looked up and laughed as he said, 'Of course, there are no roads or stock routes.'

Caroline joined in his laughter. 'Oh, William. I've heard all this before. Where were the roads when we came here to 'Bibbaringa'?'

'Maybe it's another crazy idea, but that one worked out well, didn't it?'

So he was thinking seriously about it. 'Do you know anything about the country between here and 'Nockatunga'?'

'Only what I've been told, past the junction of Strzelecki and the Cooper. I've ridden that far. You can more or less follow the creek.'

'But to bring a thousand head — and some calves among them! They will not, I imagine, be in the best condition if the place is in drought. They will have to be brought carefully if you are not to lose too many.'

'I don't think they are in too bad condition yet. That's one of the things about it. They want to sell before the cattle lose too much. It's a very tempting prospect, Caro.'

Oh, William, William. Always ready for a challenge, a new development. Some men would sit back and enjoy what they had in comfort if they had achieved Willie's assets. He so enjoyed the thrill of challenge and achievement. He was speaking again.

'I wonder where old Yuelty is at the moment? If I could get hold of him, we'd be right. He knows all this country. Great old fellow.'

He lapsed quiet for a few moments. 'Of course, he's not as young as he used to be, but he's a tough old chap. I wonder if any of the blacks camped down on the creek know where I might get word to him? I'll go down and see them this afternoon.'

Caroline could see the light of challenge shining in his face as he pushed his chair back and stood up. There was purpose in his tread as he went out whistling.

So Willie was going on another adventure,

she mused. She had no doubt he would go. He would organise, plan, weigh up the strengths and weaknesses of the project and provide as far as was possible for its successful fulfilment. Oh, there was no doubt about it. He would go.

It would be lonely while he was away. Life was empty when he was not here. And what would she do if anything went wrong? Who could she go to? There would be some of the men left behind, no doubt, but she couldn't go to them. She felt a wave of panic rise.

But perhaps it would not be for too long. She had no idea of the distance. She must be strong and positive. She would manage. Willie would leave everything taken care of while he was away. Ted would keep things going smoothly. There would be a skeleton staff left at 'Bibbaringa'.

She gathered up the dishes and cleared the table. She must plan a project of her own to keep her occupied while he was away. How long would it be?

She took the dishes out to the kitchen where Wan Loo was chopping meat for the evening meal. He was quite a good cook and a superb gardener. The kitchen garden was wonderful now under his care. The only note of discord in his presence was the constant friction between him and Minnie. It almost seemed they enjoyed this daily contest of will, wits and name-calling. Oh well, if it kept them happy, she could turn a deaf ear.

She looked down the track to the creek. Here was Minnie coming back to the house. What could be bringing her back now after lunch? The women and piccaninnies usually spent the afternoon swimming or looking for bush fruits or eggs, certainly not coming to the house where their work ended at midday.

She walked down the garden to meet Minnie, now dressed in her camp clothes.

'Where that yella chopper man, Missus?' she asked.

'Wan Loo is in the kitchen, Minnie,' she replied.

'Him give me one bad herb,' Minnie protested. 'Him bad!' She screwed up her face and thrust out her tongue. 'Uggh!' She held up her hand, clutching a small bundle of fresh green herbs. 'Put in cooking him say!' she cried disdainfully. 'Uggh! Bad! Make all bad!'

Caroline could see she was very indignant. What was this fuss all about?

'Him say pick plant right! Uggh!' Again she screwed up her face.

'Show me, Minnie.' She must try to avert a confrontation when Minnie was in this mood, or it would go on for a week.

Minnie turned back to the far end of the garden. She stopped and pointed to the herb growing by the path. 'Him!' she said disgustedly. 'Uggh!'

Caroline looked at the herb. Why would Wan Loo tell Minnie to put wormwood in her cooking? Surely he would not deliberately cause Minnie embarrassment in front of her family and the other women in the camp? The bitter wormwood would certainly ruin anything Minnie tried to cook with it. And because she worked at the homestead, Minnie tried to impress the others with her knowledge of the white man's way in cooking.

Caroline had given her a camp oven when she showed interest in these things. Why tell her to put wormwood in her cooking?

She glanced back at the house to see if Wan Loo was observing Minnie's discomfiture. As she did so, her eye fell on the plant on the other side of the path. Parsley!

'Minnie, where did Wan Loo say to get the herb for your cooking?'

'Right side track, Missus.' Minnie held up her arm with the bright bangle Caroline had given her to emphasise the point.

'Minnie, that's not your right arm. That's your left arm!'

Minnie's mouth opened. 'Not right, Missus?' she asked incredulously.

'No. Wan Loo would have meant for you to pick some parsley for your cooking. It makes nice taste. See, they look much the same. But wormwood is not nice to eat. It is good medicine. Wan Loo knows herb medicines his people use like you know bush medicines.'

Minnie dropped her eyes. For the second time today she was embarrassed. She threw the little bunch of herbs back on the growing wormwood. 'No good, yella chopper man. Keep yella medicine.' She swaggered back towards the creek, striving to maintain her pride.

Caroline returned to the kitchen. Wan Loo was just putting the boiler on the stove. 'Wan Loo, you won't be putting wormwood in the dinner, will you?'

The fat little Chinese cook looked at her in consternation. 'Wormwood no good in dinner, Missy!'

Caroline told him of Minnie's mistake and her embarrassment. His face broke into a smile. His eyes narrowed to little slits. Then he laughed. He held his sides and rocked with laughter. When he could finally speak between lingering gusts of laughter, he said, 'Oh Missy. That black jump-up gin! She think she so clever. Ho. Ho. Ho. She learn listen. She not so clever. Wan Loo show her she no good cook!'

'Now Wan Loo, you mustn't tease her. Poor Minnie feels very foolish in front of her family. You say nothing. Just make sure she understands next time you tell her how to cook.'

She wasn't at all sure he would do as she said. He was still chuckling as she left the kitchen and made her way to the store.

24

Arrangements

Caroline unbolted the door to the store. It was very dark and much cooler inside. She opened the shutters near the door to let in some light.

It was a well-stocked store. With orders being obtained only every six months, it needed to be. A line of fifty-pound bags of flour, sugar, salt and brown sugar were by the wall. On shelves above were cases of dried fruits, raisins, currants and sultanas, apricots, peaches, prunes and apples, dates and dried peas. Further along, cases of treacle, golden syrup and mixed jams filled the wide bench. Bags of rice and sacks of potatoes and brown onions leant by the wall. Spices, essences and medicines were in the cupboard.

On the other side, bolts of material, calico, threads and sewing needs vied for space with boots, trousers and shirts and a host of other things.

The other end of the store was taken up with leather of different weights for making new harness, whips, halters, saddles, bridles and all the needs of horsemen on the station. There were piles of blankets, cases of four-gallon tins of kerosene, ropes, chains and all the hardware of station needs.

She would have to get a list of what Willie planned to take on this trek, then check the supplies. It was fortunate the last order had arrived only a month ago. That gave them a good start.

Willie would go, of course. Just when was uncertain. Had he been able to get any news of Yuelty, she wondered. He was getting on. Would he still want to go?

She closed the shutters and, rebolting the door, made her way slowly back to the house, hoping this absence would not be for too many weeks. In spite of the men and the comings and goings of the blacks, it was very lonely when Willie went to the outlying areas of the property for a few days. That was when she really felt the isolation. How would it be when he was away for a matter of possibly months?

She pulled her thoughts up. She must be positive. She squared her shoulders and quickened her pace. There were things to be done.

Willie's visit to the blacks' camp had been profitable. He had found many of them gathered in little groups along the creek enjoying the shade under the trees. Most knew of Yuelty if they did not know him personally. No-one seemed to know just where he would be now.

Then, finally, he spoke to a group of young men. When he mentioned his old friend, one bright young fellow nodded. He had seen him recently at Killalpaninna, the mission station set up by the missionaries from Germany. He had been planning to spend a while there. Yes, the young man could take a message to him.

William was excited as he walked back to the homestead. He had always been on good terms with the blacks, ever since Yuelty's first introduction. He respected them and appreciated their knowledge and affinity with their environment. They had always been helpful and most willing to share this when he had sought advice. They, in turn, had grown to respect him.

He had no doubt Yuelty would receive the message and in a week or so he could expect to get an answer, or maybe even see the old fellow turn up here at the station.

He turned in happily at the gate to acquaint Caroline with his progress. He found her in the side garden. She was standing in the shade of a tree, a book and pencil in her hand. Wan Loo was beside her.

They were discussing something about the garden.

What a beautiful woman she was. The wide hat she generally wore outside shielded her fair skin from the sun. She did not seem to have aged in their years of marriage and isolation, but just grown more beautiful. She looked up and, catching sight of him waved, spoke to Wan Loo and came towards him. 'Any success?' she called as she came closer.

William told her what had happened and his confidence regarding the outcome. 'I have been talking to Wan Loo about developing this part of the garden,' she said as they went up onto the verandah to sit in the shade. 'I thought I'd make it a project while you are away.'

William looked searchingly at her. 'You don't mind my going, do you?' he asked. 'It's just such an opportunity.'

'No, no. I'm happy for you to go. It's just that it will be lonely with you away, so I thought a project to keep my mind and my hands occupied would be a good thing. It will make the time go more quickly. Between Jamie and this, I'll be right.'

'What sort of project are you planning?' said William, for the first time really considering how Caroline would feel in a personal way about this venture. She had been quite encouraging when they talked about it earlier.

'I'm going to make a bush garden. We'll bring in some rocks from the creek and get the plants from the creek and the bush. We'll look for little trees, too, and really try to landscape that whole side area. Wan Loo says we might even be able to make a pool among the rocks. It will take a lot of planning and a lot of work, but that's what I need. Wan Loo is a very wonderful gardener. He seemed enthusiastic, but a bit preoccupied. I don't quite know what's on his mind.'

* * *

The old black man moved easily over the land. This was his country. He had known every inch of it long ago, before he had come in contact with the white men and gone off to many areas on expeditions with them. He had gone to other tribal lands, entering not as an ambassador for his people bringing message sticks and observing the protocol and etiquette of their customs, but as a companion of a white man, dressed in the manner of the white man and divested of his familiar weapons.

That had been a long time ago. He still moved with the seemingly effortless grace of the bush black man, thinner perhaps than formerly, but his figure still upright. His shiny black hair and beard were now sprinkled liberally with grey, but his eyes were as keen and alert as ever.

So Willie Boss wanted to go on another journey and was asking for his company and leadership. Good man, that Willie Boss, even if he was a white man. Not many white men like him. Mostly they thought they knew all. They didn't ask black man, so black man didn't speak. Then they fall. Not Willie Boss, though. He ask. He want to learn. Could teach him, just like young boy at initiation into tribal secrets and manhood. He would go. He would go with Willie Boss.

He looked far away to the north, observing all the marks and signs of the proven bush traveller. Not many of his people had covered as much territory as he had. It would be a good time to go on this walkabout. No dilly-dally long, though. Long time get there, longer time get back. Rains come and catch them. As he neared the homestead cluster of buildings, his pace slowed. He would pay his respects to his countrymen camped on the creek. Knowing he would have been observed, he sat down a little way off in the shade of a tree until one of the party went and greeted him. He then went to wait for William to see him.

The sky was a blaze of vermillion as the sun dipped to the horizon. Yuelty sat at the gate of the homestead to wait for his presence to be noticed. He observed the sky, the movement of clouds, the turn of leaves and insects, the business of the last bees on their rounds and the movement of ants. The weather would hold.

He had been there some half-hour before William, coming from the blacksmith's shop, noticed him. 'Yuelty, you've come,' he cried. 'I knew you would.'

They greeted each other with happiness and affectionate respect and sauntered to the chairs on the verandah, William regaling Yuelty with all his plans. 'If we can do this, if we can get through and if I can buy these cattle, we'll bring back many, many cattle — a thousand cattle, perhaps.' Yuelty looked at him in surprise. 'You think we can bring many cattle through that country?' he asked.

Yuelty considered for a moment. Then he nodded. 'Can bring,' he said. 'Take many days. Must go. No dilly-dally. Him big rain come wash all away.'

'You think we go as soon as possible?'

The black man nodded. 'Rain up here,' he held his arm high, 'come where no rain here.'

He patted the floor. William realised what he meant. Rain in the headwaters of the northern rivers flowing into the Cooper could make a huge flood where rain had not fallen for many months.

The old fellow was right. There was no time to lose. To get to 'Nockatunga' to conduct the negotiations necessary, to purchase the cattle and get such a large herd to 'Bibbaringa' would be a mammoth undertaking. To get them to move together, keeping them calm, placid and moving forward would be no easy task. These were cattle from open land, not used to the sight of man or horse as most larger holding herds were. It was not for the faint-hearted, this journey, but he was confident in his men. Now that Yuelty was with him, he had few worries.

He rose and, putting his hand on the old man's shoulder said, 'Two nights, then we go.' He pointed to the men's quarters. 'You sleep men's room?'

Yuelty shook his head. It was like Willie Boss to extend him hospitality, but he preferred his earth bed. 'Me, bark bed,' he smiled.

'Right. Two days we make ready. Next day we go. We make new track for cattle. Western Queensland to Adelaide. Shorter track, good market. We do it.'

They stood up, each busy with his own thoughts. As Yuelty started down the path, William called from the door, 'Goodnight, old friend. Sleep well.' He waved and disappeared into the house.

The sun had set and night was drawing a velvet curtain over the sky as Yuelty made his way to the creek. Willie Boss good man. Not changed. He would guide them. It would be good. He lifted his head and sniffed the air. Fish cooking over the fire by the creek. He hastened his step.

25

Preparation and departure

There was a fever of excitement and activity in the next two days. William had called all his men in to a conference to see who was willing and enthusiastic for the venture and who would be happier to stay at 'Bibbaringa', keeping things going smoothly.

He had already decided that Ted Wilkes must stay and take charge. It was essential to have reliable management during his absence both for the efficient running of the property and also for Caroline and Jamie's safety and care.

As Caroline had predicted, a skeleton staff would be left behind, the others to go with William to bring back the cattle. The men all knew of the proposed sale and the drought conditions in south-west Queensland. Ted Wilkes had been bombarded with questions ever since he returned from the south.

With the keen interest of men who all their lives had lived and worked with cattle, they had plied Ted over and over for details, possibilities; who might buy such a large number, what they might bring, who would get the droving contract, what conditions must be like for the 'Nockatunga' people to be parting with so many.

For the sake of the young men who had not participated in such a trek, William spelt out the realities. 'These are open-range cattle as ours are,' he said. 'They will not be easy to handle. There are some breeders, cows and calves and a number of bulls. The bulk of the herd will be stores, steers and bullocks. They have good stock with plenty of spirit. It will be long hard yakka, especially the first week or so, to get them to move as a mob. It will mean night shifts to keep them together and from getting spooked. We don't know the country.

'My old friend Yuelty,' he indicated the black man standing quietly to one side, 'has agreed to lead us. Take notice of what he says and follow his advice. We will observe the country we go through on the journey up there and make our plans for the route we will need to use to return.

'I hope we will push along and make really good time on the way up, but the return with such a big mob will be slow. It will mean long hours, hard work and monotony.' He smiled. 'A bloke could be a fool to take it on.'

The men laughed as he paused. 'There will

be plenty of good tucker. Now who's game?'

There was a hubbub of excited voices. Eventually a coin had to be tossed to decide who must stay with Ted. And so the team was picked and the stockmen's roles assigned.

They were long days those two days before the start of the big trek: days filled with preparation; horses and equipment harness checked; whips and ropes tested, spliced, repaired; swags packed; extra boots added. The waggonette was laden with possible needs for use on the trek as well as goods for the journey. It was a bustle from dawn till dusk and after. Those staying behind were instructed on all Willie's expectations until his return.

Caroline went back and forth between the store, the house and Willie's office. Jamie darted in and out, not to be left out of the excitement.

Caroline in those days was a complex compound of conflicting emotions. She could not but be caught up in the thrill of the feverish preparations. It would be exciting to go off on a ride such as this. To visit another isolated homestead . . . what a thrill that would be. What were the women there like? She supposed there were women there. Was their life like hers? Where would their nearest neighbours be? Hers were many, many miles away.

How wonderful it would be to talk to another woman whose life resembled her own. Perhaps she should have suggested to Willie that she go, too? But that was absurd. There was Jamie. Precious, dear little Jamie. And anyway, the return journey with the cattle was not for a woman. It could take many weeks. But oh, it would be lonely without Willie. One more day and he would be gone.

Why, oh why, did he have to go at all? Surely he had enough cattle. Why go all that way and be away all that time? But then she knew his love of challenge. He had to go forward, to follow this drive. She understood, but . . .

All William's planning and organising expertise was brought to bear in those days. He had extensive conferences with Ted on all aspects of the station work, detailing the work to be done during his absence. The air was filled with the clonk of spurs and chains, the ring of the blacksmith's hammer on the anvil, the thud as yet another item was added to the load on the waggon.

At sunset on the second day, William sent for Ted Wilkes to give his final instructions. After an hour in the office, he closed the books and looked earnestly at his head stockman and friend.

'You realise, Ted, that I am leaving in your care my most precious possessions. I am leaving my wife and son in your care. I charge you to look well to their welfare. Mrs Bartlett will no doubt feel my absence acutely, but she has a great deal of fortitude and I have no doubt she will be well occupied with the garden she has persuaded Wan Loo to help her develop. I would appreciate it if you could give her any assistance that may be necessary. I know I can rely on you implicitly. I have every trust in you.'

They rose and walked out onto the verandah, standing talking for a few minutes. Then they shook hands and parted.

⋆　⋆　⋆

The roosters in Wan Loo's chookyard broke the silence in the pre-dawn the next morning. This was the morning of the departure. Caroline stifled the rising self-pity that threatened to engulf her. What would she do without Willie? She scolded herself, determining to farewell him with a smile. He must go off happily. It was for all their welfare really.

She slipped out of bed and, putting on her gown, went quietly out to the kitchen. Wan

Loo was already there, the kerosene lamp alight on the table. The little Chinese man was bending in front of the big stove, prodding the fire back to life, the kettle pulled over to boil. 'Oh, Wan Loo, I didn't know you would be up yet!' she said.

'Breakfast to get, Missy. Boss said leave by sun-up. Need good breakfast.'

'That's very good of you, Wan Loo. Thank you. They will all need a good meal to send them on their way. They'll miss your cooking the next few weeks.'

William was up and dressed when she went back to the bedroom. All was prepared. There was no rush now: all matter-of-fact.

'Don't work too hard on your garden,' he said. 'It's warming up. Have a rest in the middle of the day while Jamie has his sleep.' He put his arms around her. 'The time will go quickly and we'll soon be home again.'

For a moment, Caroline laid her head on his shoulder. Oh, the comfort and safety of his arms around her! She fought back the tears. 'I'll try to look after everything well, Willie,' she whispered.

'You don't have to worry. Ted will look after the station things. Other things you look after anyway. You know where all my papers are. You know all the business side of the place. In the odd event you should need it, you know where the money is.'

'Yes, yes.' She made a valiant effort. 'I'll be all right. Take care of yourself and come home as quickly as possible.' They went arm and arm into Jamie's room and looked at him asleep in his bed. Then smiling, they made their way to the kitchen.

Wan Loo had thick porridge and bacon and eggs ready and was just toasting thick slices of bread at the stove. The men were coming up from their quarters and all crowding around the big table in the kitchen for this early breakfast.

In no time, the food had all been demolished and only dirty dishes were left to be dealt with by Minnie when she arrived for work. Caroline looked around, these last moments etched on her mind. A heavy step sounded on the verandah and Ted Wilkes opened the door. 'Got your horse ready for you, boss. Think he's rearin' to go like the rest of you.'

He looked around the table as each of the men in turn scraped his chair back and stood up, draining the last cup of tea.

'Thanks, Ted. Well boys, let's go.' Willie stood up and the boys trooped out to a clanking of boots and spurs.

Willie turned to Caroline. 'Let's just go in and have another look at him,' he said, taking her hand and going down the hall to Jamie's room again. He leant over the little sleeping boy, his love showing in his face. He put out his hand and gently touched the fair curls around the little face.

'Take good care of Mummy,' he whispered. 'I'll be back soon.' He turned to Caroline. 'Take good care of each other,' he said. He kissed her lingeringly and went quickly out of the house.

The sky was light now. The first rays of the sun were appearing over the distant horizon as the men brought their horses into the assembling yard. Good-natured banter filled the air. The horses, sensing the excitement, swung round, frisking, anxious to be off.

Calling goodbyes to those left behind, the little party rode out along the creek track. Yuelty on the bay mare rode near Willie. Later, he would lead the way. The waggon brought up the rear.

When they got beyond the limits of 'Bibbaringa', Yuelty would guide to suitable places to camp and all would help with gathering wood and making camp. On the return journey, the waggon would go ahead and the cook and boy prepare camp in readiness for the stockmen bringing the cattle.

Caroline stood at the gate watching the

departure until even the little dust roused by the horses' hoofs blurred with the distance.

She mounted the steps to the verandah and strained her eyes to see the last evidence of them. The bees were already on the Banksia rose. She must remember to water it later.

She could hear Minnie and Wan Loo's voices out in the kitchen. She heard Minnie's high-pitched laughter. They must be on good terms today. She sounded happy.

Now, the bed must be made. Jamie would be awake soon. The first day had begun.

26

Keeping things going

The first weeks after the departure of Willie and his droving team dragged. The days seemed long and nights longer as Caroline tried to sleep in the big bed on her own.

The hours before bed after Jamie was asleep and Wan Loo finished in the kitchen were so silent and long. Sitting on the verandah, she could hear the distant voices and laughter drifting from the black's camp on the creek. What a communal life they lived. There was no loneliness there.

One night, she saw the light of a hurricane lantern coming from the creek, then turn into Wan Loo's hut. Wan Loo must have been down at the camp! She thought about the little man. Perhaps he got lonely, too. Why shouldn't he seek some company?

As the days passed, gradually she moved into a routine and focussed on the activities of the present. Ted Wilkes was very good, calling in each day to see if all was well and if there was anything she needed. Her plans for the bush garden were materialising and, with the smaller number to cook for, Wan Loo was able to give more time to the project. A plan had been drawn out on the area and now suitable rocks and plants must be found.

'Wan Loo, do you really think we can make a pond that looks like a waterhole in the creek?' she asked one day as they worked in the garden.

'You like waterhole, Missy?' he responded.

'Yes, you said we might do it.'

He put his head on one side. 'Mmm. Might take long time, Missy.'

'But you suggested it, Wan Loo,' she objected. 'Don't you think it's possible? Ted will help us get the rocks and there's cement in the store. I saw it the other day.'

'Mmm. Take very long time.' Wan Loo sounded anything but enthusiastic. What was wrong with him? He seemed a bit distracted, as though he didn't really have his mind on what he was doing.

Come to think of it, lunch had been a bit that way, too. He had forgotten to put salt in the vegetables and the pudding had been rather stodgy. He wasn't a wonderful cook, but his meals were usually better than that. Perhaps he was worried about something. She'd better try to find out. She would let the matter of the waterhole rest for the moment.

When Jamie woke from his afternoon sleep

and they had put on their outside shoes and wide hats, Caroline took him for a walk along the creek. It would do him good and he'd enjoy a scramble along the banks, his imagination working as he mimicked the blacks' throwing of the boomerang in hunt, or their spearing a fish.

They found several logs that would give a bush look to her garden and even saw some plants which might transplant successfully.

It was getting late when they returned to the house. Caroline was surprised to hear Minnie's voice in the kitchen. What on earth was Minnie doing back at the house?

She walked round the verandah and across to the kitchen. Wan Loo was speaking to Minnie in a soft voice. Minnie giggled, then, as Caroline appeared in the doorway, jumped guiltily. Wan Loo standing by the stove suddenly busied himself stirring the contents of the pot vigorously.

'Dinner not long, Missy,' he said in a high sing-song voice. 'Nice dinner.'

'Very well, Wan Loo. It's not dinner time yet.'

She turned away, mystified. Obviously she had interrupted something. What was going on? Surely there was nothing between Wan Loo and Minnie — they were always at each other. However, she realised of a sudden she hadn't noticed the same bickering of late. Did this have anything to do with Wan Loo's preoccupied manner?

But did Minnie have a 'promise' in her tribe? There would be trouble if that was interfered with. The blacks were very strict about their marrying customs and infringement of them could mean death sometimes. How could she find out? She would mention it to Ted when he called after he had finished work.

She was sitting on the verandah watching Jamie play with his blocks when the overseer came. At her invitation, he dropped into a chair beside her. All was well, he said. Everything going smoothly.

'Ted, I have something I want to talk to you about,' she confided after these preliminaries were dispensed with. She told him what had happened in the afternoon.

Ted smiled. 'I've noticed,' he said. 'I think our little Chinese cook is setting his cap at Minnie.'

'But Ted, has Minnie got a 'promise'? You know how strict they are. And is Wan Loo seriously wanting to marry Minnie anyway? Does he realise the possible consequences if he is? I'd hate to see anything happen to either of them. Does Minnie realise what she's doing?'

'I don't know all the answers to those questions, but I think there's something going on at the camp, too. I went past there this afternoon and I thought they seemed to be preparing for something. Perhaps they are going walkabout. Don't worry. They'll work it out. Wan Loo is no fool. If Minnie had a promise, he may have been an old fellow and died. She may be free. I saw Wan Loo come back from the camp one night recently. He's obviously accepted by them. Maybe they have the approval of the elders.'

After Ted had taken his leave, Caroline sat on in the cool evening air. Jamie had climbed onto her lap and was now curled up asleep, his head on her shoulder. The soft quiet of the bush night surrounded them. Perhaps Ted was right. Wan Loo had been in the country many years. He had lived with the blacks for some time and was familiar with their customs.

If he did marry Minnie, she hoped he would stay on. They had been very fortunate to have him so long since he came through looking for work. He had settled down well, finding his niche and revelling in his precious garden.

The moon was rising, casting long shadows across the paddock and the garden. Caroline sat on, content with the warmth of her son close against her body. If only Willie were here beside her, she could ask for nothing more. How was he getting on? Had he successfully negotiated the purchase of the cattle? How much longer before he was home again? He seemed very far away.

A mopoke called somewhere far up the creek, its mournful call drifting down to her in the silence. Mo-poke, mo-poke. She sighed. Better put Jamie to bed.

It was a peaceful oasis tinged with melancholy she had no real desire to break. Maybe another week and she could start looking for Willie. She smiled, thinking of the way Jamie was forever leading her out to look up the track. 'Faver come,' he would say earnestly, pointing to any wisp of dust that he thought indicated the approaching cattle.

He'll soon be home, she comforted herself. He was so keen about this venture. The thought of opening up a new stock route from western Queensland to Adelaide played a big part in it. If it was successful, he would feel he had made a significant contribution to the development of the rural industry in the colony. She must accept this adventurous side of his nature as she accepted his love. It all went to make up the person she loved so deeply.

She stirred, gathered Jamie to her more

securely, rose and, going indoors, tucked him into his bed. She bent over him, kissed him on his forehead and smoothed his curls back. What a wonderful gift he was. What joy he had brought them. He was the apple of Willie's eye. Take good care of each other, he had said as he left.

With a final action of smoothing the sheets, she turned the light down, blew out the flame and made her way to her own bedroom. Tomorrow she would make more progress on the garden. Perhaps Wan Loo would be more like himself and they could plan that pool.

⋆ ⋆ ⋆

'Go now, Mizz Bartlett.' Caroline lifted her head. Why was Minnie calling her Mrs Bartlett? This only happened when something was amiss or Minnie thought she had done the wrong thing and was trying to be extra polite to avert trouble. What could have gone wrong? She and Wan Loo seemed to be getting along quite well this morning. Minnie had put real effort into scrubbing and polishing the entrance hall, much more than she often expended on this type of work that she seemed to think unnecessary.

A movement caught her eye. Wan Loo was standing by the kitchen window. She could see his head and shoulders. He seemed to be listening.

'Have you finished already, Minnie?' She straightened her back. The sun was getting hot. Perhaps she had been gardening long enough for this morning.

'Bin go now,' Minnie repeated. 'Boss him come back soon.'

'I hope so, Minnie. Maybe next week. It will be good to have him home.' She pulled off the gloves she had been wearing. Minnie still stood there. What was wrong with the girl? What was she up to?

'Bin go,' Minnie said again. 'Tree all flower bin come back.' She waved her hand towards the tree by the gate. Whatever was she talking about?

'What do you mean, Minnie? You go back to camp now and you come back tomorrow morning.'

Minnie looked at the ground. Caroline glanced towards the kitchen window. Wan Loo was still standing there.

'Go now, come back tree all flower,' Minnie said again.

Suddenly, Caroline remembered Ted's saying there was something afoot at the camp and perhaps the blacks were preparing to go walkabout. 'You go walkabout?' she asked casually.

Minnie lifted her eyes and smiled, obviously relieved. 'Go walkabout,' she repeated. Caroline sighed. This was something she had learned must be endured when employing the women in the house. 'Come back tree all flower.' That meant they would be away some time.

'All right, Minnie. You come work again when you come back.'

Still Minnie stood there. What else did she have to say? Obviously there was still something she wanted to communicate. She scratched in the dirt with her toe. 'Bin come back, make house,' she said with something akin to pride.

'You make house, Minnie? Where you make house?' The mystery was getting deeper. She glanced again at the kitchen window. Wan Loo was watching. He saw Caroline's glance and busied himself hurriedly.

Minnie scratched her toes through the dirt again. 'Bin make house that one yella man,' she said.

'You make house with Wan Loo?' Caroline asked incredulously. In spite of her suspicion of some attraction, this announcement was completely unexpected.

'That one yella man my old fella,' Minnie said proudly, waiting to see how her news was received.

'You marry Wan Loo?' Caroline could hardly believe her ears. This must all be decided, definite, for Minnie to state this so clearly. All the discussion must have been conducted. Perhaps Wan Loo had met with the tribe the night she had seen the lantern light come back from the creek to his hut. Was Minnie saying she could live in the hut with him? It was hardly big enough for a married couple.

'That one yella man my old fella,' Minnie said again.

Caroline was trying to grasp all the implications of this. 'You go walkabout?'

Minnie nodded emphatically. 'Yella man my old fella. Come back make house tree all flower.'

Suddenly Caroline realised Minnie was telling her Wan Loo was her husband, or prospective husband, and that he was also going walkabout with the tribe.

'Is Wan Loo going with you?' she asked. There was Wan Loo at the window again.

Minnie nodded, smiling happily. 'My old fella go now,' she smiled.

Caroline realised she would now be left with no house help and no cook for an indefinite period — till the tree was in flower. And there were still the men to be cooked for. She hoped Ted could come up with some suggestions for coping with this situation.

'Boss, him come back soon.' Caroline dragged her racing thoughts back to Minnie. 'Boss come soon,' she repeated. She turned to go, hesitated, then turned back with an expression at once shy and self-conscious, yet pride crossing her smiling face. 'That one yella man like me,' she said. Then she added quickly, 'Bin go now.'

This time she did go, walking quickly and lightly down the creek track, leaving Caroline gazing after her with a mixture of emotions, amusement, exasperation and surprise competing for supremacy. She stifled the urge to laugh as she watched Minnie's retreating back.

Wan Loo was still watching, she was sure. She must go and see him and make sure she had all this revelation correct.

He would no doubt be self-conscious, too, when she confronted him. He would have to be paid up before he left. She must get it clear with him where they were intending to live. When were they going? Tomorrow? Minnie had said now. She apparently wasn't coming to work the next day. Did that mean Wan Loo would not be here the next day either? Oh, where was Willie?

Caroline walked slowly through the garden to the kitchen door. There was no sense in hurrying. What difference did a few minutes make? She was thinking deeply how to handle this interview. If she had misunderstood Minnie and confronted Wan Loo regarding this issue, it could be very embarrassing. It could be equally embarrassing and possibly lead to trouble if Minnie had been making this up.

She entered the kitchen and greeted Wan Loo. He was busy cutting salad from his garden for lunch. 'You are good cook, Wan Loo.' The little fat man looked at her, trying to determine her manner. He smiled uncertainly. 'You happy here, Wan Loo?'

'Very happy,' he nodded. What was she going to say? 'Go tomorrow,' Wan Loo said happily. 'Go walkabout, have wife, come back work for you.' He was elated by the whole prospect. His future was mapped out most satisfactorily — the holiday, the acquisition of a wife, the possibility of a family, the prospect of a comfortable home and his beloved garden. What more could a fat little Chinese cook desire?

★   ★   ★

'Blow bubbles, Mummy,' Jamie pleaded. Caroline knelt beside the round bath in his bedroom and, soaping her hands, blew bubbles. He squealed with pleasure, watching the rainbow of reflected colours as they floated down to the water.

Caroline played with him for some time, enjoying his delight in the simple game. At last, she picked up the soft towel and, wrapping him in it, lifted him onto his bed to dry.

The bathtime games were played as she rubbed him dry, rub a dub dub, this little pig. All the games must be repeated in order, word for word each night.

But were his cheeks rather more flushed than usual from the bath and the games? Caroline felt his forehead. Was he a little warm? She looked carefully at him. He seemed bright enough, though perhaps he had been rather excitable tonight.

She dressed him in his nightshirt and tucked him in bed. She knelt beside his bed for prayers. He clasped his little hands, repeating the familiar words after her, concluding with make Jamie a good boy.

Then came the nightly song sung softly as she sat on the edge of the bed. She kissed him, laid the towel over her arm and, carrying the bath, took it to the verandah and poured the water into the drainpipe for Wan Loo's garden.

The kitchen was in darkness. Wan Loo

must have gone already. He had been very happy when she paid him up before tea, vowing he would be back before long to set up house and start work again.

She would have to see Ted in the morning to decide how the men's meals could be coped with. Perhaps one of them had been a camp cook at some time. She'd see about it in the morning.

She carried the bath back inside and put it away, hanging the towel to dry.

It was a cool night, clear and starry. Back inside, she looked in to see Jamie sound asleep. He did look rather flushed. She touched his forehead again. A bit warm, too. Or was she imagining things? Perhaps she was just being over-protective. He was so precious. Any sign of illness filled her with fear.

Still, she'd look in again through the night. After a lingering look at him, she blew out the light and went to bed.

27

An illness and a dream lost

The sun was well up when Caroline woke. She had been up to look in on Jamie several times during the night. The house was unusually quiet. As sleep retreated, awareness flooded back the memories of yesterday.

Wan Loo would not be in the kitchen. Minnie would not be coming. She must dress and get some breakfast ready. She looked into Jamie's room. He seemed to be still sleeping soundly. She wouldn't disturb him yet. He'd wake presently.

She went through the quiet house onto the verandah and looked towards the camp by the creek. All was quiet and deserted — no voices, no high-pitched laughter of the women, no squeals from the playing children, no smoke curling up from a camp fire. They must be gone already.

Where would they have gone, she wondered. What did they do on their walkabout? Perhaps there was a big corroboree somewhere they were going to attend, just like that occasion when she first came to 'Bibbaringa' and Willie was building the hut. Yuelty had introduced them to the big group that had come through at that time. Then he had gone with them to the gathering further north.

All that seemed so long ago now. She had just arrived then and knew almost nothing of life on a station, or life in the isolated inland. Now she was an old hand. She had adapted. She loved this place almost as much as Willie did, but it would still be so wonderful if only there was a neighbouring woman of her own culture to visit sometimes just for a talk.

Anyway, the blacks plus Wan Loo were gone and would by now be many miles away. They never seemed to hurry, yet they covered distance very quickly. She looked towards the stockyards. Someone was working down there. She'd go and get breakfast, then keep an eye out for Ted to tell him the latest on the affairs of the heart of Wan Loo and Minnie and the predicament regarding a cook.

'Mumma.' Jamie was standing on the verandah rubbing his eyes. Caroline hurried out of the kitchen, wiping her hands.

'Here, darling. Here's Mother.' She picked him up. He put his head on her shoulder and cuddled in. He still felt hot and his little voice was very croaky. Caroline carried him into the kitchen and sat down, cuddling him. He had his thumb in his mouth, a sign of distress. She talked soothingly to him, rocking him back and forth and rubbing gently up his neck and around his temples.

'Sore,' he said plaintively.

'Have you got a headache, darling?' she asked.

He nodded slowly. Poor little man. He was very miserable. He was usually such a happy, bright little boy.

Caroline sat him on the chair and, squeezing a lemon, mixed it with honey caps and added a little fresh butter. She put a little on a spoon and was able to get him to suck a little. He liked the sweetness and came back for some more.

'Hullo, what's happening here?' Ted Wilkes was at the kitchen door. 'Jamie not well, Mrs Bartlett?'

'No. He feels very miserable and he's very hot. He has a cold or something. I'm not used to him being sick.'

The overseer came over to him and put his hand on Jamie's forehead. 'Mmm. He is warm, isn't he? Better sponge him and try to cool him. Kids can go into a convulsion if they get too high a temperature, I believe.'

Caroline's heart gave a leap. Convulsion? Yes, she had heard of this, though she had not had any experience of it. And she wasn't just imagining his condition. Ted felt it, too. She'd sponge him presently and keep him in bed so he was in an even temperature.

'What's happening otherwise? Where's Wan Loo?' Ted asked, looking round. Caroline told him of the events of the previous day.

'So, he's just gone off with a few hours' notice?' he said incredulously. He was obviously not very favourably impressed. 'That leaves us in a bit of a hole, doesn't it, especially now you've got Jamie to nurse. I'll see if any of the men are willing to take over. Snowy might be a possibility. He did that camp cooking a few years back. I can't say how good it will be, though.'

'Anything would be a help.' Caroline had stood up with Jamie. 'I'd appreciate whatever you can arrange, Ted. I'd better go and bathe this little man.'

The overseer picked up his hat and went off in search of the most promising prospect to fill the role of cook for the remaining station hands.

Caroline took her son to the bedroom, gathering towels on the way. She spread a towel on the bed, undressed him and covered him with another. Taking the washstand basin, she half-filled it with tepid water and proceeded to sponge his face, arms and body. Perhaps he was sickening for measles or something like that, though he hadn't had any contact with such things. Still, you never knew. And the blacks moved around a lot. Poor little fellow. She hated to see him so forlorn.

After a time, the little boy seemed cooler and more comfortable. He enjoyed Caroline singing to him and reading him books. At last he fell asleep again. Caroline laid him down and covered him loosely. Perhaps he would be better when he woke. The sleep should do him good. Please God, help him get better, she prayed silently.

Someone was knocking on the door. Caroline hurried out. Snowy was standing on the verandah, his hat in his hands.

'Ted said you wanted to see me about cooking, Mrs Bartlett,' he said. Caroline told of Wan Loo's departure and the reason for it and the predicament now, especially with Jamie ill.

'That Minnie!' he exclaimed laughing. 'She's a saucy little thing. She's been trying to get Wan Loo's attention for quite a while. She needled him to get him to notice her, then she's been teasing him. They'll make a good pair. Life will be anything but dull in that camp.'

Caroline laughed. 'I think you're right, Snowy. So you see, we are now without a cook. Jamie is ill and I must look after him.

Can you help us out?'

The man looked rather self-conscious. 'Well, I've only done a bit of camp cooking, Mrs Bartlett, but I can put a meal on the table, if meat and vegetables will do. I don't run to puddings, though. The blokes I cooked for on droving jobs when I was cook weren't very fussy and didn't want anything much like that. I can make bread you can get your teeth through, though, so we won't starve.'

'Oh, thankyou very much. I'll be most grateful if you'll take it on. There are lots of vegetables in the garden and potatoes and onions in the store. There's also bottles of fruit and jam in the pantry that I preserved last summer, so just use those for pudding. Perhaps I could make some pastry while Jamie is asleep — or you can cook some rice.'

With the urgent necessity for providing solid food for hungry men taken care of, Caroline went to the store to look over the medicine chest. She took out the camphorated oil. She would rub his chest and back with that after his bath tonight.

Why did Wan Loo have to go off just now? He might have been able to produce something from his herbal mixtures. She knew he used wormwood and sage for chesty things, but not the proportions. And Jamie was little more than a baby. Herbal mixtures could be poisonous if you didn't know what you were doing.

Oh, what she'd give to have Mother close by to consult! But I'm Mother here, she thought. I should know what to do. I've been too lax not preparing myself for this kind of thing. Jamie had been so healthy up till now. There weren't even any of the blacks about to find out their bush remedies. But he might be improved when he woke again.

The next twenty-four hours saw little change in Jamie. Caroline rubbed his chest and back with camphorated oil and massaged his little body gently with lavender oil.

The constant ministrations, sponging, soothing, getting him to drink, combined with lack of sleep watching over him were beginning to tell on Caroline. Great dark shadows developed under her eyes and the strained expression of worry increased. The only sleep she got was snatches of half-sleep as Jamie dozed. He was developing a nasty cough.

As evening drew on again, Caroline brought a kettle of boiling water and set it on a little spirit stove on the marble-topped washstand. Perhaps the humid air would relieve his cough. She added a little camphorated oil to the water, the rising steam sending the laden vapour through the room.

She sat by him in the rocking chair for the next hour. He was deeply asleep, hardly moving. Becoming more alarmed, she bent over him. 'Jamie. Jamie darling, suck this orange for Mother.' She tried to squeeze a segment of orange between his lips. He did not rouse. I've just got to get help, she thought in wild panic. He's getting worse.

She ran out to the cow bell hanging on the verandah and rang it vigorously. It clanged out through the silence. Ted had suggested this call for emergencies.

She waited only a few seconds before she saw a light appear in the men's quarters, the door open and the lantern light approaching quickly. 'Oh Ted, I want someone to go for help. Jamie is getting worse,' she cried. Her voice caught in her throat. 'I'm not making any impression on his illness.' Tears were only just held at bay.

Back inside, Caroline found an old flannel shirt and tore it into wide strips. She prepared a poultice and spread it on the warmed cloth. She carried it quickly to the bedroom and, turning the bedclothes back, placed it gently on Jamie's chest.

Please God, make him better. Surely God would answer her prayer. He had given her this child. Surely he would save him.

She sat by his side watching the little

flushed face and the glazed eyes when he did open them. He seemed to be having bad dreams. He was whimpering in his sleep, calling out several times in a choked voice. Caroline tried to comfort him, but realised this was no ordinary dream and he was unaware of her presence.

The lamp burned low as the hours passed.

Ted Wilkes went back to the quarters. The men were all awake now after the noise of the bell and Ted's hurried exit had jerked them from sleep. The overseer told them of Jamie's condition and Caroline's request that some help be sought.

'Might be someone that could help at 'Blanche Water'.' It was Jacko who spoke. 'Ought to be able to get there by midday tomorrow. Otherwise there's only the German mission and that's as far again.'

'There's no doctor even there,' said Ted. He thought for a minute. 'Don't suppose any of you know anything about how to break this fever? Seems to me the little bloke might have pneumonia, from what Mrs Bartlett said.' The men looked more concerned than ever. If a little kid had pneumonia, he'd be pretty lucky to pull through. What a terrible shame if anything happened to him! None of them knew anything more to do by way of treatment. Couldn't very well give a little bloke like that a good swig of rum — a good many swigs, actually.

Jacko stood up and pulled on his clothes. 'I'll go to 'Blanche Water' and see if anybody can come and help her. Poor woman must be about exhausted.'

Young Danny was disappearing out the door, pulling on his boots. 'I'll get yer horse, Jacko,' he called.

It was decided. Jacko would go to 'Blanche Water' and bring back anyone who could help in this emergency. If there were no women there, or no-one likely to fill the need, he would ride on to Killalpaninna to seek possible assistance from the missionaries. Even though there was no doctor or hospital, there may be someone with nursing experience.

In less than fifteen minutes, the hoofbeat of Jacko's horse could be heard galloping over the paddocks and down the creek track south towards Lake Blanche. The moon was rising. Lucky it was a full moon, Ted thought. It would be very light later. It would make Jacko's night ride much easier if he could see his way. And quicker.

Every half-hour till dawn, Caroline changed the poultice and renewed the steaming kettle. If only he could breathe more easily. She could hear each rattling breath as he battled with the infection.

Her own endurance was waning. She felt her mind waver. She had to concentrate consciously on anything she did for him, afraid that in her exhausted state she might do something to harm him.

The room was spinning round. She jerked herself upright. She mustn't go to sleep. She had to watch him, to sponge his little face. She mustn't allow herself to fall asleep. What did she have to do now?

The bed wavered before her eyes. Why was she sitting here in the rocking chair? O yes, Jamie my little darling. Should she blow out the lamp? No, no, she must be able to see him.

Her head dropped. Her eyes closed. Caroline having had almost no sleep since Jamie first became ill had reached her limit. She slept the sleep of the exhausted.

She started awake just an hour later. Where was she? Jamie! Was he all right? She bent over him. His forehead was burning!

Oh, how could she have gone to sleep when her little boy was so ill? What sort of mother was she? Totally negligent and careless! Oh, what would Willie say? He trusted her to care for his son. To fall asleep! It was unthinkable that she could do such a thing.

He was worse. She was sure he was slipping away from her. His breath was now coming in great gasps. Oh God, what would she do? What more was there to do?

She must get more water to bathe him. He might go into convulsions. Ted had said children sometimes had convulsions when they had a too high temperature.

She picked up the dish and hurried to the kitchen. Oh, she was thirsty. She'd just get a glass of water. Filling the glass at the tap, she drank deeply then, taking the dish, went back to the bedroom.

The air was heavy with the scents of lavender, camphor and the poultice. She set the dish down carefully on the washstand, squeezed the washer out of the lukewarm water and turned to the bed.

Towel in one hand and washer in the other, she leant over the bed to sponge the little head, trying yet again to bring him cool relief. As she reached out her hand, she was suddenly aware the noise of the heavy breathing had stopped.

With horror she realised that Jamie was not breathing at all.

28

Self-accusation

Blackness! The awful horror. No Lord. No! It can't be. Oh, don't let it be. He's so little, so full of life and joy. His precious little body, Lord. Bring him back. Bring him back.

Caroline's mind reeled, pushing back, refusing to accept the awful reality. Jamie couldn't be dead. Not her baby, her gift. She rocked back and forth in a paroxysm of grief. Her whole being cried out in denial. Why, Lord, why? When you gave me this child, why let him die? She tried so hard to look after him well. But it hadn't been enough.

Why, oh why did she stop to have that drink? He had slipped away when she was not with him. What sort of mother was she that she couldn't even be with her little boy when he died? He might have opened his eyes and wanted her just when she was outside. He might have called for her — and he died without her comfort.

She had failed him. She had failed Willie's trust in her, too. Where had she gone wrong? She had thought of her own needs, that's where. Even when she sat beside him earlier, she had gone to sleep.

How had he got this illness? It was her fault. She had taken him for that long walk down the creek. He had paddled in the water after running along the banks. He had probably got a chill after being so hot. It was her fault. She hadn't thought.

But then she left him sitting in his bath while she blew bubbles for him. He might have got cold then. Wasn't it easy for a little child to get a chill? Her fault again.

She should have known better. She was a mother, wasn't she? Where was her care for her child? Why, even a mother bird risked its own life for its babies. And here was she, neglecting hers. Willie, oh Willie, I failed you, too. I failed. I've been no good as a mother, no good as a wife. My baby, my baby. Blackness descended.

★   ★   ★

Jacko had ridden hard all night. The full moon had made it possible to push along, making good time.

At mid-morning, he approached 'Blanche Water', the stone homestead in its cluster of trees beside the creek. A station hand came to meet him, aware that something was amiss.

Both horse and rider were exhausted. The long, hard night ride had tested the endurance of both. Jacko quickly explained his mission and the stockman galloped back to the homestead to give the alert. When he arrived, hands were ready to unsaddle his horse and rub him down. Jacko was taken inside and sat down to food and drink.

He told his story again: his ride for help, Caroline's despair and the urgency for some further assistance for Jamie. 'Is there anyone here who can help?' he asked. 'If not, I'll rest an hour, then, if I can borrow a horse, I'll go on to Killalpaninna. Maybe the Germans have someone with them. Thing is, I don't know how long the little fellow can hold out.'

'If he is as you say and it developed so quickly, I think he may have pneumonia,' Mrs Williamson said. 'We have no doctor here, but I have some nursing experience. When you have finished your tea, you sleep on one of the bunks. Bert here will look after you. I'll prepare and wake you in an hour and we'll head back. Do you think you can make it back again, or should I get one of our men to accompany me? We'll get you a fresh horse, of course. You can pick yours up later.'

Jacko assured her he would be right to set out again after a short sleep. 'That meal has done the trick and picked me up no end,' he said.

* * *

Caroline lay on her bed, her face on her arms. Exhausted, she could cry no more. The well of tears and grief dried up and expended, she felt numb.

Only her great sense of guilt consumed her. Jamie. Jamie. She had failed him. She had thought more of her own bodily needs than of her son. She ranked with the lowest of mothers. She did not deserve to be a mother. That was why God had taken back this great gift of a son to her. But God, Jamie was William's son, too. He was his pride and joy. Now Willie had no son, either. Her negligence had brought that about. She deserved to have no children if she couldn't look after them.

How Willie must hate her. Oh Willie, I love you so much, she thought. I'm so sorry, Willie. But that doesn't bring him back, does it? Oh, she deserved for Willie to hate her. He'd probably turn her out and want nothing more to do with her. What man would want a wife who couldn't look after his children?

He must have sensed something to say take good care of each other. He meant her, of course. Perhaps he was doubtful even then

281

that she would take care of his son. That's why he said it. He knew she was selfish. How he must hate her.

Oh Willie, I'm sorry. Forgive me, Willie. Forgive me. Don't hate me, Willie. Love me. Please love me. As she lay tormented with her condemnation of herself, Caroline became aware, as through a haze, a fog, of a knocking, a voice, a woman's voice calling her.

She was imagining it. There were no women here, not even any black women any more. She must be going mad! That's it! She must be mad. She was incapable of caring for her son. She had let him slip away from her. Now Willie would hate her. She was no use to anyone.

Through the maze of thought, the voice and the knocking sounded again. Perhaps she should go and see. But what was the use? She was only imagining it. There was no-one there. And what did it matter anyway if there was someone there?

'Are you there, Mrs Bartlett?' Mrs Williamson stood by the front door where Jacko had brought her.

Ted Wilkes had met them with the news of Jamie's death and of Caroline's devastation. They stood now waiting for a response. 'Better go in and see if we can find her,' Ted said. 'I'm sure she hasn't left the house. I kept an eye out, because she was so cut up.'

'Poor girl. What a terrible thing to happen. He was their only child, wasn't he?' Mrs Williamson's kind face was creased with compassion.

'You go in,' Ted said to her. 'The bedroom is the front room.' Mary Williamson stepped hesitantly into the vestibule. What a lovely room! She turned into the long central hall and followed the way Ted had indicated. She looked in the door.

Caroline lay on her bed, unaware of all except her great sense of guilt. 'May I come in?' The voice came from the door. It was a voice. Surely she wasn't imagining this. She turned and, raising herself on her elbow, saw her visitor standing in the doorway.

'May I come in, my dear?' Mary Williamson asked again. 'Can I talk with you?'

Caroline nodded.

Mary came quietly in and sat on the edge of the bed beside her. 'I'm so sorry, my dear. I came as quickly as I could. Most likely I wouldn't have been able to do anything to save him if I had been here.'

'It was my fault.' She turned her head away.

'Oh no, my dear. I'm sure it wasn't. But let me get you a cup of tea, then I want you to tell me about it.' She stood up and went in search of the kitchen. In a short while, she returned with a tray with a pot of tea and two cups and a plate of toast. The poor lass probably hadn't had anything to eat since the death. She must get her to have something to eat and drink.

She set the tray down on the bedside table and, sitting on the bed said firmly, 'Come now, dear, sit up and have a hot cup of tea.'

Caroline sat up. How dreadful she looked. Her eyes were sunk in two black chasms in her face. She poured the tea and passed a cup to Caroline. She took it and raised the cup to her lips. Mary talked quietly while she plied Caroline with the toast, talking about her coming to 'Blanche Water' — where it was and how they must visit when it was possible.

When Caroline had drained her cup and leaned back against her pillows, Mary took her hand and covered it with her own. 'Now tell me all about it,' she said simply.

The sad little voice went on for some time, telling of the sudden cold, fever and how quickly one thing had followed on the heels of the other. 'It was my fault. I can't ever face Willie.' She turned her face away. 'He'll know it was my fault. I'm not worthy to be a mother.'

There were no tears, just the tragic eyes.

Mary's heart went out to her. 'You must not allow yourself to think like that. Pneumonia, which I believe it was from what you have told me, is a very serious thing. Not many people recover from it — certainly very few old people or young children. In doing all you did, you followed the treatment that anyone would. You are not God, you know. All your love and care could not save him. You must not blame yourself like this.

'I'm sure your husband won't think that way. Your overseer Ted has told me about him and how devoted you are to each other. He said Mr Bartlett would be so upset not to have been here with you at this time. You are fortunate in that you have each other and your love. You must comfort each other.'

'But even so, I let him slip away from me when I wasn't with him, just because I was looking after myself. I wanted a drink, so I wasn't there.' Her eyes closed and her head dropped onto her arms.

In a few moments, Mary saw exhaustion had taken over. Caroline was asleep. She would snatch a rest herself while the girl slept. She realised suddenly just how tired she was. The urgency had kept her going during the long ride, receiving the information when she arrived with Jacko and then finding Caroline and attending to her immediate need. Now her legs started to tremble.

She covered Caroline with the quilt and, after taking the tray to the kitchen, returned to the bedroom with a blanket. She lay down on the couch to be near this young woman she had come to assist. She drew the blanket over herself and almost immediately was asleep.

29

A welcome and a business transaction

Nockatunga station perched on the crest of a wide ridge above the river. It was an ideal place for the homestead and other buildings. Plentiful water was close, the river having wide, lengthy holes and the ridge providing a vantage point from which could be seen the whole of the surrounding country for many miles.

William Bartlett and his party approached the settlement. The ride had been long, through difficult, unfamiliar country. Yuelty, in spite of his aging, had led them successfully to water and camp sites and finally to 'Nockatunga'.

Urging his horse forward, William led his men up to the homestead. Their approach was heralded by a chorus of barking from the homestead dogs.

A young woman emerged from the house and met William at the gate as he dismounted. 'Welcome to 'Nockatunga',' she called.

William slipped the bridle over his arm and

approached her. 'William Bartlett, Mrs Hunter. I sent word to your husband some time ago of my interest in your cattle for sale.'

'I thought you must be Mr Bartlett. Tom is just coming now.' She pointed to a rider approaching the rear of the homestead at a canter. 'He had some matters to attend to on one of the outstations. He has timed it well to return so close to the time of your arrival.'

She opened the gate. 'Perhaps your men could take the horses to the paddock over there,' she indicated with a nod, 'then freshen up and make themselves comfortable down at the quarters. Dinner will be after dark. We try to avoid the annoyance of the flies.'

William directed the men. They moved off, glad to be at the end of the track for tonight and eager for the prospect of a freshen up.

'Do come in, Mr Bartlett. We have been expecting you this last week.' She led the way onto the verandah and offered one of the chairs. 'It is so seldom we get visitors. You are most welcome.'

'Thank you,' William replied. 'I regret the reason for my visit — or rather, the reason for your sale of so many cattle at this particular time.'

She nodded solemnly. 'We regret it, too. Very much. These are some of our good breeders we are parting with. However, we believe it is the best thing to do in the circumstances. We shall have to build up again when the seasons change and become more favourable.'

'The country is certainly in a bad state at present.'

'Would you believe, Mr Bartlett, that in good seasons this is the most wonderful fattening country? Further out,' she waved towards the setting sun, 'it is absolutely bare now. But when the rain comes, or when they have rain up north and the water comes down, it floods out over the channels and, as it soaks away, a miracle happens.'

She sat upright. 'We will recover. It will come again. I hope you can arrange things satisfactorily with my husband for the purchase of the cattle. We can't let them starve.' She paused. 'They are not near starving yet, but certainly not at their best.'

Tom Hunter had reached home and now met his guest. The two men took an instant liking to each other. Dinner was a pleasant meal. The Hunters' hospitality left nothing to be desired.

'And do you have a family, Mr Bartlett? We are all so far apart in this country that we know little of each other.'

'Yes, I am married. My wife Caroline and I have a two-year-old son. Of course, he is the apple of our eye. But he really is a bright little chap — full of life.' He paused then continued. 'As a matter of fact, he's particularly precious because we were married ten years before he arrived.'

'Oh, that was a long time,' exclaimed Lucy Hunter. 'I can well see why you say he is particularly special.' She smiled at her husband. 'We had four children by the time we were married ten years. They are all having a holiday with their grandparents at the moment.'

'And now, you are interested in purchasing all the cattle, the one thousand head I have to sell?' Tom asked Willie. 'You believe you can take them successfully all the way to your station?'

'Yes. If we come to a mutually satisfactory agreement on price. Yes. I feel quite convinced we can take them.' He had been speaking confidently, but now he added with a smile, 'I'm not saying it will be easy.'

'I hope you have good men with you,' Tom said. 'You'll need them.'

'Yes, I have good men. There are two fairly new ones amongst them. The others have been with me for some years, so I am confident in them.'

'You had one of the blacks with you,' interjected Lucy.

'Yes, that is my old friend and guide, Yuelty. A wonderful old man. He served me well when I first took up my place. Now he has led me again, to here. He is a very reliable man.' He leant back in his chair. 'I have ridden as far as the Cooper previously. But there my knowledge of the country ceased. Water, as you know, is the sometimes elusive necessity in unfamiliar country out here.'

His hosts nodded agreement.

'When Yuelty was available to lead our party, I thought it far wiser to rely on his superior knowledge.'

'You are very wise,' Tom agreed. 'But tell me, what is the country like between here and your place? Obviously you are having a much better season than we are.'

The conversation turned to details of the area covered. Two days' ride back was where conditions had started to deteriorate. Until then, it had been reasonable, better the further you went south. Much of the intermediary country was covered lightly with a low scrub. The clay pans between the ridges were lush in the southern area.

'That is why I am in a position to be interested in your stock. I have heard of their quality and think it would be to my advantage to introduce some of your strain. I am

291

anxious to see them in the morning,' William said.

'I'm sure you will not be disappointed. They are not in the best of nick, but quite reasonable as yet. That is why I want to sell these now. I also want to keep our reputation high,' Tom explained.

'Some of those we are selling are calving, you know,' Lucy Hunter ventured. 'I hope you can get them all safely to your place — if you buy them, of course. There is no stock route, is there? This scrub area you mention may prove a problem for so large a herd.'

'That is true, but I think it can be handled. I must admit the challenge stimulates me.' He leant forward, his elbows on the table. 'I believe if I can carry this whole venture off successfully, it could open up a new route to Adelaide markets for this part of the country. It is an exciting challenge to me.'

His hosts could see in his countenance and shining eyes the degree of excitement and challenge this venture offered.

'Then I wish you the best of luck,' Tom said. 'I had not thought of that. But yes, it would provide an alternative market, to take stock to South Australian markets.'

So this was also behind Bartlett's scheme. He seemed to be an enterprising sort of

fellow; the first to venture out into uninhabited country in his part of the colony, too. He
was a man after his own heart, really
— probably a bit more daring, though.

The wicks were burning low in the lamps
before they rose from the table and William's
hosts showed him to his room. 'I suppose
your wife will be anxiously waiting for your
return,' Lucy said. 'She no doubt has
someone attending to your station affairs
while you are away.'

William told her of his confidence in Ted
Wilkes in keeping things going with the other
men left behind.

'She has Wan Loo, our Chinese cook and
two black girls who help in the house. They
keep her amused and are great company for
her. Then, of course, there is little Jamie. She
is busy making a new section of garden while
I am away. Even so, I shall be happy to get
home and make sure they are well and happy.
We, as are you, are a long, long way from
outside assistance should anything go wrong.'

He bade them goodnight and entered his
room. They were a nice couple. Four
children, eh? Would he and Caro ever have
four children? They might. Now they had
started and had Jamie, they might. He
thought of Caro and her envying the cows
with their babies every Spring all those years

ago. It would be good for Jamie to have brothers and sisters, too.

How were they, Caro and Jamie? His heart filled with love as he thought of his little son asleep in his bed when he saw him just before he left. As he turned the bedclothes back and climbed into bed, he felt an aching longing for Caro. What was she doing now? Was she all right? Was all well at home?

He felt a sudden shiver of apprehension. If anything should happen to them . . .

He pulled himself up sharply. All would be well. Ted would look after them. They had plenty of people about. It wasn't as if they were alone. If anyone got sick, Wan Loo knew lots of Chinese treatments and even the blacks down at the camp had their own bush remedies for illnesses. He turned over and closed his eyes resolutely, determined to go to sleep.

William was awake early. The day was as so many days before it, bright and sunny. It was hot already. He dressed quickly and went out onto the verandah.

The sun beat down on the parched paddocks from a sky devoid of any semblance of a cloud. The bare red ground seemed to vibrate in the sunlight. 'No sign of rain yet, William.' His host was behind him.

'Must break your heart when it's like this,'

William responded.

'It will come good again,' his host responded. 'Shall we go and look at the breeders now — and after breakfast I'll take you out to look at the others.'

William was impressed with the quality of the breeders. These were what he was really interested in. The Hunters had to sell the others and he was willing to buy the lot if the price was good.

He couldn't take advantage of the poor fellow's misfortune, though. He was willing to pay a fair price. He would be able to fatten them at 'Bibbaringa' and 'Onavale' and sell for a profit. But the breeders he would introduce into his herd.

After breakfast, they rode out to see the rest of the stock to be sold. They talked for some time. Eventually, reaching an agreement, they turned the horses for home.

'Well, Mr Bartlett, do you like our stock?' Lucy asked as they gathered around the lunch table.

'I think you have some fine animals, Mrs Hunter,' William responded. 'I have decided to take them. We will bring the stores in closer this afternoon and head off at daybreak tomorrow. It will be a slow journey — at least until we get them away from their own familiar territory.'

When they had finished the meal, William rose. 'If you will excuse me now, I will go and alert my men to our movements.'

He went out feeling glad to have been able to make the purchase and to be able to help his hosts in their vulnerable position. Once again, he was thankful for having been able to purchase 'Onavale'.

The men were in the quarters playing cards. William gave them the news. They rose with alacrity to saddle the horses and round up the cattle as directed. The next day, the work would really begin.

30

The challenge of the return

At first light, the 'Bibbaringa' men were rounding up the cattle. It had been decided to start with two mobs, the first and closest to the homestead being made up of the breeders. William appointed one of the new men, Oliver, in charge of this first mob for the initial part of the journey. They would head off as soon as they were able. The other mob, the stores — those ready for market — were further away and it would be later in the day before they were mobilised and under way. These would travel more quickly and would soon catch up to the leaders.

Yuelty led the first party. They would not be able to travel quickly with young calves. As Lucy Hunter had pointed out, some of the cows were still calving, so this would slow things down.

During the day, newly-born calves would be slung into a canvas hammock under the waggon and returned to the mob to be claimed by their mothers when the cattle caught up.

The first party led off early. 'Take them slowly,' William cautioned Oliver. 'They are not in the best of condition and quite a few of the calves are very young. Just ease them along and keep moving.' He left them then, urging his horse to follow the men already well on the way to the area where the store cattle were to be mustered.

They were scattered far and wide. With shortage of feed, they searched for any pick they could find. The sun was getting hot. William looked at the sky. It would be a scorcher before the day was out.

The men were out wide around the cattle. Range cattle, without fences, they were not going to be evicted from their territory without a struggle. The crack of stockwhips and the pound of hoofs filled the air. The bellows of beasts, turned where they had no desire to go, rent the air. But experienced men on good stockhorses eventually won out and the reluctant steers and bullocks were mustered into a mob and moved off down the tracks.

William now left them to follow and set off in pursuit of the earlier mob. It was evening before he caught up with the breeders. The men were constantly watching them. These first few days would be the worst.

Stars appeared in the dark sky — a

dry-weather sky, clear and crisp. Nights in the inland sandy country were always cool. Soon the moon would rise to full. William lay back against his saddle. It had been a long day. The campfire burned brightly. He would catch a bit of shuteye now and keep watch a bit later.

The eerie howl of a pack of dingoes woke him. He started up, alert at once. The full moon was rising, casting a flood of light over the land. The cattle were restless. He called his horse softly and, saddling him, rode out quietly.

Again the howl of the dingoes wafted out. The cattle moved nervously. They started up at any movement in the bush, at shadows, their long, low bellowings rumbling monotonously. It was an uneasy night.

At daylight, they moved off again. There were now three new-born calves slung under the waggon.

Riding behind the mob, William came upon Oliver standing by a calf which had obviously been abandoned. The mother was nowhere to be seen. 'Well, might as well finish this one off,' Oliver observed.

'What do you mean?' William asked.

'Knock it on the head, of course,' Oliver replied.

'Knock it on the head?' William said incredulously. 'We'll do no such thing. I've just bought these cattle and I intend to get them all to 'Bibbaringa'.'

'But you've got three new-borns under the waggon now — and they've got mothers to feed them. This one hasn't even got a mother, as far as I can see. I've no idea which one is its mother. She's not interested in it, anyway.'

'Well, I am.' The reply was brusque. 'We've got the goats. We'll give it goat's milk.'

'Well, don't ask me to feed the thing. There's enough to do keeping these cattle together without poddying calves.' He flung onto his horse. 'Leave it to the dingoes. They were looking for a feed last night.'

Fury surged through William. Who did the fellow think he was? Why was he in the game of cattle if he didn't care more than that for any beast? He hadn't noticed him being overly zealous last night, anyway. Won't last long in my establishment, he thought.

He picked up the little calf and set it on its wobbly feet. Poor little creature. It hadn't had anything in its stomach for hours. If it was going to survive, he'd better get it in and give it a drink. It was weak. He looked a nice little fellow, though. Hoisting the calf over the horse, he rode back to the camp fire. The cook was packing up, preparing to move off.

'Got any goat's milk left, Cooky?' William asked.

'Yes — there, at the back of the waggon, boss. What? You got a calf to feed? What happened to the mother?'

'I don't know. He was abandoned, poor little chap. His sides are very hollow. I think he might be all right if I can get something into his stomach, though.'

Between packing his supplies and harnessing up ready to move off, Cooky watched the boss. He had taken some of the milk and added some hot water from the billy over the fire. Now he was trying to get the calf to feed. 'Your finger can't be the right shape, eh, boss?' he joked.

William was wetting his finger with milk and trying to draw the calf's nose down into the milk. 'Perseverance usually wins,' William joined.

This boss certainly nursed his cattle along, Cooky thought. Like a mother to them, he was. They mustn't be hurried along too much. Give them plenty of time to drink at the watering places. Call a halt if a cow was calving. Wait for her. Pick up the new-born calves and carry them under the waggon when you moved off. Make sure they found their mothers when you made camp for the night.

He thought of the new member, Oliver. He didn't know how he would like all this. He didn't strike him as being very concerned about looking after them. He certainly couldn't see him feeding a calf like this. Belt 'em along and get his pay at the end of the trip and head off again: that's how he struck him.

At the end of the second day on the road, the mob of stores had caught up. Now they had the whole mob to move. The nightwatch was kept constantly alert, turning stragglers back into the herd.

They must be careful they were not spooked. Any sudden movement — a flare-up of the camp fire, a sudden noise from some bush creature in the scrub — could send the cattle in an instant plunging away — through the scrub, over the camp fire, through the camp, terrified, panicked, making a wild stampede, meaningless in direction or purpose. There was danger in such events.

The full moon rose again. The large herd settled. Howls of dingoes close at hand — but out in the scrub, out of sight — indicated that the pack was following, looking for a new-born calf unprotected, or a cow caught down in calving. They weren't fussy. It all made a good meal — and possibly for their pups back in their lair.

William again rose and rode round the cattle about midnight. They seemed fairly quiet, though that could be deceptive. The night watch rode up to him. 'Seem quiet, eh, boss?' he said quietly.

'Yes. Doesn't take much to change that, though.'

They talked in undertones for a few minutes, then he moved away. William continued his rounds. His thoughts wandered. How was Caro? How was her garden progressing? She'd just about have flowers blooming by the time he got home. He was realising just how slow this trip was going to be.

The little bull calf was doing well. A bit of perseverance paid off. He only had to take out the bucket now and it would come looking for its feed. Cooky had been amused and intrigued by the little thing and its response and offered to feed it the rest of the way. He was a nice fellow — and quite a good cook, too. He'd have to remember him for the next big droving team to Adelaide.

A stealthy shadow slunk out of the scrub and approached the herd by a circuitous route. Two cows with young calves lay clearly visible in the moonlight. Instinctively, William reached for his revolver, then checked himself in time. A shot would send the whole mob crashing through the scrub. He nudged his horse in their direction. The dingo retreated silently, lost in the shadows of the scrub.

By the end of the first week, the team and the cattle were falling into a routine. Cookie now had the calf following him everywhere when its feed time approached. 'You've got yourself a mate,' one of the boys called as the calf bunted him.

'Yeah. You'd better call this one Cooky, eh, boss?'

William laughed. He looked around the team tucking into their meal. They were a good crew — except that fellow, Oliver. He was out on watch at the moment. He wouldn't trust him on night watch, though. You never knew what a fellow like that would do if he thought he could get away with it.

His eye fell on Yuelty. The old fellow looked tired. He hoped that was all it was and he wasn't ill. He went to the fire, filled his pannikin from the billy of tea and took it back to sit down beside the black man. 'How are you, old friend?' he asked.

Yuelty shook his head 'Get old,' he said solemnly. 'Not young man. No more.'

'Mmm. You've got a few grey hairs there — not like when we went with Stuart Boss that first time, eh? You strong young man then.'

Yuelty smiled, his face lighting up at the memory. 'Good time then. Good man. Make good friend then.' He looked down, then poked William with his finger. 'You,' he said and laughed.

'Good friend. You been good friend to me,' William replied. There was silence for a few minutes as they gazed in the fire, each thinking of the years that had passed since their first meeting.

'When we get back I go my people,' Yuelty said. 'I lead you home. Then I go. I lay down soon.' He nodded gravely.

'We all get old. My time will come one day.' William stood up to go. 'Goodnight, my friend,' he said, resting his hand on the old man's shoulder.

'Goodnight, Willie Boss,' he replied.

Willie Boss! Was that what Yuelty called him privately? He'd never said that before. Just 'boss' was what he always called him. Willie Boss. It had an affectionate sound.

A tightening came in William's throat. He had great affection as well as great respect for the old man. This would be their last journey together. It had been good, though, the times they had journeyed and explored and ventured out together; those times had been good.

What a debt he owed the black man for his guidance in all his ventures with 'Bibbaringa', thrusting out into the unknown. He had shared his knowledge, his wisdom, his judgment willingly — and their friendship and love had grown.

He's the whitest man I know, William thought as he settled down with his head on his saddle.

31

The last leg of the trek

They headed the cattle west. The parched country around 'Nockatunga' had been left far behind.

They relied again now on Yuelty to guide. The old man went on confidently. He knew this country well. Many times as a young man he had been over this land. The vast distances with no distinguishing features held no fears for him. Somehow, somewhere he found his markers and navigated skilfully. He saw signs — portents — where no sign existed for the white man's eye.

He led them to water each day. Sometimes it was a large waterhole, sometimes a string of shallow holes or a billabong. Pastures had improved. The herbage at least was green and the bushes provided some substance. The big mob left unmistakable evidence of its passing.

'Won't be long now before we meet up with our creek,' William observed. 'Then we turn south.'

'Have to keep this way till then,' Yuelty

said. 'No water that way now.' He pointed to the south.

'How far no water, Yuelty?' one of the men asked.

'Long way,' the old man said. 'Man, cattle die that way. No water.' The subject was closed for him.

They were moving now through the far reaches of the greater channel country, the country where floods occurred at times when no rain fell, where the creeping orange water snaked its way slowly south, meandering for miles, spreading out to cover the countryside, far from its source in the north.

The cattle were holding well. Their losses had been minimal, thanks to Yuelty's guidance, William thought. It would have been a different story if he had struck out on his own.

His eyes turned towards the horizon. There was a haze far out. It looks as though we could possibly get a storm, he thought with alarm. It would be disastrous to be caught here if they had any amount of rain. An inch of rain could mean the loss of a great proportion of the herd in the bog of the wide channel.

He urged his horse back towards the drovers bringing up the rear. The cattle were getting restive. They kept lifting their heads and sniffing the air, looking to the north. He must heed the warning. 'Could be a storm building up out there,' he called. 'We'll move the cattle on more quickly. I want to reach the far ridge before it breaks. It's about ten miles wide, and we haven't come far.'

Oliver lifted his head and looked around. 'Can't see any clouds, boss. Think you're wrong about the storm,' he observed.

William felt his irritation rise. This fellow would try his patience too far yet. He'd be glad to be rid of him. But he couldn't let him go yet. 'I'll be the judge of that,' he said calmly.

Oliver watched him move off. 'If it rains, they'll just get a good bath,' he said, waving a hand.

'A mud bath, probably, up to their bellies.' Splinter had come up behind him.

Oliver whipped around. 'What do you mean?' he asked.

'Look, Oliver, you're new to this country. It's not your coastal land. Even half an inch of rain can play havoc for drovers here. These clay pans become impassable. This will be one tremendous bog across here if we get a decent storm.'

Splinter had alighted and was tightening the girth of his saddle. He looked up at the man seated on the grey horse. 'Can you imagine this mob of a thousand head trying to squelch its way through mud when they sink deep in it?'

His girth was right. He flipped the reins back over the horse's head. 'Ever tried to pull two or three beasts out of a bog?' Oliver shook his head. 'How about a thousand? Be some job, eh?'

Splinter mounted and wheeled his horse round. 'The boss knows what he's doing.'

He moved away at a canter, out on the wing, bringing the strays in and moving them along. The rest of the men were doing the same.

Oliver shrugged his shoulders. It would be good to be finished with this God-forsaken country and be back down south where the jobs were shorter and conditions a lot better. There is a bit of life there, too. He spurred his horse.

All afternoon, they kept the mob moving. They had stopped in relays for only a few minutes at midday for a slice of damper and a cup of tea. Then it was back on the horses, keeping the cattle moving.

The clouds were visible now, building up way out. Hopefully, it would veer away or spend itself before it got to them. But they couldn't chance that.

The cattle could smell the coming storm.

The leaders were out in front moving well. They were making for the ridge themselves now. By sundown, the clouds were approaching, the first almost overhead. The sky was darkening. Just a bit further. The calves were tiring and the mothers were anxiously calling them, falling back, searching when they got behind. Several had been picked up and put in the sling under the waggon.

Cookie's little mate was trotting by the waggon. It was doing well.

As the first beasts reached the bottom of the ridge, a flash of forked lightning seared the sky. Thunder boomed out and rolled away over the distance. They were scrambling up the ridge, slipping on the loose sandy areas, slipping back, losing their footing. How are we going to get the calves up there? William thought.

'Keep them going, boys,' he called urgently. Back and forth around the back of the herd, the men set their horses. The whips whirled out, cracking lightly behind the stragglers.

As the last beasts reached the foot of the ridge, the heavens opened. Great drops of rain started. Then it became a deluge. Cookie had just reached the top of the ridge. The cattle, exhausted, were breathing heavily as the rain poured down around them. They had spread out now, waiting for the storm to pass.

'Well, we did it,' William cried. 'We got them across. But only just.' He laughed happily, the water pouring down from the edge of his hat. The wall of rain made it impossible to see more than a metre or two. Thunder rolled overhead. It was over in half-an-hour. The storm passed on its way.

'Wonder if they got any of that at 'Nockatunga'?' Henry called.

'Too far east for that storm, I reckon,' Splinter ventured. He had been watching their route, placing their direction by the sun. He even sat with William, asking questions about the stars and charting a course as they sat around the camp fire at night.

As the clouds rolled on south, they looked back across the claypan they had crossed. It was a wide sea of water, already turning muddy brown. It would be impassable for days.

Tea was a jocular meal. With no wood of any kind at hand, let alone dry wood, Cookie had done his best. 'Think we'd better get a new cook next trip, boss,' one man called as he tucked into a slice of corned beef and damper.

'This is pretty poor. What, no puddin'?' another contributed.

'There's a tin of cocky's joy here to spread on your damper if you want puddin',' Cookie replied, taking it all in good part. 'That's golden syrup, if you don't know what cocky's joy is, Oliver.'

The night watch went out after tea. The cattle were grazing on the saltbush or lying down. There wouldn't be much trouble tonight. They were tired.

Only hope we've left those dingoes behind, William thought. The calves would be sitting ducks tonight after the day's happenings. He'd have to mention it to the night watch to keep a sharp lookout. The men were tired, too, and wet. Boots squelched as they moved. Thank goodness it was not cold. There was no wind now.

Everything was washed. The atmosphere was clear now. They settled down. William warned those taking over the late shift about the extra vigilance for dingoes, then went to alert those already on watch.

The stars were bright as he made his way from one to another. They would be glad when their watch was finished and someone else took over.

'We'll rest them here today,' William told his men next morning. 'By tomorrow, the higher ground on this side will be dry enough to travel.'

They moved off. The cattle, rested for the day, moved along contentedly. The herbage was getting better. The cattle had not lost too much condition.

Soon be home with you, Caro, William thought as he followed along. What would Jamie be doing? He would have grown in the weeks he had been away. What a fine little fellow he was; a real boy. Brave for his two years, too. He was a tough little chap, really. He didn't go into tears every time he hurt himself.

Just wait till I can take him on a trip like this, he thought. He smiled at the thought. That would be the day. Maybe they would have some more children, by then. The Bartlett and Sons Enterprise. Caro laughed at him about this. He laughed at himself. But what a thrill it would be. He was working towards it. He wanted to have something great to hand onto his children, just as Grandfather Bartlett had left him that legacy. The Bartlett and Sons Enterprise would be a fine thing to hand on. He would go on working on it.

At last, they turned south down their creek. It had dried somewhat since they had left. That storm couldn't have reached this far. The feed was still good, though. The cattle would soon fatten here. Then he would move the stores to 'Onavale' and thence to Adelaide.

If things were right at the end of this year, he would start looking for another place on the route to markets. There was even talk of a railway extending further north into the inland. If this eventuated, he would investigate the possibility of taking stock the shorter distance. It could halve the distance for droving to market. He would have to look to the availability of water, though. If it was feasible, a place in this direction could be a possibility.

The Bartlett and Sons Enterprise was well in his mind.

32

What must be done

'We'll have to do something.' He jerked his head towards the house. 'She's just not capable of deciding anything. I tried to talk to her earlier, but I can't get through at all. She doesn't seem to even hear or see me. She looks at me, but right through me. It's just been too much for her, poor little woman.'

Ted Wilkes, Snowy and a little group of the hands sat on the men's quarters verandah with their mugs of tea. 'Can't wait much longer,' said Jacko, looking up at the others. 'It's not mid-summer, but it's not the South Pole either. Can't wait much longer.' They nodded agreement. They considered the situation for a few minutes.

Ted pulled himself up and hitched his trousers. 'Well, the lady from 'Blanche Water' did what had to be done inside, boys. Looks like we'd better get on with the rest of the job.'

He took a few steps off the verandah. 'Danny, get the shovels and a couple of crowbars.' Then he called over his shoulder.

'Bring them down to the corner of the yard.'

He went off towards the house. 'Better get a mattock, too,' Bill said, following Danny.

Ted knocked on the door. Mary Williamson answered the knock. She felt somewhat refreshed by her sleep, but deeply concerned about Caroline. 'I thought I'd better have another go at talking to Mrs Bartlett,' Ted said. 'Can't wait much longer. It's been a while now. We'll have to go ahead. It would be way too long to wait for a parson to get here. With the boss away, we'll just have to take over. Said he left 'em in my care when he was going, you know.'

He stood awkwardly, turning his hat round and round in his hands. Mary looked searchingly at the overseer. There was a great deal to this man, she was coming to see. The more she saw of him, the more she was impressed by him. 'I was thinking the same thing,' she said quietly. 'I'm afraid Mrs Bartlett is just so shocked, she is unable to bring her mind to these things. As you say, I think we'll just have to go ahead. But go in and see her and try to talk to her. You never know. If she'll only face up to the loss and stop blaming herself, she'll be all right. But her mind is set so completely on that. She doesn't really seem to have realised her own loss. If we can just bring her out of this terrible feeling of guilt she has.' She paused momentarily. 'Go and see what you can do.'

Ted went through the house, trying to step lightly, his boots still heavy on the polished boards. He stopped at the open bedroom door and knocked. Caroline, sitting by the window, turned her head. 'Can I come in and talk to you, Mrs Bartlett?'

She nodded, looking back out the window. Ted walked over and sat in the chair beside her. How could he put it? The thing was to get her to respond, but yet not upset her further.

He took a deep breath. Here goes. 'Mrs Bartlett, we've got to get on with the funeral.' He watched for a reaction.

She nodded vacantly.

'Boys are looking to things outside. Thought you might like it up in that corner of the garden.' He pointed in the direction where the men were busy digging. 'We'll fix it all up properly,' he comforted.

Caroline nodded again, but didn't speak.

'We'll have to go ahead. You see, we can't wait for a man of the cloth to get here. You understand that, do you?'

Caroline looked at him, not really comprehending what he was talking about. What was it he was talking about? It was too hard to concentrate on what he was saying. Willie trusted him and relied on him. He'd do the right thing, whatever it was he was asking her about. Willie, Willie, oh Willie.

She looked vaguely at the overseer. 'Do whatever you think Mr Bartlett would want you to do,' she said quietly, then added, 'It was all my fault, Ted.'

No use talking to her any more, Ted thought. She didn't seem to be grasping the situation at all. He'd have to make the decision. He'd have to decide about a burial service, too. He had been to plenty of funerals, of course, but this was a bit different.

The parson always read out of a book, didn't he? Well, the boss or Mrs Bartlett probably had a book like that — a prayer book, he supposed. We sure want the little fellow to have a Christian burial. Wonder where he'd find a book like that?

'You got a prayer book, Mrs Bartlett?' he asked.

Caroline looked at him, surprised from her introspection. 'Of course,' she said, her brows drawing together. What on earth would Ted want a prayer book for? He wasn't a very religious man, was he?

'Could I borrow it, please, Mrs Bartlett?'

'Borrow? What do you want to borrow?' She had slipped back.

319

'A prayer book, Mrs Bartlett. You said you've got a prayer book. Could I borrow it for a while, please?'

Caroline pulled open the drawer in the little table beside her and took out a smallish book. She handed it to the overseer. Why did he want a prayer book? It was too much trouble to find out.

Ted took the book from her. The Book of Common Prayer. Of course, that was what it was called. He stood up, his hat in one hand and the book in the other. 'Thanks, Mrs Bartlett.' A man of few words, he searched for something to comfort her. He swung his hat. What could he say? 'We'll do our best,' he finally said.

Caroline nodded. He'd be able to fix it up, whatever it was. Willie. Willie.

The boys had finished their job when Ted came out again. He went up to the corner of the garden and they all stood there, surveying their work.

'Looks all right,' Ted said.

'Measured the box Sam's been fixing up,' Jacko said.

'So everything's ready. I tried to talk to Mrs Bartlett, but she doesn't seem to realise. Anyway, we can go ahead. You blokes have all been to burials. You know what to do.' Ted held up the prayer book. 'I've found what's been used at most of the funerals I've been to. 'Burial of the Dead' it's called. I can read that.'

'Got nothing for you to put on like the parson wears, Ted,' Snowy interrupted.

Ted looked quickly at him. Was he trying to be funny? Embarrassment made Ted's face flush. No, he decided Snowy was serious.

'Can't see that's necessary,' he replied. 'Anyway, I suppose there's some meaning connected to them. I wouldn't be entitled to wear them anyway.' He paused, not knowing what to say. 'I can't see myself in that get-up. I'll just read what it says here. We'll all have to pray as best we know how. We'll go and clean up and when everybody's ready back here . . . ' He left the last words unsaid and tramped away towards the quarters.

The men stood for a few minutes. No doubt about old Ted — big man, all right — good bloke. Not every fella could do what he was taking on. He'd had to face the Missus, too, to get permission to go ahead. That couldn't have been easy.

Oh, well. Better go and do as he said and get back here. The lady from 'Blanche Water' was still here. She'd come. They'd better spruce up a bit and do the best they could.

The little group gathered around the grave. Ted stood awkwardly at the end, book in hand. Mary Williamson stood near. Should she have persevered with Caroline to have her here for her son's funeral?

She had finally decided it was pointless to continue. Caroline seemed unaware of what was happening. She sat staring into space, unable to bring her consciousness to bear on the present for more than a minute. The only thing to do was to leave her where she was for the moment and see what could be done tomorrow.

Ted had started reading. 'I am the resurrection and the life,' saith the Lord. 'He that believeth in me, though he were dead, yet shall he live, and whosoever liveth and believeth in me shall never die.' Ted's voice went on reading. Those standing by listened as they had never listened to the words before.

There was a lot in those words. They made a man think. None of us was here forever, was he? We all had to go some time. Pity about this little bloke, though. His life had only just started.

Ted was reading. 'We therefore commit his body to the ground.' This was the cue two of them had been waiting for. They stepped forward and cast some earth on the coffin.

Ted's voice continued: 'Earth to earth, ashes to ashes, dust to dust, in sure and certain hope of the resurrection to eternal life, through our Lord Jesus Christ . . . ' It was over. Ted turned aside, visibly shaken.

Mary went to him and, placing her hand on his arm, squeezed it. 'Well done, Ted,' she said huskily. 'Well done.'

A week passed. Mary Williamson, torn between her compassion for Caroline and the knowledge of the need for her at home, at last decided she could stay no longer.

She had written at length to Caroline's parents, telling them of Jamie's illness and death and the present condition of Caroline. When they would receive it she did not know. She would take it home with her and send it off at the first opportunity of finding someone travelling south. With the date of William's return so uncertain, it was no use leaving it here.

She departed in company of Jacko who would escort her home, return the horse he had borrowed and pick up his own. Mary farewelled the men who all saw the two riders off. The experiences of the last week had welded a bond amongst them. Mary shook hands all round before mounting. As she shook hands with Ted, she clasped his hands between both her own with an added pressure. Words were not necessary.

Caroline descended into a mist-shrouded

world within herself. She ate mechanically something of the food placed before her. Voices came and went, but the voices in her head went on and on incessantly.

What sort of woman was she? She was no use to anyone. She couldn't even look after one little boy. Some women had ten or more children and helped their husbands as well. She didn't have to do that and she only had one little boy. No wonder God had taken him back. He had taken him back, hadn't he?

She started up. 'Jamie. Jamie,' she called. Perhaps this was all a nightmare, a terrible nightmare. She staggered to Jamie's room. Where was he? She looked wildly around. Was he hiding?

Of course he's not hiding! You killed him. The voices again. Battering in her head. You. You. You . . . killed him. Killed him . . . Killed him . . . You're to blame. It's your fault.

She clamped her hands over her ears, trying to shut out the voices. But they went on just the same. You killed him. You couldn't look after him. What use are you? Willie will never forgive you. Why should he? You couldn't look after one small child. You're no use to him or anyone else.

Stop it! Stop it, she screamed silently. I can't bear it. Willie, love me. Willie, forgive me. Willie, I want you. He won't want you.

He's finished with you. The voices again hammered in her head. You're done. Finished. God won't forgive you, either. You wanted a child and when you got one you couldn't look after him. You'll go to hell. Hell! This is hell!

Caroline groped her way back to her room. Willie. Willie did love her very much. She wouldn't listen to the voices. They shouted at her, but she'd try not to listen. She'd fill her mind with Willie. She wouldn't give the voices a chance to be heard. She'd concentrate on Willie. She'd go to Willie. She'd find him. She knew the direction he went. She'd tell him all that had happened. He'd understand because he loved her.

Who are you trying to deceive? You couldn't find your way to the creek. The voice scorned her. He won't want you. Next thing you'll be saying that God will forgive you, too. You know he won't . . . He won't . . . He won't . . .

Her head reeled. With a great effort, she slipped out of her skirt and pulled on a riding skirt. 'I'm coming, Willie. Love me, Willie. I'm coming. I need you, Willie. Oh, I need you.'

She ran wildly, staggering with weakness, to the saddle room, pulling her saddle off the rest and struggling to the horse paddock. Star would take her.

You won't even be able to get on the horse, let alone stay there. You killed your son. Willie won't want you. Won't want you . . . Won't want you. He will. He will. She leaned her head against the fence rail.

Oh God, give me strength. Help me.

Huh! God won't help you! You should know that! You don't appreciate what he gives you. You let your son die! Let him die . . . Let him die . . .

A soft nose nuzzled her shoulder. She looked up. Star was before her, his ears lifted in question. What was she doing? Did she have something in her pocket for him?

She reached up and stroked his forelock. Dear Star. He knew she needed him. She slipped his bridle on and, with a great effort, saddled him. She leant against the fence, exhausted. The world reeled around her.

That's right, take your time. You won't find Willie anyway. And even if you do, he won't want you. The voices again. She closed her eyes, stretching her endurance and trying to hold on. She must get to Willie. She must get up into the saddle.

The horse whinnied softly and nuzzled her again.

Yes, Star, I'm coming. She led him out of

the paddock, put her foot in the stirrup and pulled herself up. She sat limply, the reins loose, her breath coming in great gasps.

Then, gathering the reins and herself, she rode out of the house paddock and with mounting urgency towards the creek and track Willie had taken.

Star, sensing her urgency, broke into a gallop as they came to the track. The activity had helped to silence the voices momentarily. The wind blew through her hair, soothing her forehead and the aching in her neck.

Willie, Willie, love me, Willie. I need you, Willie. Please forgive me. Please God, help me to find Willie. Make him understand. I tried to look after Jamie.

You let him die! Oh, the voices again . . . You let him die. Why are you talking to God? He knows all about it. He won't forgive you.

She grasped Star urgently. Hold on. Don't fall. Don't listen. She struggled inwardly to free herself of this torture chamber. The walls closed in on her. Prison. The voices screamed from every side, condemning her. She clutched the reins desperately and closed her eyes. The horse galloped excitedly through the scrub.

Nibbling the fresh grass beside the track, the 'roo did not anticipate the approaching horse and rider. Suddenly aware of danger, instinctively he leapt up and across the track. Startled, Star shied.

Caroline, thrown from the side saddle, hit the tree with a sickening thud. Under the spreading roots, the washed-out hole trapped the horse's leg. He crashed to the ground, rolling on the soft body beneath him.

33

Found

Great shafts of fire slashed the sky. The glow extended from the west, reflected again from the eastern horizon. The heat of the day was waning. The men working around the homestead paddocks were finishing work for the day. It was just about time to clean up and have some tucker.

No sign of the missus today. Ted had taken her meal at midday, but the door was closed, so he knocked and left the tray outside the door when there was no answer. Poor woman. What were they to do?

Danny unsaddled his horse and put the saddle and bridle on the fence. He slapped his horse on the rump. 'Off you go, old fella, go and see your mates.' The horse trotted off, whinnying to the other horses in the paddock. Danny watched, grinning at the antics of the reunion.

Suddenly he frowned. Where was Star? Surely Mrs Bartlett hadn't been out?

He walked up the fence towards the horses, then looked around the paddock. No doubt about it. Star was not with the others. He went back to the gate and picked up his saddle and bridle. The horse couldn't have got out of the paddock. In any case, he was not the kind to try to get out.

Danny dropped the saddle onto the rest and hung up his bridle. As he turned, his eye ran along the wall. Mrs Bartlett's side saddle was missing!

Ted had finished the job in the blacksmith's shop. He'd have to get out soon to the lake outstation and check things over. He wondered when the boss would be home. What a homecoming for him!

The boys had been all right through all this business — a terrible thing to have happened. He'd better see if Mrs Bartlett had eaten anything. He'd have to try to get her to have some tea. Awkward, it was, trying to look after a woman. It wasn't so bad when Mrs Williamson was here, but now . . .

And she wouldn't open the door when you knocked — he couldn't very well go barging into a woman's bedroom.

'Ted.' It was young Danny's voice. What was wrong? He was running down the road. 'Ted, Star's not in the horse paddock and Mrs Bartlett's saddle is gone. Do you think she's saddled him and gone out?'

'She'd never have the strength!' Ted's stride

quickened as he headed for the saddle room. Maybe Danny was mistaken. The lad was beside him as he turned in the door. Sure enough it was gone, all right. They left the saddle room and made for the horse paddock. He was right. Star was gone.

'Ted,' a voice shouted. 'There's a horse coming down the creek track. I'll go and fetch it in. Looks like it could be Star. He's limping.' The man galloped away.

Ted whipped round the building, Danny at his heels. He strained his eyes to see the approaching horse. He was limping badly.

'Better go and saddle the horses again, boy. Looks like something's up.'

His long strides soon brought him to the house. He knocked, knowing there would be no answer. He went quickly through the house. The tray of food was still on the floor beside the door. It was untouched. He opened the door. A skirt was lying in a heap on the floor. The room was empty.

Star was limping badly as Sam met him. His left foreleg was badly scraped, the bone exposed where the tree roots had ripped the skin away. Sam lifted the hoof and examined the damage. Poor old fellow must have come a real cropper. The leg was swelling badly.

But where was Mrs Bartlett?

He gathered up the reins and led the horse

in. 'Get the lanterns from the store — and a rug, too,' Ted called. 'Looks like she must have been thrown.'

Danny hurried away to prepare the search equipment. Ted was by the gate as Sam rode in, leading Star. 'Had a bad fall — looks like he must have put his foot in a hole.'

'Thing is now, where is Mrs Bartlett?' Ted looked over Star's injuries. 'You go and see to him while we get ready. Wonder how far she went?' He looked at the darkening sky. 'Be dark before we go too far.'

The light was fading fast as the little search party rode out and turned their horses up the creek track. They would need to travel as fast as possible to make the most of the remaining light. Once they were in the scrub, if they didn't find her before that, it would be a matter of slow going.

They'd have to be careful not to miss her if she'd been thrown off the track. In the thickest scrub, it wouldn't be hard to ride right past in the darkness without seeing her. They'd brought the lanterns, but their light didn't go very far.

There was no sign of the rider. They had reached the edge of the scrub. It was almost dark now. 'Have to light the lanterns now, boys. Won't see much when we get in the thick. Go steady and look carefully. She could be on the track. We don't want to ride onto her if she's unconscious. Then again, she might have been thrown as the horse fell and be in the long stuff near the track. Let's hope she's sitting somewhere waiting for us to find her and not too much hurt.'

The lanterns lit, they entered the scrub steadily. They spread out, scouring the undergrowth on each side. The search went on.

It was young Danny who eventually gave a shout. He had somehow got in the lead. 'Over here.' The others spurred their horses. Danny was on the ground, bending over something. Ted was beside him in an instant.

The form lying in the undergrowth didn't move. 'Bring a lantern here quickly,' Ted jerked out.

He turned her head and pushed back the hair that the wind had released. The gentle face was scratched and bruised. Dried blood caked strands of hair to the skin. The body was twisted grotesquely.

'It's no good. We can't do anything,' Ted said shakily. He put her head down.

They stood, dumb before the enormity of the discovery. 'Looks like the horse rolled on her when he fell,' Sam said quietly. They nodded.

The horses moved restively. They were

anxious to be back in the paddock, free. It had been a long day.

The lantern light fell softly on the figure on the ground and on Ted and Danny stooping beside her, then merged into the thick darkness beyond. An owl hooted somewhere in the scrub. A mopoke called mournfully away up the creek.

'How will we take her back?' It was Jacko speaking.

'She must have been gone some hours. Probably killed when she fell. Didn't have a chance when Star rolled on her, poor lady.' Ted was silent a moment. 'Bring the blanket. We'll take her back over the horse. Can't hurt her any more.'

They were mounted, ready to go. Ted's eye moved over the ground where she had lain. 'There's one of her combs,' he said. 'Better pick it up. She put great store by those combs. Think the boss gave them to her or something.'

It was a silent little party that made its way back down the track. The moon was rising, casting long shadows as they emerged from the scrub.

What was to be done now? When would the boss be home?

Here was another funeral. Someone would have to be notified. Who? They'd better try to get word to the boss. So the thoughts of each of them ran as slowly they plodded back to the homestead.

They carried her in and laid her on the bed. Young Danny proved himself, getting water in a dish and washing the caked blood away. 'I helped my mother when Granny died,' he said. 'I know what to do.' They were glad to leave it to him.

It was almost daylight when the last ones blew out the lamp and left the room, closing the door softly. They'd get a few hours sleep now, if that was possible. They'd done what had to be done now. They'd face the next step later.

The sound of hammer nailing wood to wood penetrated into Ted's consciousness as he woke. The events of last night surged back into his mind. Sam must be busy already. What should he do now? It was possible the boss could be back at any time, depending on how the mob went on the trip. How long should he wait? Fancy coming home and finding both your son and your wife dead!

He couldn't wait too long. He'd better make preparations anyway. He'd send Jacko up the track and see if he could meet up with the boss. He'd forewarn him of happenings at home — try to soften the blow a bit. He'd have to register the death, too. Anyway, first things first. He pulled on his boots and clomped outside.

Sam was busy near the blacksmith's shop. 'Go into business soon,' he said grimly as Ted came up.

'You've found all you need?'

'Yes. It'll be right.'

Ted walked away. How was young Danny? He'd proved himself top class last night. Not many young fellows his age could do what he had done. It was a bit of luck having him on hand like that and knowing what to do. He'd be a man worth knowing when he reached manhood — a man worth knowing now, even if he was only a lad.

Ted made his way to the men's quarters. It was empty. He found the others at the stable, tending Star's injuries. 'He'll be all right,' Snowy said, rubbing liniment into his leg. 'Had a nasty fall, but there's nothing broken.'

'Pity we can't say the same for the rider,' Jacko said quietly.

They were silent a few minutes, awed by the presence of death and the sequence of recent events. 'We do the same as we did for the little fellow, Ted?' asked Jacko. 'When will we have this funeral?'

'I've been thinking about it.' Ted stood up and hitched his trousers. 'We've got to notify somebody about the death. That can wait a bit. The boss could be home any time, but we can't wait past tomorrow. Get the place up in the corner of the yard ready — next to the little fellow. If the boss isn't back tomorrow, we'll go ahead.'

The others nodded agreement.

★   ★   ★

Sam had done his work well. All was done decently. The casket was ready. Danny had been to the garden, picked a red rosebud and laid it on Caroline's breast.

'Mother did that for Granny,' he told Ted solemnly. It was the right thing to do — added a little bit of something. The others were impressed.

Jacko and Harry offered to carry the casket, wanting to be involved, to contribute something in this situation where they felt so helpless, so ill-equipped. It was a far cry from the droving, roping, branding of cattle that they knew so well. This world of little kid, women, death and all that must be done was utterly alien to them. They clutched at any straw to bring action and normality into it.

They gathered round the grave, bare-headed in respect, clutching hat in hand.

Ted began again, the second time in such a short while: 'I am the resurrection and the life saith the Lord. He that believeth in me, though he were dead, yet shall he live, and whosoever liveth and believeth in me shall never die.'

They followed the service through. It was finished. Each felt he had done what he could.

They even started wondering who would be next. These things often went in threes, you know.

The question, why, could not be answered. First a little kid, then a young woman. Why?

Of course, she hadn't been in her right mind when she rode out. Maybe that was a death that could have been avoided. She was so beside herself, poor lady. She probably didn't have any control over the horse, or any chance of staying on his back, whatever caused the accident. But the little bloke: why did he have to die?

Oh well, these things happened. Nothing you could do about it. What was that Ted had read? 'He that believeth in me, though he were dead, yet shall he live.' Have to think some more about that. They sauntered back to the quarters. Snowy went to make tea.

They sat on the verandah, their tea steaming in the mugs. Cup of tea helped: strong and plenty of sugar. 'Well, we've got to meet the boss and prepare him before he gets home.' Ted sipped his tea. 'Any volunteers? Not much of a mission.' There was silence for a minute.

'I'll go.' It was Jacko.

Ted heaved a sigh of relief. Someone had to go. He should stay and keep things going. All this made a man nervous. You never knew what might happen next.

He stood up. 'Right. Get some tucker and gear together. Take Paddy as pack-horse and set out first thing in the morning. Get a good night's sleep.'

He walked off to think his own thoughts and to take out his pent-up feelings on the woodheap.

34

Carved words

The sun beat down mercilessly on the figure bent over his work. It did not seem to bother him. In fact, he seemed oblivious to all around him.

He sat tapping with hammer and chisel on a slab of pink-grained sandstone on the ground beside him. His hat was pulled well down over his face. The only movement, the only sound was the tap-tap as he worked.

A Willy wagtail, emboldened by the silence and stillness of the man, danced and flipped his tail some centimetres away. The bees droned on the Banksia rose behind him.

William Bartlett was home. Jacko had met the mob on the Strzelecki Creek track. A few more days and they would have been home. It was not an easy job to tell the boss his sad news. How could you break that sort of news gently to a man? What could you say? How could you gently say you've lost everything that means most in the world to you?

He'd done his best. He'd tried to comfort. But what comfort was there?

The boss had taken it like a man, no doubt about that. After the first rush of shock and grief, the only indication of his sorrow were his eyes and his flared nostrils. He'd taken the blow right on the chin, no doubt about it. He'd gone about the mob and the men, giving orders. He left Blue in charge. Then they set out — Jacko and the boss — for home.

It was a forlorn homecoming. Ted had met them at the homestead paddock gate. The men came tentatively from the quarters. They were anxious to express their sorrow, to offer some sort of comfort, but the right words did not come easily to them. William was aware of the sentiment behind their clumsy efforts. He appreciated the sympathetic expressions, the mumbled condolences.

A week had passed now since he got home. They had gone — Ted, Jacko, young Danny and he — to find rock for a headstone for Caroline. They took a dray and tools and went to the section of the property where the stone for the house had come from. They had cut a slab, a beautiful section of pink-grained stone, and carefully brought it back. William had now begun work on it. He smoothed the stone. He would polish it when it was finished.

Caro, his Caro. How could he express the

love he felt for her? All her beautiful dear presence gone. What was life without her?

He mustn't think about that. Not yet. In time perhaps. But not yet. He chipped away at the stone. The Willy wagtail danced closer to him, chirping his sweet pretty creature.

William looked at him. He was a happy little fellow. No doubt he had a mate close by, lucky little bird.

When he had the stone ready, what would he carve onto it? What could he put after her name and that sort of thing? What could he say on the stone?

She was a wonderful wife. If only he had not left her alone, he might have still had them both. If only he had been here to comfort her when Jamie had died. What a terrible thing for her to have to bear alone.

It was no use going on like that, though. He had thought he was doing the right thing for all of them with this venture. You couldn't foresee the future. Caroline would know that.

If only he could have seen her before she died. What a good wife she had been. Good wife! That was it. That bit about the good wife in the Bible. That said just about what he wanted to say. He put down his tools, stood up and stretched. He'd go and look up the words.

In the bedroom, William picked up the

Bible on the table by the bed. Now where would that bit be? In the Old Testament. He turned first to Genesis and the story of creation: the story of the creation of woman. Bone of my bone, flesh of my flesh. That's what Adam had said.

He would say that, too. They had been one, he and Caro.

But the bit about the good wife. Of course! Proverbs. He skimmed through, looking for the words he sought.

A virtuous woman. That was Caro. Her price was far above rubies. Yes, his heart safely trusted in her. She was a blessing to him. She was never idle. All these things she did. She looked after her household well. She ran the whole place well. She worked and looked to the welfare of everybody on the station — and she was his, his beloved, just his.

But he couldn't put all that. He'd say it in a few words. That was how he felt about her. Yes, that was it.

His step was purposeful as he went back to his work. He picked up the tools and set about the smoothing of the stone again. As he worked, William thought of the letter he had written the night before to Caroline's parents. What a shock it would be to them, too.

Jacko the messenger had again been sent

on an unenviable mission. He would carry the news to the family and also do the official things that had to be done. It was good to have fellows like Ted and Jacko and Snowy — and young Danny, too. What a good lad he was turning into!

He'd have to get rid of Oliver, though. A fellow who thought the way he did had no place on 'Bibbaringa'. He'd pay him off and let him go when the droving job was finished.

Ted had taken over getting the cattle where he wanted them. The calves had survived well and should thrive here along the creek. He'd have to start work branding soon and get the castrating done before they got too big, too.

He'd give himself a bit more time yet, though. He'd have to pull himself together and face the future.

What future? He'd think about that later. For now, he'd just work quietly on this stone.

The sun was a great golden ball close to the horizon as William straightened up from the stone. He stretched and looked to the horizon.

It looked as though he had a visitor coming — a lone horseman and approaching from the south. He didn't look like a stockman, though.

He went indoors and washed his hands. It would be a while before the rider arrived. He didn't look as though he was in a hurry. William rose from his chair on the verandah and went to meet his visitor as he drew near the homestead.

By goodness! What a surprise. It was certainly no stockman. His clothing was distinctly unusual for this part of Australia. Surely he must be German. The visitor dismounted and greeted William in heavily accented English, an accent that reminded William vividly of his grandmother. There was no doubt he was German.

He spoke to him in German and the man visibly relaxed. He was one of the missionaries from Killalpaninna, the German mission to the Aborigines in central inland Australia established a few years ago. He had heard word of William's loss and had come to comfort and console him, and to pray with him. He was obviously not an experienced horseman and the journey was not short or an easy one.

As the evening wore on and the meal was over and the two men sat on the verandah, William was more and more impressed with the courage and dedication of Heinrich, as he discovered his name to be, and his party. This small group, fired with zeal, had left their homes and security for life in harsh, unknown conditions, in great isolation, not for any personal gain, but to do what they believed God called them to do: to bring the Christian gospel to this tribe of Aborigines of the Australian inland. It was not an easy mission.

They sat on in the cool of the evening. As bedtime approached, Heinrich spoke the words of comfort to William. They prayed together and, after a brief goodnight, retired to their rooms.

William lay for some time, going over all his visitor had spoken of. Some men had never known a marriage of love. He had experienced that. Some men had never had the joy of a child. He had experienced that great joy of a son. He must concentrate on that.

In time, perhaps, he could pick up the threads of his life. He had 'Bibbaringa'. The cattle purchase and trek had been successful. There would be something at least to fill the days.

It was just that the motivating force was gone.

Sunlight was streaming in the window when William woke. He could hear his visitor already up. He would want to get away early to make halfway today on the trip back to Killalpaninna.

The farewell was brief. The handshake said volumes.

William stood at the gate and watched Heinrich's departure till he reached the creek. Then he turned and made his way back to his work on the slab of sandstone.

The bees were already busy on the Banksia rose. He put his tools on the verandah, fetched a bucket and, filling it at the well, poured the water around the roots.

He must make sure it endured.

35

Conviction

Angela groped for understanding. Why did this girl have such antipathy towards the woman Caroline? Why this strong, fiercely emotional involvement with something that had happened so long ago? In any case, surely Caroline wasn't responsible for her son's death?

She could not let this pass. All her research, her reading, her interviews with family members told her otherwise. 'I don't believe for a minute that it was Caroline's fault that Jamie died,' she said definitely. 'I can't imagine why you feel so strongly that she is responsible. She nursed him day and night, all alone. Remember, she was all alone with the responsibility, the physical toll of his care. She was utterly exhausted.'

'But she went to sleep! Sleep! When her baby was almost dying! How could she?' The girl's tone was vehement. 'How could any mother go to sleep with her baby in that condition?'

Her sunken eyes flashed. Her lip curled in

contempt. How could she be so hard, so condemning and so vehement about something that happened over one hundred years ago? And where was her understanding, her compassion for a woman in Caroline's situation?

Angela searched for words to convince her of the pathos of that situation. Caroline was hundreds, thousands of kilometres from civilisation, from advice — and alone in this vast country, with no Willie to support or consult; not even the Blacks, who may have had some bush remedy.

The enormity of it filled Angela's mind. Thank God for modern medicines — and the availability of medical treatment. Of course, there were still areas of isolation in a country like Australia with such vast distances. Thankfully, services like radio and the Flying Doctor bridged these distances today, making it very different from the early days.

'Oh, you must see. You must understand,' she cried. 'Caroline must have been utterly exhausted! No-one can go on and on without sleep or food and drink. We all have our limits. Can't you see that?'

'But Willie,' the girl persisted. 'She let Willie down. Willie idolised Jamie. He was his son. He loved him.'

'Of course he loved him. But Willie didn't

blame Caroline,' Angela interrupted. 'Willie loved her, too. He knew she did all she could.' She paused. 'There are some things that are beyond human control. Pneumonia, which it probably was, is a very serious illness. And more so back then, before we had antibiotics and things — especially for a child.'

'Yes. She tried,' the girl conceded. 'But she didn't try hard enough. Then she let him slip away when she wasn't there.' After a moment's softening, the condemning hardness was back again.

'She couldn't do any more than she did,' Angela reasoned softly. 'Willie knew that. He understood.'

She longed to convince her companion whose picture of Caroline was far from Angela's own perception of a woman of courage, of self-sacrifice; a loving, giving person. How could she convey the love and heartache Willie had suffered when he learned of the accident that killed her just days before his return?

It was important to put this girl right. Why, she did not know. Angela just knew it was imperative, perhaps just for her own peace of mind. She had a picture, a concept of the people, the events, the outcome. She didn't want that to be upset. Her work would be an important addition to available information.

She had to believe utterly in its authenticity. Was this girl upsetting that certainty?

'Willie adored Caroline, his beloved, his cherished wife. Haven't you seen his work on the beautiful stone out there?' She pointed to the little graveyard. 'He did that himself. He was not a stonemason, but he smoothed and polished that slab of sandstone. It must have taken the greatest patience and perseverance. Then he set about carving her name — and the words that came from his heart. He chipped and chipped. He laboured over it to put his great love into words.'

She looked back from the graves to her companion. 'He adored her,' she said quietly, but with deep conviction. 'He was heart-broken when he got home and found he had lost not only his son, but his beloved wife, too. Remember, the idea of going to 'Nockatunga' to get these cattle and bring them home was his idea, not hers. Can't you see how this must have made him feel?'

She at least seemed to have the girl's attention. 'He left her alone and wasn't here when she needed him. Maybe he even felt he needed Caroline's forgiveness, leaving her like that and not thinking of her needs.'

There seemed to be a little less rigidity about the girl's stance. However had she come to this perception of Caroline? Was there some personal link? Some involvement?

'Willie didn't blame her,' she repeated. 'Jamie was a healthy little boy because of Caroline's care of him. She did all she could when he became ill. The illness that developed so quickly was just too much for him. Can't you see that?'

The girl didn't answer.

'Willie didn't blame her. Don't you blame her, either.'

There was a silence which seemed to go on for a long time. She waited. Had she been successful? Had anything she said penetrated this girl's hard crust? Whatever had been her experience? And why does it matter so much to me, she thought.

The moments ticked by. Yet at the same time, time seemed not to exist. She seemed suspended in the now. Then the girl lifted her face. It was a contorted face. 'But it was more than that. Oh, it was more than that. Don't you see? It was much more than Willie. Don't you see?'

Passion was in the girl's voice. 'She prayed for a baby. She wanted a baby so much. She pleaded, begged God to give her a baby. She could think of nothing else. She begged for Jamie. And God gave him to her. He gave her the baby she longed for.' Her voice faltered. 'And she let him die. She was granted her prayer, her great desire. And she let him die.'

She paused, then continued in a fierce whisper. 'God won't forgive her.' What a strange creature she was: so fiercely involved — and so condemning.

'How can you say such a thing?'

'Because she didn't look after him well enough,' the girl interrupted. 'Mothers have a great responsibility. And she didn't do all she should have. She thought of herself. She can't expect forgiveness when she did that — especially when she was granted the baby she wanted so much.'

Angela was frustrated. The girl's unreasonable hardness was upsetting her. 'Don't you believe in the forgiveness of sins, in Christ's death on the cross so that we don't have to pay the price for sin? Don't you believe that?'

The reply came hesitantly. 'Yes, I believe that.'

'I don't believe Caroline did neglect Jamie. But even if she did, there is still forgiveness.'

'But she doesn't deserve it,' the girl insisted.

'No-one deserves forgiveness. You can't earn it. It's a gift. God's gift. We just have to accept it.'

There was a silence after Angela's words. She tried to see her companion's expression. It was difficult. Was there a softening in the grim lines around her mouth? Was there a relaxation in her bearing? Could she have touched a chord of memory buried under goodness knows what?

Pressing her point, she continued softly. 'I believe no-one is beyond forgiveness.'

'But if it's so very bad?' the girl ventured in a different tone.

Angela sighed. 'We can think we are *above* forgiveness, I suppose — it's an upside-down sort of pride.'

She looked again at the girl, trying to see her response. 'Surely you must have been taught these things,' she appealed.

The girl nodded almost imperceptibly. 'Yes. But sometimes you forget. Things happen — and you forget. Thank you.' The answer was almost inaudible. The drone of the bees on the Banksia rose filled the silence in the room. The two occupants were still.

At last, Angela broke the silence. 'I know that God is my father and I only have to lay my head on his shoulder and feel his arms and his love around me.'

The silence descended again. Still the girl did not move.

Angela's eyes searched again the far horizon. This land was timeless, as was this place; this old house and its ghosts. If the walls could speak! She felt somewhere between the people whose lives she had come to research and the present. And yet she felt part of it all. It all mattered.

'Perhaps you are right. Yes. Yes, you are right. Thank you.'

The girl's hand which had been holding the bottom of the ragged curtain dropped by her side. She walked the few steps and stood in front of the glass panel and looked out. Her head lifted, her hair again falling around her face. Then she turned and, smiling at Angela, walked out of the room. Her bare feet made no sound on the floorboards.

Her emotions gradually subsiding, Angela stood for a few moments where she was. Then suddenly, regaining her alertness, she moved swiftly into the hall. She must find the girl. She must talk with her. She looked both ways, up and down the hall. She had gone. She hurried along, looking into each room. There was no sign of her. Breaking into a run, Angela went out onto the verandah and around the house. There was no sign of anyone.

The plain stretched in every direction devoid of tree or hump, bare everywhere. No girl. Angela's mind reeled. She couldn't just disappear! Surely she hadn't imagined her presence. They had been together for some time. She went around the verandah again, searching: not a clue.

Re-entering the house, she retraced her steps to the bedroom. As she re-entered the bedroom, her eye was caught by a small object on the floor by the French door. She walked quickly towards it. Reaching down, she picked it up and stood staring at it.

36

Peace

The light in the room had faded. The quietness was almost tangible. Except for the bees, nothing stirred. Even their droning had lessened. It was the silence of the plains, the vastness, the isolation. It was a silence as only the far distant places from civilisation, from habitation or human intervention, know.

A strange aura of peace seemed to have settled over the old house. A door down the hall creaked as it moved in a breath of air. The tattered remnant of curtain swayed slightly.

Angela groped for thought; for coherence; for reality. Yet what was reality? Was it simply the present, the visible? Or was it a certain concept of the present in present experience? Was the past not equally reality? Could the past and the present exist together in reality?

What of the future? This present that seemed to encompass the past and yet the future . . . Was this infinity? The thought came unbidden to her mind. Was this a glimpse of eternity?

She looked out over the paddocks, away and beyond to the north-east, the direction in which Caroline's eyes had turned so often and so longingly, searching for the first sign of dust on the horizon to tell her Willie was coming with the great mob of cattle.

She recalled all she had learned: the joys; the sorrows. She recalled the conflicts of the woman whose plight she felt so deeply and whom she had championed so whole-heartedly. When her gaze came back to the room, she realised her fatigue, the emptiness of the house — and her aloneness.

She must get back to the camp. Robert would be looking for her. She stirred and turned into the hall and wide entrance that had been the scene of so many happy times, with friends and family coming and going — and so much heartache.

She walked slowly down the crumbling steps and along the old stone pathway, now overgrown with weeds. A peewee lighting on the leaning headstone in the corner of the little graveyard opened its beak and gave its last piercing call for the day, pee-wit, pee-wit. A late ray of light across the darkening sky fell on the stone, highlighting the contours of the carved letters.

She thought again of the words so painstakingly carved there:

Bone of my bone, flesh of my flesh,
My heart doth safely trust in her.
Her price is far above rubies.
My wife — my beloved — my own.

She turned and looked back at the house, at the room she had come from, at the wide verandahs and at the Banksia rose still twining its way around the verandah posts.

She uncurled her fingers and looked at the small carved ivory side comb in her hand. With a little shake and a quick indraw of breath, she whispered almost inaudibly, 'Peace be with you, Caroline.'

Then she turned and walked quickly away in the direction of the camp.

We do hope that you have enjoyed reading this large print book.

Did you know that all of our titles are available for purchase?

We publish a wide range of high quality large print books including:
Romances, Mysteries, Classics
General Fiction
Non Fiction and Westerns

Special interest titles available in large print are:
The Little Oxford Dictionary
Music Book
Song Book
Hymn Book
Service Book

Also available from us courtesy of Oxford University Press:
Young Readers' Dictionary
(large print edition)
Young Readers' Thesaurus
(large print edition)

For further information or a free brochure, please contact us at:
Ulverscroft Large Print Books Ltd.,
The Green, Bradgate Road, Anstey,
Leicester, LE7 7FU, England.
Tel: (00 44) 0116 236 4325
Fax: (00 44) 0116 234 0205

Other titles published by
The House of Ulverscroft:

SKIN DEEP

Catherine Barry

Finn has felt unhappy with her chest size since she was a girl and decides that her dysfunctional childhood, failed relationships and poor job prospects all come down to the fact that her image is lacking. Indeed, post-operative Finn's life changes dramatically, but is it all she imagined it would be?

PRAIRIE FIRE

Patricia Werner

In 1887, in the ranchlands of the Oklahoma territory, the beautiful Kathleen Calhoun is ready to start a life of her own. A chance meeting brings the handsome Raven Sky into her life. Sky is gentle and educated, but he is also a Creek Indian . . . Kathleen's attraction to Raven Sky is undeniable, but her dreams are haunted by the Indian savages who brutally murdered her parents. Torn, Kathleen flees Oklahoma and the arms of her beloved. Deep within, she knows she must return to the firm embrace of Raven Sky to feed the flames of her desire . . .

THE DECENT THING

C. W. Reed

David Herbert lives a privileged life in Edwardian society but is dominated by his sisters, Gertrude and Clara. At public school he suffers bullying and at home his only friend is Nelly Tovey, a young maid . . . Living on a pittance in London after being disowned by his family, he becomes seriously ill and is nursed by the devoted Nelly. Although certain of their love, Nelly is aware of the gulf between them. David must find the courage to defy convention and breach the barriers to their happiness.

FLYING COLOURS

Heather Graves

With a broken romance behind her and a promising future ahead Corey O'Brien intends to concentrate on her chosen career. She certainly doesn't expect to come to the attention of someone like Mario Antonello, a racehorse owner and heir to a fashion house ... Their first meeting isn't friendly so she is surprised by the interest he shows in her later. It all seems too much and it will take a while for Corey to find out the truth. Then she discovers a shocking secret and feels she must turn her back on him forever.